Julius Stinde, Harriet F. Powell

Frau Wilhelmine

THE CONCLUDING PART OF THE BUCHHOLZ FAMILY

Julius Stinde, Harriet F. Powell

Frau Wilhelmine
THE CONCLUDING PART OF THE BUCHHOLZ FAMILY

ISBN/EAN: 9783741112607

Manufactured in Europe, USA, Canada, Australia, Japa

Cover: Foto ©Andreas Hilbeck / pixelio.de

Manufactured and distributed by brebook publishing software
(www.brebook.com)

Julius Stinde, Harriet F. Powell

Frau Wilhelmine

FRAU WILHELMINE

THE CONCLUDING PART OF THE

BUCHHOLZ FAMILY

BY

JULIUS STINDE

TRANSLATED BY

HARRIET F. POWELL

NEW YORK
CHARLES SCRIBNER'S SONS
1887
[*Authorized Translation*]

CONTENTS.

FRAU WILHELMINE.

REPOSE.

On a contemplative old age—And travelling nerves—Why work of sterling quality commands its price, and business depends on patterns—On competition and the Tower of Babel—Why a wager is made and Frau Krause is pleased—Why Felix cannot rebel.

IF any one wishes to attain an object, he must not only choose the proper moment, but grip it tightly as well. Even a senseless mouse-trap is aware of that fact, for whatever has once escaped from it does not return. How much more therefore ought deliberating man to ponder the question of time, when it is of import to him to carry his point and to reduce probable opposition to a state of nullity!

Fortunately I am to some extent acquainted with my husband's inner life, even though it be not quite devoid of hidden corners, and I wait for a favourable opportunity of presenting for his approbation wishes that I have in view. Of course it must be before he has been to his office, where the correspondence nuisance claims his entire attention, and it is just as necessary that it should not follow a sleepless night. For many years I have tried the state of the barometer by breakfast. If, for instance, he takes great gulps of boiling hot coffee, without scalding himself, it is best to leave him quite to himself: for sheer hurry and worry prevent his giving his attention; but if he only sips it, and butters another half roll for himself, and then a quarter, and lastly a tiny piece, then his cup may be tenderly replenished, and he stays and listens quietly.

After our Betti had become engaged to Herr Felix Schmidt, I discovered that my Carl carried secrets about with him, which naturally had reference to the business, as he did not let them come out. Such had ever been his way. He never laid his cares on my shoulders when business came to a standstill, when woollen goods gaped at each other, or such-like conjunctures occurred. No; I only discovered how we stood when everything was quite clear once more, and always after an interim of one day's post. Therefore I did not bother him with questions on this occasion, for my Carl does not belong to those speculators who risk everything that they may drive on india-rubber tires for a year, and get along on clogs for the rest of their existence.

However, if he carried secret designs about with him, why should I not have mine? Emmi was provided with a husband, and Betti next door to it. I could therefore fold my hands in my lap, and look passively on at the march of events. Why should I go on toiling and moiling, and make my life a burden to me? The young people were big enough to commit their own stupidities, and independent enough to learn wisdom without assistance. Why, there are many parents who give their children no other education to take along with them than two strong arms, and the non-cultivation that goes with them; but mine have had something of everything. They have been taught the sciences, as well as deportment, culture, and domestic economy. This being so, I said to myself, "Wilhelmine, a contemplative old age is most adapted for you. You have done your duty, and may fitly lay claim to a comfortable state of repose."

In saying this, however, I did not depict for myself an absolutely hermit-like mode of life, with nothing but carrots and such-like roots of the woods ; but rather I contemplated merely a withdrawal from everything that did not concern me, by means of which much vexation and worry may be avoided; for discord and annoyance really only arise from the fact that the good which one wishes to do is misunderstood. On the other hand, for any evil-doing there is always a prompt and intelligent comprehension.

As soon as my ideas began to be matured, the time came to present them to my husband and to snatch the right moment for doing so. "Carl," said I, "have you thought at all yet about how we are to keep our silver wedding?"—"Not so far," he answered; "but it shall be jolly—that is as fixed as an old poplar."— "You meant to say rationally amusing, did you not, my Carl? You know surely that noise and bustle do not suit me!"—"But who is going to make a noise and bustle?" he asked.—"It cannot be avoided. Before dinner, certainly, they are anxious to behave like people of the world and speak as though they were shod in felt ; but once let the fish course be over, and all fear of fish-bones be rendered groundless, then free course is given to the vocal chords ; and the redder people get as the wine warms them, the more noise they make, until each one must strain his voice more than his neighbour is already doing, simply in order that he may be understood ; and so it goes on, one outbidding the other, till one fancies that the deaf are holding a quarterly meeting. Such acoustics are trying to my nerves."

"Wilhelmine," said my husband, smiling quietly, "your nerves are as good as new."—"But, Carl, I do possess some."—"I dare say they will be all right again by then. The day on which you became my dear wife, five-and-twenty years ago, cannot be allowed to pass without celebration; I owe that to you, and you to me."

"We might start off on a little journey," I suggested casually, and filled up his cup afresh in order to keep him in his place.—"So you don't possess nerves in travelling?"—"Carl, the matter is too serious for you to dispose of it with cool derision. Travelling is strengthening—that is a generally recognised fact."

"And where have your cogitations determined that we are to go?"—"If you take up the map, Switzerland hardly seems to be any distance."

My Carl did not answer at once, but took a great big gulp from his cup. "Aha," I noticed, "obstacles are towering aloft here," and continued therefore at once: "The police-lieutenant's wife went to Switzerland when she took her daughter Mila to a boarding-school, and she behaves as if the Rigi had been piled up solely on her account; and if you speak to any one on the subject, they make a boast of their travels in Switzerland. Assessor Lehmann and his wife skimmed across Switzerland on their wedding-tour, and even Herr Pfeiffer is on familiar terms with the most out-of-the-way mountains. Do you think you will be able to endure for a continuance people asking you with a sort of contemptuous pity: 'What, you have not been to Switzerland yet?'—'Really? Why, it is incomprehensible.'—'One certainly ought to have seen it, if only on account of Andermatt, and all those places spoken of in Tell.'—I don't want to be exposed to that any longer. And we can manage it, my Carl. The festivities for the silver wedding would run into more money than a little trip to the eternal heights, with their real glaciers. Do be reasonable."

) My Carl had got up while I was talking, and lighted
'his morning cigar, after which he seated himself again on
the sofa. He was therefore disposed to entertain the
idea—a fact that aroused considerable gleams of hope.

After he had drawn some fragrant puffs, he began
in a very explanatory tone : " I am of your opinion in
many respects, Wilhelmine, and should have no objections to take to your idea of a trip, if it were compatible with business engagements."—" Well ? "—" Let
me finish, child."—" I am hardly moving ! "—" In these
days competition is a very different thing from what
it used to be. The worth of the goods no longer turns
the scale, but rather their cheapness ; and the public
favours this underselling by reason of its ignorance."—
" Of course the whole lot is rubbish," I exclaimed in
interruption, " and not worth half the price ! "

" Quite right ; the purchaser deceives himself. Good
materials and proved workmanship are not to be had
for nothing ; they always command their price, and
will continue to do so in future. But one must follow
the leading features of the time."—" Carl, you are
surely not going to make arrangements for a constant
sale of riff-raff goods ? "—" No ; but I shall manufacture certain articles myself, and rely on them against
all healthy competition. The man to whom Betti is
engaged possesses exceptional abilities, his knowledge
of manufacture and his youth will join itself to my
business experience and age, and result in fresh and
profitable activity."—" I do not doubt that in the least,
my Carl ; wherever you are, things are sure to go
right. If you are really about to get such reliable
help, you will be able to tear yourself away splendidly, and to travel with all the greater peace of mind."
—" Travelling is not to be thought of. We are going
to build."

"To build ?" I repeated in horror.

"Certainly ; with bricks and mortar."

"I can vividly imagine that you don't intend to use chocolate-cream for the purpose !" I exclaimed angrily. "A pleasant partner, an excellent son-in-law, to beguile you into such follies ! Build indeed ! Just think of it—to build ! You had better brick in both your wife and daughter in the foundation, that their bodily eyes may not see how everything goes topsy-turvy, while nothing sensible results from it. Oh, Carl, why did you not tell me something about it earlier ? But now of course it is too late—worse luck! —and nothing can be altered."

"Wilhelmine, that I should make any communication to you about my plans is contrary to my usual habit, and has only been done on this occasion to convince you of the impracticability of your project for travelling."—"I do not see it at all, as yet."—"Patience ! You soon will. In our branch, business is done in certain articles according to the novelty of the pattern. Whoever is the first to place a successful pattern on the market, skims off the cream; the next comer, after the principal demand has been satisfied, must content himself with less; and lastly, he who only gets a conception of the pattern after it has been already imitated and made common, in order to lend the most abominable shoddy a saleable outside, stands quite at the bottom after the race is over. Now if we manufacture certain articles ourselves, we make not only the manufacturer's gains, but as sole possessors of the pattern we pocket the largest profit, before imitators take forcible possession of it and send the business to the dogs by putting goods on the market that resemble it, are less valuable, or have even been manufactured for purposes of imposition."

"Carl," I asked in astonishment, "if you invent something, surely nobody else is allowed to imitate it?"

"He is not allowed, but he does it."

"Is there no prohibition against it?"

"We have laws relative to patents and the protection of patterns, which are a sort of safety-hedge to prevent burglarious entry on mental or industrial territories, but they only ward them off in part. Any one wishing to cheat and swindle, will spy out holes in definitions that honest people look upon as a most unassailable covering. A swindler like that, does not imitate the pattern servilely—for then he would very soon be seized upon—but he repeats it with certain, of course, unimportant alterations; he reproduces it, as people say, by means of his perceptive faculties, and there is no legal method of proceeding against it."

"Why does he not invent something for himself?" I asked angrily.—"Because he is without talent, and finds annexation a less laborious process than inventing something novel, and incurring the risk of the first bid."
—"Carl, is he not ashamed of himself?"—"No, he is impudent into the bargain, the better to impress the public. Besides, every one wants to live—the one in this fashion, the other in that."

"It is true," I corroborated him, "nobody gives his neighbour a hundred-mark note, but then he need not set to work at once to rob him."

"It is not called robbery, but competition. The same causes induce German manufacturers to affix English and French labels to their best goods, because the German purchaser considers a '*haute nouveauté*' better worth paying for than a '*neuheit*'; and so the old superstition that all foreign products are superior to ours, is artificially kept up. In token of their gratitude, the English send miserable articles with the stamp of German

manufacturers affixed to them to those places where
they fear competition ; by this means they bring our
industries just as slowly and surely into bad repute as
we, in our love of foreign articles, have helped theirs
to a reputation that, all things considered, is not deserved by all of them."

"That is a nice state of things, Carl."

"And therefore, it is necessary to make a stand
against it.   Open your eyes while purchasing, and
look to the quality of the goods instead of their label.
Then this cheating will come to an end.   Competition
is forcing building upon us.   If the manufactory ac
complishes what we expect of it, I will travel with you
wherever you want to go, Minchen,—to the Blocks-
berg, or wherever else it happens to be pretty."

"Carl, a tombstone has more tact than you—it would
not even mention such localities !   Have you considered what discomfort and dust building brings with
it ?   Surely nor even now you would say that you
had better leave it alone."

"The piece of ground bordering on our court-yard
has been already acquired, and the buildings upon it
can be easily adapted to our purposes.   The architect
Krause has already begun on the plans."—"That is
a consolation !" I exclaimed ; "I have confidence in
him—he has a sense for the practical and the solid.
If the people of long ago had employed him for the
Tower of Babylon, it would have been in existence
to-day."—"You ought to see, Minchen, that the building will afford even you pleasure."—"Most if it tumbles down again.   Ah, and I had such delightful fancies about devoting myself entirely to repose !"—"To
whom ?" asked my husband, placing his hand behind
his ear.—"To repose.   It seems to me that I spoke
sufficiently plainly."—"Wilhelmine, you and repose !

May I ask since when ?"—"Carl, if you have kept your seat for the sole purpose of hurting my feelings, then you had better say so straight out, instead of dissembling and torturing me by inches. I don't consider it high-minded."—"The astonishment was too great," he made excuse ; "I could not take it in at once. Just explain one thing to me, Wilhelmine : how are you to set to work to look on quietly when things are going crooked, without giving advice ? how will you fold your hands quietly in your lap, without helping where it is necessary ? "

"I shall not trouble myself further about anything that does not concern me," was my answer ; "I will not burn my fingers any more for other people. 'Don't meddle with what does not concern you,' shall be my rule of life from this moment ; and if you really choose to understand me, you know exactly now what I mean. But you are one of those people who can only see through a brick wall when there is a hole in it."

"I have understood you perfectly," answered my Carl, "and I can only approve of your programme."— "Carl — programme ! What sort of expression is that ?"—"Let us say holiday arrangements, then, as you wish to give yourself a holiday."—"Carl, I consider it extremely immoral to make game of me; and now, of all times. You shall see that I will carry it out. So far as our private relations are concerned, I shall be at my post now as always—that is my duty, of course—with avoidance of all superfluous interference ; but so far as outside matters and all relations to them are concerned, I have ceased to exist under any condition whatsoever. Make a note of it, Carl; for such folk Wilhelmine Buchholz is an unsubstantial void, now and for ever."—"If I might be permitted to entertain certain doubts——"

"You are not permitted."

"Your repose begins well—you flare up at once about a nothing!"—"A nothing, Carl? A nothing? I want to go to Switzerland, and you want to build; do you call that a nothing?"—"I thought you were specially bent on repose."—"For what other reason do I propose the journey than to get away from the bustle of the silver wedding here?"—"As if you would find repose on the journey! Where is your logic?"—"Do you think I am as variable as a chameleon, that changes its mind every five minutes? Oh, no; I keep to what I have undertaken!"—"Will you wager that you do?"—"I shall."—"For six months?"—Being wounded in my deepest feelings, I was prepared to hurl back a remark that was two-edged, to say the least of it, when a sly idea that, so to speak, fell from the clouds, prevented my doing so. "All right," I said, "let us have a wager. If I win we will go to Switzerland."—"Done," laughed my Carl, and gave me his hand upon it; "but what are you going to stake in return, in case you lose?"—"I lose? Not a thought of it!"—"Name your stake, Minchen."—"If I lose, I will acknowledge that you are right in everything, whatever it may be."—"And you won't contradict if I build? Done."

I shook hands on it. "That's settled," exclaimed my Carl.—"What is settled? I bind myself to nothing."—"Are you inclined to break your contract already?"—"Carl, I beg of you not to be abusive."— My husband got up, as it had now become high time for him to be at his office. "The journey depends upon yourself alone," he said. "If in the course of six months you have made persons with whom you have nothing to do neither happy nor unhappy by forcible measures, I shall acquiesce in the journey to

Switzerland; but if you forfeit your word, then we shall stay at home and build."—"Carl, I swear to you."—"Wilhelmine, consider that consistency and obstinacy are two very different things."

"You shall see how consistent I can be," I called after him. As if men had made a general compact of steadfastness! On the contrary, whenever there is a question of real energy, people turn to us women. That may be found in every Universal History as often as one turns over its pages.

As soon as I was alone, many things occurred to me that I might have said to my Carl; amongst others, that too large a measure of confidence has never yet been a wise gift, and that he stakes wife, children, and grandchildren unscrupulously on the plans submitted to him by a young man, who, even if he does possess some fortune, may yet be sufficiently ill-advised to use up our small amount of money. Buchholz's thalers can be made to fly—they are not leaden. Can he look back on a steady life without any break? But why stir up old stories?—for then Betti would discover that the man whom she loves with all her might, in whom she sees the prince of men, was very near engaging himself to a worthless woman, and then there might be an awful bother. She is quite capable of it. And so one must be as dumb as the Bible on the altar.

Now I certainly had absolutely asserted to the police-lieutenant's wife, in the course of conversation, that I and my Carl would positively go to Switzerland, and the others knew it also, although she had talked more about it than I. Frau Bergfeldt must have heard about it through her, for she said to me the other day, " Good gracious, Frau Buchholz, I thought you were on the top of Mont Blanc, and here you are dancing up the Dorotheen-strasse in person!" And

then Frau Krause, who so pointedly remarked that
one ought only to speak of a journey after it had come
to a happy ending, it was so easy for something to
interfere with it. If she discovered that the journey
was an over-hasty vision, which my husband refused
to make a reality, her delight would be the death of
her; for she snatches at every opportunity for making stupid and unkind remarks, that people like myself
must swallow, because this time there really is a tiny
grain of truth lying at the bottom of them. Such an
old cat as she is !

Perhaps I may succeed in inducing Dr. Wrenzchen
to dissuade my husband from his building fad. Building costs money—a great deal of money ; and as the
Doctor is tolerably eager about his inheritance, he will
probably express his undisguised doubts about em-
ploying capital for its destruction. As the father of
twins, he must have a care that the bit of inheritance
is not squandered ; and then again, it is desirable that
some one should form an opposition against Herr Felix
and my Carl, for if the three men hold fast together,
they will put me aside in skat. I certainly wish for
repose, but I shall not let myself be relegated to the
garret beside the rocking-horse. If I have the Doctor
on my side, Herr Felix will be unable to rebel ; for as
soon as he shows signs of doing so, I will give him
gently to understand that I know something, upon
which he will become amenable. As soon as this point
has been reached, we can easily out-vote my husband:
the building goes overboard, and we go to Switzerland.

The prospect would doubtless have been more
cheerful if my Carl had said Yes at once, instead of
refusing my request, hesitating, and opening hostilities with a stupid wager. If neither means to lose,

there must of necessity be warfare. Switzerland is inevitable, if only on account of the talk there has been about it. I wish to sit in the refreshing shadows cast by the mountains and to breathe Alpine air, instead of climbing over heaps of sand and broken bricks at home, and swallowing the dust from the walls that have been broken through. If I have to call all sorts of intrigues into being in order to attain my end, the fault belongs to my Carl, should my character get spots and excrescences; but for the rest I shall take great care not to lose my wager.

As if men were always right! At the very utmost, just now and then. ·

IN THE "ZOO."

Why everything is forgiven to money—Why my Carl was to search the wide world through—How Natural History gets changed—About the vessel of wrath—And Noah's ark—About rapid atonement and New Years' eves—About clever women and revelling in moonlight.

In former days, when it was still customary to exhibit the sciences in the booths of our annual fairs; civilised man had to dispense with all sorts of conveniences if he wanted to be instructed on the subject of wild beasts, which generally, it is true, dwindled down to some monkeys ; or if a high pitch of excellence was aimed at, it ran to a desert king in a cage— an endeavour to represent the desert being made by strewing some sawdust about, which, however, did not take in the connoisseur. But now one takes a seat on the town railway and goes to the " Zoo," where everything is concentrated ; knowledge, nature, instruction, and refreshments. And then the concert on Tuesdays, with the public moving backwards and forwards to its strains, when the ladies array themselves in spring in the gorgeous apparel that they will wear later on in the watering-places. Those people who do not go to Heringsdorf, may, in the Zoological Gardens, get a taste of the general colouring of the picture that will be on view on the shores of the Baltic.

However, this was not the circumstance that led us thither on this occasion. We were rather urged on by the intention of holding an afternoon family gathering in the place, which was to consist of my Carl and myself, Dr. Wrenzchen and Emmi, who were desirous of enjoying once more a larger allowance of fresh air, Felix and Betti, and Herr Max, with his *fiancée* Frieda, who intended to join us.

Herr Max and his *fiancée* had paid their visits, and also received their invitations. I cannot yet say whether she is the right person for him, for she speaks but little, and behaves rather awkwardly. Indeed, I should be sorry if he has made a mistake, for he is such a nice fellow, and deserves a wife who would be a fitting counterpart for him in every respect; for there can hardly be anything more depressing for a man than to be saddled with a wife who is a lifelong wedded enigma to him, and to have every one who sees her marvelling how such a man could have come by such a wife. Money is an excuse for everything in the present day, but she is said to have as good as nothing.

However, I will not be the person to draw attention to the beam in her eyes, for perhaps she has her estimable qualities incognito. Besides, we did not go to the concert to criticise our fellow-creatures, but to enjoy what was offered to us in an appreciative and gentle spirit.

And even if she does inspire me with much anxiety, I will keep my fingers out of the pie ; for firstly, she is a stranger to me, and secondly, she is far too much my inferior for me to feel the slightest inclination to imperil my journey on her account. Herr Max possessed unclouded eyes when he became ambitious of matrimony ; why, why did he shut them ?

A large concourse of polite society presented itself to our gaze when we arrived, so that there appeared but little prospect of obtaining a table for four couples in a good position ; but Dr. Wrenzchen soon made an arrangement with waiter No. 93, who reserved an excellent place for us ; and as soon as fingers had met over this matter of obligation, we were able to join the general promenade, which extends from the bandstand, past the refreshment-rooms, as far as the vultures. On the other side, there is the lake with the big fountain, and water-fowl on it, which form into picturesque groups.

The pleasure-seekers, immersed in conversations full of courtesies, pass each other in two broad processions. Those who are acquainted greet each other with charming expressions of delight ; while those who are not, devote their attention to each other's costume ; and when one lady does not look just as she ought to look, the observer feels herself quite superior, although she, on her side, does not know by whom she may be surpassed in the very newest novelties. Fashion is not only expensive, but unfathomable, as well.

Betti felt an indescribable pleasure in being able to show herself with her intended among so many people ; and she was quite justified in doing so, for as I sauntered behind them I could easily see what an excellent impression the two made, and how many a one thought to herself, " Ah, if that handsome young man did but belong to me, how proud I should be—how quickly my heart would beat!"

As a matter of fact, Felix did look very attractive. Being possessed of a good figure, his new frock-coat sat as if it had been electro-plated on him, and the cut of the silver-gray trousers was faultless ; besides, there was a white waistcoat and a tall hat of dazzling black, which had scarcely been worn twice. Betti's appearance was not less tasteful. She was simply dressed in a pea-yellow satin, with a small red-brown pattern, and a pointed hat of the same colour, trimmed likewise with red-brown plush and yellow wild flowers. I admit that pride is a weakness, but still I could not refrain from whispering to my husband—

"Carl, are they not ornaments to the human race? You may seek the whole world through, and not meet their equals!"

We could also regard the Doctor and Emmi with a certain amount of pride, when we reflected how many, whose fingers had already pointed towards eternity, had had their plebeian existence restored by means of his prescriptions. Being a University man, and possessing his doctor's degree, he starts by being worth ever so much more than Felix, especially when one reflects on the difficulties that have to be overcome before one attains to being a Councillor of Commerce— a title that is not conferred until it is ascertained that it will be worn with due dignity.

After listening to a portion of the music, and taking a sufficient survey of humanity, I made a proposition to devote a small half-hour to the zoological beasts as well. "Dear son-in-law," I said distinctly, for divers inexpressive physiognomies were looking at us with a certain amount of freedom, "you, being a doctor, will surely know the names to which the animals respond.

I think it would be most interesting for you to explain
to us of what use they are, and in what way they influence us for our instruction." He at once expressed
his readiness to do this, so we went from enclosure to
enclosure, and made reflections on natural history.

The ordinary European has, generally speaking, but
feeble ideas on the subject of animals and their special
qualifications. Many take the form of furs and muffs
after their death, or call branches of industry into
being, as for instance the glove dog ; and others are
really only created that they may be stuffed. I have
always been highly amused when people in the " Zoo "
affect to have had a University education at the very
least, but cover themselves with confusion when the
labels on the rails are turned the wrong way, and
make mistakes in their natural history as regularly as
do people of a normal standard. On such occasions
they do not know whether the cassowary really is
the cassowary, or something similar from the same
country; are brought to an utter standstill when several animals are railed in together, and are not a whit
the wiser when they see an old friend such as a horned
owl.

I admit that the Doctor for the most part gave a
side glance first towards the tablets bearing the animals' names, but I expect it can only have been to see
whether they were in their right places; for what he
knows, he does know.

We saw some young tigers in the house of the car-
nivora, which had been nursed and brought up by a
dog. The Doctor told us that it had been specially
ordered from the Spreewald, and it was not until I remarked that this was a presumptuous proceeding on
the tiger's part, that he laughed, which showed me
that he had been poking his fun at us. I requested

him to stop making such jokes, as they caused science
to be depreciated. However, he merely remarked as
usual, "It is only external, dear mamma-in-law !"

It can be imagined that I declined with thanks a
continuation of reflections which degenerated into the
absurd, and we left the house of the beasts of prey,
my Carl and I in front, then Felix and Betti, followed
by Herr Max and his *fiancée*, the Doctor and Emmi
coming last, who to my vexation were tittering together, and had chosen one of us as the butt of their
mirth. This I could not endure, a mysterious gig-
gling being really too despicable ; and in my just indignation I was on the point of expediting a repri-
mand, albeit addressed to his wife, to my doctor son-
in-law's sense of hearing, when I was prevented doing
so by a person, dressed in some faded-looking summer material, raising his straw hat and greeting us.
It was Herr Kleines *in propria persona*. This piece of
impudence dashed the vessel of wrath, which had been
filled to the brim on the Doctor's account, from my
hand. Herr Kleines behaved as if nothing had ever
happened between us, and he made use of my astonishment to address us, and to question me in especial
about my health. In the first bubbling-up of my
anger, I was on the point of requesting to have the
pleasure of his company at a greater distance ; but I
reflected that we might perhaps require his help at
skat during the winter ; and besides, as our daughters
are in firm hands now, he can do no further damage
within our four walls.

I therefore merely threatened him with my finger,
and said, "You are a nice sort of person!" "How
so ?" he asked, as if he knew nothing about it.—
"Mila, the police-lieutenant's daughter, had to be sent
to a boarding-school in Switzerland on your account,"

I said reproachfully.—"I am delighted if I have been the cause of it," he answered courageously, "for she was sadly in need of the assistance that other young ladies "—he bowed sideways towards where Betti and Emmi were standing—" never have required."

I could not say that his idea was altogether wrong, and so permitted him to join our party. "Did you not feel at all frightened when you saw me again suddenly just now ?" I asked him.—" No," he answered. " When you and your dear ones left the tiger-house a little while back, I was forcibly reminded of Noah's ark."—"Why so ?"—"On account of Shem, Ham, and Japhet," he said slyly. And now I was suddenly enlightened by a whole gasometer. " I don't suppose you mean to insinuate that you take me for a Mrs. Noah ?" I flew at him ; but he played his part seriously, and remarked indignantly: "Excuse me ; I thought that you understood a joke ! "

I was silent, and cast a glance towards our party, which certainly might have attracted attention, owing to the way in which it was made up of couples, although I had just been rejoicing over our numbers. And now Herr Kleines' remark gave rise to the fear that perhaps others had had the same spiteful thoughts about us as he, while we were unsuspectingly walking about.

In such wise may the most mirthful ease be changed into a by no means elevating feeling of undefined wrong-doing by one single relentlessly-dropped word, and therefore I turned over in my mind how we were to reach our reserved table, with avoidance of our double goose-walk. Fate lent us her assistance here as she has often done during my life, but without my feeling that any special thanks were due to her for it, for even the remembrance is not what may be called a pleasure.

The children were anxious to go and see the bears, which have extremely funny attributes for the amusement of young and old, and which are allowed to be fed. So up we clambered to the top of the den, from whence an insight into zoological depths may be obtained, and small morsels be thrown to the bears, which they catch with very droll demeanour. It was pretty full, but we pushed our way through and stood close to the parapet, to see the performance thoroughly.

Herr Felix had brought some cracknels, and Betti was amusing herself by apportioning small pieces to the bears, which she threw down into the water, the clumsy creatures taking the morsels out of it with their paws. While this innocent entertainment was in full swing, Frieda wanted to see something of it too, and endeavoured to squeeze herself in between Felix and Betti. Naturally Felix looked round to see who was pushing in like that, whereupon she knocked him with one of her clumsy elbows, and down tumbled the beautiful new hat into the cage. This was fun indeed for the spectators. I screamed, " The hat—the new hat ! "—which was followed by another outburst of mirth.

Meanwhile the biggest bear dragged himself across to where the hat was lying, sniffed it all round, belaboured it so with its paw, that in an instant the hat was crumpled up into the shape of a concertina. The spectators, so far as they were not composed of our family, were inordinately delighted, for now the bear proceeded to take the hat, stuck one paw inside it, and then surveyed it to see what else he might be able to do with it, and sat down while doing so just like a Christian. Every one's attention was strained to the uttermost. Suddenly a voice exclaimed quite

loud, " He is going to iron it now," and that at the
very moment that the monster rushed at the hat again,
and so to speak split it up into several fractions with
its vile claws. Such shouts of derisive laughter as
followed upon this !—they are still ringing in my ears,
together with the offensive remarks of a plebeian multitude. May I never hear the like. But the fun did
not come to an end until the beast had worried the
brand-new stately beaver into a scandalous mass of
tatters. Herr Felix had to look on bare-headed at the
sacrificial rite, and feel uncomfortably conscious, in
which latter pleasure Betti helped him. She was very
near crying.

But who was the author of the contemptible excla-
mation which had unloosed the mocking jeers of the
multitude ? Need it be said that it was none other
than Herr Kleines, who never considers what he is
doing.

However, on this occasion he may have seen that
his behaviour needed a quick atonement, if he did not
wish to destroy his chances with us for ever and ever ;
therefore he hurried off at once to acquire as a loan a
head-covering from one of the waiters. Herr Max
made excuses for his *fiancée*, and offered his hat to
Felix ; but as Frieda's face exhibited great repug-
nance at this, although she had been the authoress of
the mischief, Felix refused it. She is a silly thing !

It was just like the girl ! Generally speaking, if a
girl is staying with one for a lengthy period, even if
one does not love her, still she becomes bearable, and
one grows callous to her defects ; but one can only get
disaccustomed to this girl. Her face is not ugly, the
colouring is healthy, although complexion is the most
evanescent of marriage gifts. Her figure inclines
pretty much to breadth, but then that is pleasing to

many. But the little bit of beauty and figure fade away, while the disposition remains; and as soon as that is worthless, it is little marvel that marriage should degenerate into discomfort, and the husband feel happiest everywhere, where she is not.

Herr Kleines came bustling up after a while, and he really had fished up a hat; but as might have been expected, it was unusable. When Felix put on this object, which certainly must have been through a hurricane or a New Year's night somewhere or other, he looked a pitiful sight. The rest of his finery was annihilated; he could not let himself be gazed upon by men in such a disfigurement. Betti was furious, but she choked down her wrath, in order that Max's *fiancée* should not notice her weakness.

There was no amusement to be got out of loitering for ever and a day about those generally objectionable bears, which are also quite superfluous in nature, as they only serve to populate the jungles. Could not creation have taken something more civilized instead of wild beasts?

The supper-hour drew near, and so we determined to make a start, although we should have liked it to be rather darker, especially as my Carl was beginning to get hungry. Herr Felix intended trying to reach our table along unnoticed bye-paths, and that rather hatless than in the waiter's helmet, which I am almost inclined to take for a practical joke. I divided the remainder of our party into four retiring companies, so as to get rid of the similarity to the ark, but Betti insisted on remaining with Felix. I said to my Carl, "If she bears an annoyance that has drifted down upon her path so well while she is only a bride elect, she will remain steadfast to her husband in later life, should misfortune overtake him; which God forbid."

—" The right people have come together," answered my Carl, " and that is well." Upon this I wished to express my opinion concerning Max and his flame; but I was dumb, in order not to break my oath and lose my journey to Switzerland.

After the lapse of some time we all met together at our table, and Betti and Felix arrived just as the orchestra was trumpeting the arrival of Lohengrin. She had advised him to hold the old hat at his side, as if he had just taken it off on account of the heat, and it really looked very well. The public had noticed nothing, and the two were immensely pleased with Betti's idea. " I am getting a wise woman for my wife," Herr Schmidt remarked politely.—" Just like her mother," said the Doctor.—" And Betti is not getting a dealer in personalities," I returned his gibe.

Everybody consulted their own taste in looking through the bill of fare. I decided in favour of a tench with dill; * and when I asked, " I suppose, Herr Felix, that you will take a tench too," he chose the same. The Doctor ordered a baked pike, if possible one whose head extended beyond the dish, and endeavoured to convert Felix to his choice likewise; but he did not succeed in stirring up a spirit of rebellion. My husband looked through the bill of fare with constantly growing irresolution, until at last I asked him, " Well, what are you thinking of, my Carl ? A fowl with cucumber salad, and a well-ripened Harzer † to follow, I suppose!"—and that really was what he had been thinking of.

The rest of us had finished long before Herr Max's

* A herb much used in Berlin cookery for purposes of flavouring. —TRANS.

† A cheese manufactured in the Hartz Mountains.—TRANS.

fiancée stopped picking about on her plate, as if the food was not good enough for her; and then she sprawled in such an unmannerly fashion over the table, and spoke never a word! Neither did Herr Max say anything, but there was a reason for that—he was ashamed of the chosen one of his heart, and grief and vexation gnawed away the words from his tongue; but Frieda took it quite coolly. I fear that it will not come to a happy end.

As we intended taking a little turn in the Park in the enchanting moonlight, we had meanwhile left the table. When Herr Max rose, I saw that he had come to some resolution. He was trembling with excitement, and his voice sounded as if his throat were parched, when he said with forced quiet, "Felix, give me the old hat and take mine instead."—"I beg that you won't make an exhibition of yourself!" screamed his *fiancée.* —He only exclaimed, "Frieda!" but there was something in the way he said it, and she held her tongue.— "Many thanks, my boy," answered Felix; "but don't make troubles for yourself on my account. One may go through the country hat in hand, and the Park as well."

As we were dawdling along the shady side-walks and revelling in the moonlight that seemed to dot the paths and trees with whitewash, I said to my husband, "How can he misunderstand his gifts so utterly and engage himself to such a girl?"

My Carl was silent.

"There will be a tragedy there," I recommenced after a pause; "the best that could be done would be to kill her at once."—"Who?" asked my Carl.—"Frieda," I answered testily; "who else should it be?"— "Are you troubled concerning Herr Max's future?"— "Yes, that I am."—"Very glad to hear it," retorted

my Carl ; "according to my calculations, your journey
will come to nothing."

I was silent from this moment.

A LADIES' COFFEE-PARTY.

About worn-out wheels and boasting—Why life is full of debts and
Frau Krause does not sit on the sofa—About gymnastics, music,
and the picture of Sais—Why experiences are interesting and
Augusta rushes to the rescue—About universal plaster, counts
and barons—About social niceties and pasted-up clocks—Loving
judgments.

IT is years since I have left off getting enthusiastic
about single-row parties. I mean those where only one
sort of human beings meet each other, either only
ladies or only gentlemen. And why so? They all of
them amount to the same thing. And how soon one
comes to an end of one's subjects if quarrels are to be
avoided !—though indeed these are fairly inevitable if
Frau Bergfeldt is to be found in the same circle, or
any one akin to her, such as Frau Beckmann. First
of all they ask about my recipe for cooking carp in
beer, and after I have explained it exhaustively to
them, one or the other grumbles on the next occasion
that after all her husband prefers them as they have
always been served, and that the children did not care
about them either. Disagreeable little brats !

And what was the reason for it ?

Why, naturally, that she listened with both ears
while I was telling her about the laurel-leaves and
peppercorns, and with a lazy effort of memory took
both hands full of them afterwards. If one tells her
that she must have seasoned it much too highly, she

insists that she had not put in a mite more than she had béen told ; upon this I convict her of a mistake, which she in turn disputes ; and so retort follows upon reply, until the grandest discord is reached. Any one possessing knowledge of the world will agree with me herein ; and whosoever sucks reason from life as the bee sucks honey even from such flowers as really do not possess any, will give up at last trying to convince other people.

Therefore the invitation to a coffee-party with which Frau Bergfeldt had honoured me, was not likely to cause me much pleasure in anticipation, and I would gladly have given it up, had my Carl not lent it a helping hand. "Wilhelmine," he explained to me, "you may perhaps hurt her more by your refusal than you think. It is unfortunately true that the Bergfeldts have gone back in the world, since they have had to make shift to live on his wretched pension, given after his superiors recognised in the old man, a played-out wheel of the bureaucratic machine, out of which no amount of repairs could wrest further use. Will you make their downtrodden position more palpable to them by your neglect? Will she not be forced to interpret your absence as an intentional rupture, by which you intend giving her to understand—You are not good enough for me, now that you have less to live upon than formerly ?"

"Carl," I interrupted him, "what Frau Bergfeldt assumes is certain not to coincide with nature, therefore it may be all one to me."

"But supposing she hits the right nail on the head this time, and says, Herr Buchholz has been doing a good business, and his wife has set herself up on the strength of it. I should not have thought her so stupid ?"

"Carl !"

He passed his hand over my forehead, as if he wished carefully to brush away some dust, and looked kindly into my eyes. "Pride and stupidity grow on the same tree," he said.—"I know people of whom that may be said," I answered. "What but pride has been the ruin of the Bergfeldts? And the branch upon which this fruit flourishes, is she, the wife. No factory chimney was too high for her—she wanted to soar above them all. Did she cast a glance towards us at the time that she thought her Emil was going to make her mother-in-law to a millionaire? No. Were we invited to the wedding? No. Did she make one step towards us so long as her boasted parade had not come to a terrible end? No."—"But when you were in trouble owing to the law proceedings, she visited you with all her old cordiality."

"Carl, do you call it cordiality if a person glues herself to you, and terrifies you with the gallows and the wheel?—that too when I was as innocent as could be,- and the whole thing nothing but a vile proceeding on the cook's part."

"But she meant it well."

"And therefore I went to see her again with all due propriety; but I will not encourage her boastfulness by my presence. As it is, she has barely room to move in. The front rooms are let, and the back* room in which she and her old husband fiddle-faddle about is no suitable place for society, even when it only consists of a small addition. Where then is she to spread out her coffee feast?"

"I see that you mean to be obstinate," said my Carl, crossly, "and so you must just do as you please; but

* "Berliner Zimmer" (back room) is a room running along and borrowing its light from the passage; commonly used as bed- or dining-room.—TRANS.

remember that you will grieve Augusta too, who pro-
vides for her parents, so far as in her lies, with such
touching affection."

I reflected for a little, and then yielded the point.
" Well then, for Augusta's sake I will plunge into the
mess of chicory ; but I shall only stay for one short
hour at the very outside, according to the ways of polite society, which consist in leaving early."

" You can arrange that as you like," said my Carl ;
"the principal thing is that you should not embitter a
small pleasure to those whose life has become very
poor in pleasures."—"Is that my fault? Oh, no ; but
they——"

My husband cut short my sentence with the door,
and had left the room before I was able to refresh his
memory about bygone days.

By paying ten pfennigs and taking the town train
from the Alexander-platz to the station in the Fried-
richs-strasse, one single bend round the corner will
lead you directly into the Dorotheen-strasse, where
the Bergfeldts have settled down in the fourth story,
because that is a good locality for letting, although
the young folk frequently change, and move out with
their trunks as easily as they move in. Frau Bergfeldt
told me that a new lodger frequently came in before
she had cleared away the ashes of the last man's tobacco ; but then too the room often stood empty, and
when that happened she had to try and drag something more out of the next-comer, for life is short and
full of debts.

And now, instead of stinting, she must make her
calculations to give a coffee-party, so that one has the
feeling of working towards the enlargement of the
family deficit with every mouthful, and this causes
the intended feast to result in smiling offering and

pressing, and just as smiling thanking and declining, and to make one heartily praise one's Creator when the mutual hypocrisy comes to an end. But my husband wished it, and I submitted. It is just the same to men whether women suffer or not ; they are wanting in our more delicate organisation !

I arrived with a considerable amount of distaste, and with apprehensions which were quite justified by former behaviour ; but on her side Frau Bergfeldt received me with a wealth of affection to which she seemed to have habituated herself, especially for this day. She greeted me with a tender embrace which would have degenerated into a kiss of welcome had I possessed less powerful arms to ward off all who approached me too nearly.

The back room had been turned into a ladies' room, the beds serving as receptacles for bonnets and cloaks while the society assembled in the best room, where her best things were kept, and which was let with the dressing-room. "Well," I thought, "if it just happens to be free, it may as well be used," and I entered.

The remaining ladies who had been invited were already present, and the accommodation for sitting, with the exception of a sofa-corner specially reserved for me, had all been laid claim to. Everybody spoke to every one else, and was introduced. Most of the people were known to me, as Frau Krause, Frau Beckmann, Frau Helbich, but I now made the acquaintance of Frau Schüler and Frau Stahl. Frau Stahl sat in the other sofa-corner, and was the owner of the house, so that she and I occupied, so to speak, the places of honour, a fact that stuck in Frau Krause's throat; for, first of all, her usual smiling society face was puckered into very ill-tempered looking wrinkles, and secondly, she repeated several times,

without any one wishing to know it, "No, I dislike
sitting on the sofa ; I am glad to resign that honour
to my elders and betters."

As if she had reason to pride herself on her youth-
fulness ! Why, judging from her attenuated appearance, it is by no means impossible that Schliemann
excavated her certificate of baptism at Troy, near
where Priam's was found, on the third door to the left.
If a person behaves like that to me, I behave the same
to her !

Giving her the benefit of my back, I addressed myself to Frau Stahl, and asked her if she had had spring
cabbages already.—"They are still too dear for me,"
she grumbled. "I cannot afford sixty pfennigs for a
bushel, with husband, four children, and a serving
girl."—"We only pay five groschen for them in the
market on the Alexander-platz."—"Everything is a bit
dearer with us here in the Dorotheen-strasse," she
groaned; "though most things ought to be cheaper
now in these hard times. Duties and taxes become
larger every year. They calculate to the last groschen
what we householders have, and when rents are not
duly paid up we come to grief."—"Are you satisfied
with your tenants ?" I questioned, in order to discover
exactly how matters stood with the Bergfeldts ; for
people who have something to get are pitilessly communicative.

To my astonishment she did not complain, but informed me with great satisfaction that Frau Bergfeldt
had always brought the money before nine o'clock in
the morning. Therefore she was on very good terms
with her, and allowed her to have musical instruments
in her rooms without raising the rent—a thing that
she did not generally permit in her house, as those
who practised usually drove away the other inmates ;

and indeed, if they all began making a noise on them, she would be forced to look out for a dwelling for herself under one of the railway arches. Too much music gave her neuralgia. "People played in my younger days, too," she said; "but nowadays they thump more furiously than ever." ;

"It must be the result of gymnastic exercises," remarked Frau Beckmann; "that strengthens their muscles so much."

"I allow no one to bring a violin into the house,' continued Frau Stahl; "it sounds as if they were sawing one's bones. Violin-players may go to Weissensee and scrape a measure for the tadpoles; and as for singers, who clear their throats in the early morning with a shake, I simply drive them away."

The communication about the Bergfeldts' pecuniary circumstances tranquillised me somewhat, and had a favourable effect on the coffee that was now being offered to us, which would, however, have been better if she had not made it quite so strong. As for myself, I was obliged to ask for some hot water to add to it.

She had also used the good cups which dated from former years, and had preserved their gilding astonishingly. The coffee-pot had been broken on some previous occasion, for which reason the pouring-out had been done in the kitchen, and she brought the tray in with full cups upon it. In addition to the pound-cake, there were sponge-cakes, crisp pastry, and apricot-jam on small glass dishes, which I at once recognised as belonging to Augusta.

"And where is Frau Weigelt?" I asked.—"My daughter is coming directly," answered Frau Bergfeldt quickly, "as soon as she has attended to the kitchen."—I knew enough now. Augusta, who let herself be attended upon hand and foot and run after

by her mother during her objectionable bread-and-
butter days, now took the work off her shoulders with
devoted willingness, strained the coffee and washed
the cups, while old Herr Bergfeldt was pottering about
her in the kitchen. Indeed, they could not have hidden him anywhere else, for we did not discover him
behind the bed-screen when we were taking off our
things in the back room.

While I was still considering how sadly the old man
was situated, and how difficult it would be to turn the
conversation upon him without destroying the very
communicative disposition which now prevailed, Frau
Krause asked loudly, " I say, Frau Bergfeldt, is there
any truth in what folks are telling each other, that
your husband has to go to the hospital, to the third
court, where the incurables are ? "

The angel that now suddenly passed through the
room was no common one. Frau Helbich looked as
if a hailstone had shot down immediately beside her,
and the fright caused my hand, in which was a tea-
spoon full of preserve, to remain stretched out like the
petrified image of Sais. Wrath caused Frau Stahl to
assume a perpendicular position, and say, with a look
of rebuke directed towards Frau Krause, " Goodness
gracious, what a question ! "—Upon this Frau Schüler
remarked, " And what is the old gentleman doing ? "
Frau Beckmann got a fit of the hiccoughs, the angel
withdrew slowly, and conversation once more resumed
its course, though only in driblets.

As Frau Bergfeldt did not make up her mind at
once how best she could serve Frau Krause out, I undertook the office of retribution, and said, " You have
made a most ridiculous mistake, my dear ; Herr Bergfeldt has improved immensely since last winter, so no
doubt you will wish to withdraw your remark about

the incurables. Providence often works in a marvellous way, and can make him quite strong and hearty again in a short time."—"Providence is merely a figure of speech," she retorted; for her husband, being a master and enlightened to the last degree, a reflection of his glory falls upon her.—"Indeed?" I questioned; but this "indeed" was written in capital letters. "If Providence had not possessed sufficient insight to devote its attention to the lake at Tegel some years ago, I wonder what would have happened then? But people have tact, and do not discuss the question."—"He-he!" Frau Krause gave a short snappish laugh, but she had difficulty in smiling her parched lips away from the teeth that were pressed against them. "He-he! There is not a word of truth in it!"—and glaring at me like a viper gnashing its teeth in its wrath, she continued with ill-timed scorn: "Frau Buchholz gets more and more peculiar. For years she has been imagining something utterly incomprehensible to me, that is supposed to have happened at Tegel; and being unsuccessful in her imaginings, she now calls Providence to the rescue. Who is there that still believes in Providence in the present advanced age, which has provided us with steam trams, telephones, and the electric lighting of the Leipziger-strasse?"

Before I could level a well-directed ace of trumps against her persuasive eloquence, Frau Beckmann interposed and delivered herself as follows: "I am against it too—I mean as touching Providence; for I don't suppose that any one will dispute what I have experienced myself." We all held our tongues and turned our heads attentively in the direction of Frau Beckmann, in order not to lose a syllable of her experiences, for they are always the most interesting things to listen to, though they are mostly only a tissue of inventions; and on this occasion we were obliged to listen more carefully than ever, as hiccoughs interposed continual commas in her speech.

Meanwhile Frau Helbich had recovered, and began to put in her word against Frau Krause and Frau Beckmann. "I have experienced Providence too," she exclaimed bravely, "just as well as other people, and I say that there is one." Absolute excitement sent water to her eyes, and her little podgy body quivered with inward·indignation. "Don't—excite yourselves," hiccoughed Frau Beckmann. "What I am about to tell you, happened—to the very letter. When, some two years ago,—or it may perhaps be three,—we wanted to go one Sunday to Steglitz, an unforeseen impediment hindered our doing so. I cannot remember whether visitors came to us, or whether we were unexpectedly invited by friends—enough, a——"

"You really should do something to stop the hiccoughs," I interrupted her, for her everlasting commas were abominably trying. "It is a capital remedy to eat three morsels of bread slowly, or to hold a sharp knife against you."—"It is all-but gone," she answered.

Frau Schüler, who is an intimate friend of Frau Beckmann (nothing very refined, and makes sad work of her vowels and consonants), got up suddenly, and taking a sharp grip of Frau Beckmann's shoulders from behind, she shrieked in an awful voice, "Fire!"

Frau Beckmann flew up from her chair and screamed, the rest of us jumped up too, and were not behindhand with our shrieks, each one being paler than the other with terror-stricken surprise. Augusta, too, who had remained on the other side of the door till now, rushed in in a fright, and asked: "Good heavens! what is the matter?"—"Nothing!" answered Frau

Schüler; "Frau Beckmann had a fit of the hiccoughs, and so I just gave her a bit of a fright. Is it gone now?"—"As completely as if it had been blown away," said Frau Beckmann. "A thorough fright is always effectual."

We gradually recovered, and were able to give a smiling opinion on what had happened. Augusta, who was aware that we required something to strengthen us, fetched some bitters which Frau Bergfeldt had concocted herself, and which are said to be a very good stomachic, from the cupboard; but after tasting it, I arrived at the following decision : Rather an hour's suffering than another drop of that. It appeared to be methyllated spirit distilled from some poisonous trash from the druggist. And she is able to stand it !

"What really did happen about Providence?" asked Frau Stahl during a pause in the conversation.—"You shall hear all about it," Frau Beckmann recommenced, "one thing after the other, just as it happened to me." —Augusta whispered a few words to her mother, who cast a glance towards the clock and shook her head, upon which it became clear to me that there must be something below the surface. Had I only known what it was, I would have made a move to break up the party; but as Frau Bergfeldt did not explain herself, I let Frau Beckmann twaddle on, as we were curious to know how Providence had behaved itself.

"I must tell you that we did not go to Steglitz, and it was a real stroke of good luck; for the next day we read in our papers, that the train had gone over ever so many people, and that several had been killed. Had we been on the spot we should certainly have come back home as dead corpses."

"Now do you see," I exclaimed triumphantly, "who else but Providence protected and cared for you?"

"I said just the same," retorted Frau Beckmann, "and was positively certain of it. But just imagine, three days later I fell backwards down the cellar steps with a full bucket of ashes, and dislocated my right shoulder. What was Providence about then? I was laid by with it for a fortnight, and even now I can hardly raise my arm to do my hair."

"You should have got a groschen's-worth each of lard and oil of St. John's wort," said Frau Stahl. "It did an acquaintance of mine an immense amount of good, and she recommended it strongly to me."—"For a dislocated shoulder too?"—"No; her trouble was more in her leg—something of rheumatism, I believe; she called it *hiskias.* But the remedy has been useful to many; you simply rub it in with a woollen rag, and fasten wadding over it to keep it warm."—"But allow me," I interposed. "Dislocations and bruises ought not to be kept warm; on the contrary, they have to be kept cool with ice or lead lotion."—"I know nothing about that," answered Frau Stahl; "but so much is certain, a groschen's-worth each of lard and oil of St. John's wort is the thing."—"We always use spirits of ants," remarked Frau Helbich; "it softens the body and disperses the blood from the veins."

"Universal plaster disperses too, and draws as well," said Frau Schüler. "Frau Beckmann might have saved herself doctor and apothecary had she followed my advice. There was a little girl in our neighbourhood with a horribly bad finger, and as the doctor said that he would have to use the knife, her parents did not let her go to him. Who wants to be cured by being made a cripple? So accident brought her to me, and as soon as I looked at tne nnger ı saw that it had festered to the bone. 'Good gracious, child,' I said, 'why did you not put on universal plas-

ter at once?' Well, I gave her some, and it really and
truly would have cured her, if the doctor had not insisted on taking off half the finger. I have had that
plaster in my house for ten years, and never once required a doctor. They are as ignorant as any one in
such matters."

I was angered by this woman's uplifting of herself
above the medical profession, to which my son-in-law
belongs, and by which he must live; I therefore permitted myself the question : "Do you use the plaster
internally when you are ill ?"—"It draws all unwholesomeness to the surface," she answered, undismayed.
"There was a woman in our neighbourhood who had
four doctors to see her——"—"Oh, I know that story !"
exclaimed Frau Stahl; "so will the ladies kindly excuse me for a moment?—I just want to see whether
the girl is doing her work or looking out of the window. As soon as ever one's back is turned, they do
nothing but idle, and then demand wages high enough
to ruin us."

She had scarcely gone out of hearing before she was
pulled to pieces. "I shouldn't like to be her servant,"
said Frau Beckmann; "she has a fresh one every fortnight."—"She is in bad odour in every registry office."
—"The servant is not even allowed time to sew for
herself."—"And the food ! Why, she gives her the
water she rinses out the pots with, instead of the fat."—
"If one could thrive on scoldings, her servant would
have been fattened long ago."—"You ought to see her
in a rage ! I can tell you that green fire flashes from
her eyes."—"Is she any different towards her husband ?"—"Only since the house has been entered in
her name."—"And what a fuss she makes about her
daughter ! She says that she might mix with counts
and barons."—"I suppose she means with their photo-

graphs."—"There is nothing whatever in the daughter."—"Torn under-clothing trimmed with lace."—"No one who knew her would have her."—Oh, goodness me, what did not the ladies know about Frau Stahl !

My original intention had·been to break up the party with a courteous leave-taking immediately after Frau Stahl's departure ; but when I saw how absent friends were set upon, I determined straightway to remain to the very last, in order not to get my share of abuse. Rather let me be guilty of a breach of social refinement than be so hacked to pieces. Besides, according to the clock it was only five. But I do wish that I had gone. Augusta took no part in the conversation, which was clearly objectionable to her. I therefore asked quite loudly, " How are matters going on at home, Augusta ? how are the little ones? why did you not bring them with you ?"—" They are within there," she answered hesitatingly.—"And won't you let us see them ? Do bring them in, Augusta."—" I am afraid of their touching the things ; this room is let."—" But the gentleman will not be in before tea," said the old lady gently : " we shall not be disturbed."

Augusta let herself be persuaded, and brought the children in, their entrance being a happy signal for the gossip about Frau Stahl to cease. Franz is a splendid boy, obedient and modest ; little Käthe, the second, a pretty girl ; but the third, on the contrary, is a mere atom of a child, weak and puny as if it had as many cares already as grown-up people. The little ones were given cakes and preserves, and a little bit of pastry from the confectioner's. I find it very hard to say No when I see imploring children's eyes, and know that their heart is set upon it. But when naughtiness, overeating, and kicking are shown, I come with the stick—that is to say, figuratively. Correction need not be applied at once, if only there is no giving in.

As, according to Augusta, the youngest child was very fond of music, and there was a new cottage piano in the room, a suggestion was made to strum a few bars, but none of us were sufficient *virtuosos* to do so until Frau Stahl returned, who remembered a thunder-and-lightning waltz from the days of her youth, and settled herself down to the instrument : first she rumbled a bit with the left hand in the bass to produce the thunder, and then performed delicately on the high notes at the other end : dum, dum, dum, dumdidi, dumdidi, dum di ; very sweet.

Pleasure brought a real colour into the child's cheeks, and Frau Stahl was greatly commended, as if nothing but pleasant remarks about her had been spun together during her absence. This flattered her ; and as she could not get through a second piece, and Frau Bergfeldt stupefied her afresh with her stomachic bitters, she repeated the same waltz until she became unconscious of what she was playing, and found that the instrument had a very charming touch.

We other ladies fell once more into an animated conversation ; the children too felt more at home, began to rush about pretty vivaciously, and to touch the piano. Augusta alone became more disturbed from moment to moment. "Child, what is the matter with you ?" I asked her privately.—"It must surely be later than ten minutes to five," she said fearfully. I cast a careful glance towards the time-piece on the console table, and sure enough, the glass covering was broken, and the crack pasted over with a strip of paper that Frau Bergfeldt must have got the post-office official to include when she was buying a post-card. Im-

mediately behind the strip the hands remained point-
ing to ten minutes to five. To paste up clocks and
leave them unwound is as thoroughly Bergfeldtian as
anything could be.

"The clock has stopped," I said quietly, as if it were
a matter of everyday occurrence.—"How late is it,
then?"—I looked at my watch: "Half-past seven."
Augusta gave a start.—"Already!" she exclaimed,
and went to her mother, to whom she again whispered something, more urgently than before. "Nonsense!" said Frau Bergfeldt aloud; "he would have
been here already in that case."

But the explanation came before I had really com-
prehended what the matter under discussion was.
What with the noise the children were making, the
conversation, and the thunder-and-lightning waltzes,
no one had heard how somebody had opened the door
into the vestibule, which somebody was the gentleman
to whom Frau Bergfeldt had let the room in which we
were holding our session; and when this gentleman
suddenly tore open the door and remained standing
as if he had made a mistake, the consternation on
both sides was about equal.

"Pray excuse my taking the liberty of taking possession of my room," said the gentleman sarcastically.
We were quite dumbfounded. "I hope the ladies
have no objection to my wishing to be alone!" While
saying this he bowed with perfectly cool amiability,
and pointed with his hands towards the door.—"Let
us be off," hissed Frau Beckmann. What came to
pass now was a bowing out of the room *en masse*.
Frau Bergfeldt wanted to begin a scolding match, as
if she were absolutely in the right, but the gentleman
merely said, "Excuse me!"

We had to march past him as the vanquished ones,

a circumstance that was attended by very humiliating feelings. Each of us carried off something—cups, tray, glass dishes, cakes. Augusta drew the children away, and before you could turn round the place was vacated.

Frau Stahl remarked that she never had turned her heart into a marl-pit, but she must acknowledge that she had never met such an ill-bred person in the whole course of her life. This was when we had established ourselves in the back room. Frau Schüler thought him impertinent. Frau Beckmann said, "Why did the fellow come back so early? It was extremely rude of him." Frau Krause said that the young man was a churl. But that was because he had looked scoffingly at her while she carried off the coffee.

While we were holding forth against him, he rang his bell. We all jumped, and were as quiet as mice.

"What can he want?" asked Frau Bergfeldt; "I am not going in."

There was a knock. "Come in!" The gentleman ordered politely: "Would you have the kindness to wipe the keyboard of my instrument with a damp cloth? It is so sticky that I cannot play upon it." Augusta followed him.

"Was such vulgarity ever met with before!" exclaimed Frau Stahl. "To be a householder, and have to put up with such insolence!"—"I should find a way of giving it back to him," instigated Frau Beckmann.

When Augusta returned, she said: "Mamma, if you had asked the gentleman, he would willingly have placed the room at your disposal for the afternoon; now he is angry at your having behaved so independently, and gives notice to leave on the first. And you know how difficult it is to let the room in summer."

"He may go at once, as far as I am concerned,"

answered the old lady.—"You can get people like that at the rate of ten a day," Frau Stahl seconded her.— "He always pays regularly on the first," Augusta suggested. "Mamma has lost enough by doubtful gentlemen."

"I should speak to him," I remarked.—"I will do so at once," exclaimed Augusta, and went bravely across.

Her doing so pleased me extremely. What would become of the whole family without Augusta?

After a while Augusta returned. "He will stop," she said; "but he expects mamma to give him a promise not to give any more parties in his room." Frau Bergfeldt grumbled a few objections, but seemed satisfied all the same.

I had had quite enough of it. Frau Helbich left with me, and on the way we talked about what had happened. She too acknowledged Augusta's worth. "Life educates many people," she said, "if they refuse to accept instruction in their youth."—"Unfortunately, good guidance is wanting to many," I returned.

We parted. I returned by train, and was glad to find myself in the Landsberger-strasse.

"Well, what was it like?" asked my husband.

"Carl, as it always is at the Bergfeldts. You will not worry me to a ladies' coffee-party there again. They are not up to our level."

FRIEND MAX.

Hemlock used by mistake—Why the doctor is in the wrong box,
and Herr Buchholz chops wood—About virgin lilies and secrets
in letters—Frau Schulz appears and Wilhelmine sprinkles gentleness—Why Max is of age and Venus like the end of a cigar
—Why nobody can live without love and Max gets blamed—
Why further consideration is necessary.

IF it has hitherto been a mystery to me how thinkers
find time to arrive at subjects difficult of comprehension, I know all about it now as accurately as if I had
been doing nothing but the same work all my life
long : they make use of sleepless nights for this purpose. No cow's hide could contain all the things that
may be thought out in a single one, and had it not
been Frau Bergfeldt who once—of course, when it
was utterly out of place—expressed herself to the
effect that, "Thinking makes one stupid," I should be
almost inclined to agree with her; for after one such
night of thought one's head seems to be filled to the
brim with all things incomprehensible. But Frau
Bergfeldt may talk for a long time before anything
she says pleases me.

For to whom were thanks due for this sleeplessness
but to her? If she possesses a stomach impervious
to fire, she surely need not imagine that the stuff concocted by herself would be good for others, and it is
only to avoid making a sensation that I do not send
for the doctor. If he discovered at once that I had
been poisoned by her ignorant use of hemlock, or
whatever else she may have put in by mistake, he
would be forced to give notice of it, and the Court
would get hold both of her and her bottle. But I
should object to such harsh measures, for what would

become of the gentleman meanwhile, if she were shut
up for three weeks, or a fortnight at the very least?
Less than that would be contemptible.

What would become of the old man, with his brittle bones?

And supposing he died, what would become of her,
Frau Bergfeldt? She would be sure not to get on
with her gentleman lodgers for a continuance. Then
she would be a burden to Augusta.

Her I value more and more. What Herr Weigelt
may want in energy, she makes up for by having her
head put the right way on her shoulders. They will
all get the benefit of that later—her husband, the
children, old Herr Bergfeldt and her mother; although the latter never tires of rubbing destiny the
wrong way and so courting failure.

To what could the fevered state of my blood, my
beating heart, the difficulty I found in breathing, be
ascribed, if not to her coffee mixture, which ought to
be avoided, as there is peat amongst it? The doctor
said that there was a tendency to asthma whenever
hurry reduced me to a state of breathlessness; but
like many another doctor, he has got on the wrong
track. It is from nothing in the world but Frau Bergfeldt's hospitality.

Some of the ladies absolutely allowed themselves to
be persuaded to take several glasses of Rachenputzer.*
They must either have been born impervious to its influence, or else they have gradually grown so accustomed to it that it can do them no more harm.

Merciful Heavens! Supposing my husband had had
a wife like Frau Beckmann or Frau Schüler! How
awful! How they would have embittered his life for
him! Both would have been equally disagreeable,

* A sort of sour wine.

powerless to appreciate his worth, the soup would have been unpalatable—over-salted water, with lumps of grease floating about in it—the vegetables without flavour or relish, and always prepared with mutton fat—a thing he can't abide. What would he not have had to endure! How he would have longed to get away from it all, and sighed for the advent of the noseless man who was to envelop him in the wooden dressing-gown and carry him away from all his misery!

This thought aroused such grief and misgivings within me, that I did not know what to do with myself. I should have liked a good cry best of all; but dared I give way to that? Was my Carl not sleeping as splendidly as if a good conscience *in propria persona* were in the bed beside him?

And how he did snore! It was not a mere simple grunt, but an intermittent snore of fibrous nature. Usually my habit was to call out, " Carl, Carl, stop snoring! Others have paid their money as well as you. Do you hear me, Carl? It is impossible for me to close my eyes. Carl, am I to get cross in earnest?" After this he was generally quiet long enough for me to slip off to sleep, or if he woke up more thoroughly, he denied his misdeeds *in toto*, which resulted in mutual hilarity and interchange of reproaches.

No, I could not be a woman like Frau Stahl or Frau Krause, whose husbands positively miss something if they are not kept in continual abject terror. I lay there patiently, and hoped that from moment to moment he might turn in bed, and give up the wood-splitting business.

But it was all in vain. He was so tired that he was in a dead sleep.

Therefore I had the most splendid leisure foi

thought, and who else could I think about but Frau Bergfeldt?

Before her marriage she understood the art of hiding her disagreeable qualities behind the mask of a most amiable exterior; but since her wedding placed a household at her command, she has perfected herself in unsupportability. Thus she has spoiled her husband's life for him.

Whatever he did, she found wrong; and if he had done what she preached at him, it would have been absolutely certain to be all wrong. She expended the least of her pains on him, and by her keeping him regardlessly in the background the remains of his youth became mildewed.

Of what avail was it that he worked overtime? They got on none the better. His salary was never sufficient; and by the time that he thought he had plugged up a hole, she had torn open a fresh one; constant in borrowing and unceasing in squandering, as the saying is. Then there were the daily trivial quarrels which fed on him like a canker; and when his pride, his Emil, on whom all their hopes were set, came to his sudden end, his measure was full. Then the old man began to break up by slow degrees. It was first noticed at the office in his writing, in which he put small letters where he used to use capitals, and no admonitions could break him of the habit. Then while speaking he could not recall certain words, or if he did they were wrong ones. They began by finding it very funny; but when the doctor explained that it was a symptom of incurable disease, they did not laugh at him any more.

Augusta feared the worst at once, nor did she dissemble her trouble from her mother; but she thought it would yield to treatment—that the old man must be held in more tightly. She carried out that idea too. Now he is bereft of will, and such a sad sight ! And yet he was once young and lusty like my Carl !

They were good friends too, just as Herr Felix and Herr Max are nowadays.

My Carl now made a pause for vespers in his sawing ; but it was quite useless, for the thought of Max sent the fever flying through me. Is not Frieda a horribly life-like image of Frau Bergfeldt in the days of her youth ? No, she is still worse ; for even as *fiancée* she heaps disagreeables upon him.

I can see a little further than just in front of my nose, and what I see is likewise a life full of disappointments, full of inward grief, vexation, and bitterness, until he too will have had enough at last, and wish that this vale of tears might come to an end.

Those two must be parted.

But supposing I say to him, " You have not found the right correspondence in your life's time-table," and he breaks with her ; what will then become of the girl ?

For it is possible that she loves him according to her fashion, knowing no better, and then I shall be the cause of her unhappiness.

A young man is sure to find an opportunity of getting another bride, but a has-been-*fiancée* is in sad case. She may be as innocent as a virgin lily, and yet suppositions will be rife among the circle of her acquaintances ; and the more presentable a wooer may be, the more they malign her, and interfere and gossip and hurry and worry them, until at last he withdraws to the place whence he came, and no one wipes the stain off her. Her heart may break, and no one will see it. She may sob out her grief to her pillow ; no one will hear it. And should they perchance become aware of it, no one will confess to it.

My poor Max, I cannot help you ; I cannot, I cannot.
The girl has her right to happiness and a future as
well as you.

But is he not in the same case as the boy who wants
to cross over a frozen river, in the middle of which a
tiny rivulet is still glistening, where the ice has only
just been formed, and is as thin and brittle as glass ?
Now he is leaving the bank, the ice bears, and he has-
tens merrily forward, sliding and slipping on his way,
on towards the middle. The people on the bridge
shout and gesticulate. What do they want ?—the ice
is quite safe. He goes on, not seeing the open water,
on in glad security. Then one single loud shout from
those upon the bridge. A piece of ice has loosened
and floats on the water. How did the ice give ? who
knows that ? Each one who is forced to look on, help-
lessly closes his eyes.

In the morning I was sore all over. If any one has
ever got up very late with his brain all in a whirl, he
can have a conception of what I felt. But only a feeble one.

While I was in this frame of mind Herr Felix
Schmidt came across from the office with a letter
which had been delivered there. Although it had my
address upon it, written in the most legible of hands,
it had already been torn open at the top—a thing for
which Herr Schmidt excused himself, on the plea of
business zeal.

"Herr Schmidt," I said jestingly, but with an under-
current of reproach, " the inviolability of a letter is a
very sacred thing, and I think I might become unpleasant if anybody took to sniffing through my correspondence with a view to satisfying his curiosity.
The reason that I write so rarely, is, that I do not like
people to leave my letters lying carelessly about for

the benefit of the young women when they are sweeping out the room of a morning."

He regretted having been so thoughtless, and promised to look at the address more carefully in future.
Had this occurred with my son-in-law the Doctor, he
would have asked what all the fuss was about, as if
my letters were of no importance, or something of
that description. But Herr Felix does not permit
himself such liberties, because I know his former
course of life, and he may well fear that reproaches
would be showered down on him if he contradicted
me. It never occurs to me to speak about it, for all
that is forgiven is forgotten as well; still it is extremely agreeable to a mother-in-law's feelings to
know that she holds her daughter's husband, so to
speak, by an invisible thread.

However, he had to listen to my story that Max had
entered into an unwise engagement, which he might
better have done a thousand years hence. He answered that Max's fate lay very near his heart, but
that the time for altering it had gone by. Max had
entered into an engagement with the girl, and would
certainly marry her. He was given to keep his word.

" You are his friend ; can you not advise him and
help him ?" I asked.

" Max would rather come to grief than behave dis-
honourably. He is true as gold—I have made trial of
it—and as honourable as he is true ; that is the reason
of our friendship, which is as close as if we were real
brothers. He would rather endure to the bitter end
than blush for shame at having betrayed the confi·
dence of a girl."

"It would have been no harm if you had exercised
a more wholesome influence over your friend. However, that remains between ourselves."

He might put that into his pipe and smoke it.

Felix took his leave with a few words. As soon as he had gone, I opened the letter.

The beginning was remarkable : "You have never heard about me, but I have heard of you. Do you know that it is your belauded humanity alone that makes me venture to address these lines to you ? You only amongst hundreds of thousands are the one single person."—"What can be the meaning of this ?" I questioned, and looked at the signature, "Therese Schulz, *née* Western," I read. And the letter came from Zehlendorf.

I discovered by degrees, while continuing to read it, that she had a daughter Edith, whom she wished to place under my care for the purpose of further education, giving in return payment of expenses and her eternal gratitude. Further, she buttered me with such an amount of praise that I really felt embarrassed. The letter ended thus : "Will you not accede to my request ? To know that my Edith is in such an excellent household, guided by your wisdom, introduced by you into the cultivated circles of the metropolis, will make the happiest mortal of one who esteems you above everything," etc., etc. End.

I was to some extent taken aback when I had the four pages of handwriting behind me. "It is too much of a good thing," I exclaimed. "Now that I want to settle down in peace, a woman I don't know from Adam expects me to receive her gawky girl into a sort of housekeeping convalescent home. That is the last straw. No, certainly not."

I knew neither the mother nor the daughter Edith. Supposing the one was just such another as Frieda !

I suddenly sprang to my feet. It was as clear to me as daylight. How could it have come to pass that I had not thought of it long ago? How can one be so stupid, and bother and worry oneself and never find the simplest remedy?

I knew now what I wanted. "You will take Frieda into your house and draw her near to your heart; you will sprinkle upon her gentleness and yielding which will loosen the rust on the bolts of her disposition, so that it may open and absorb friendliness into itself."

'Twas thus I spoke unto myself in much delight. "Wilhelmine," I jested to my solitary self, "Wilhelmine, fancy having such a lust for enterprise in your old age! I expect you are not in your right senses. Do you know what you are taking upon you?"—But scruples got no power over me. I heard again and yet again the words, "He is true as gold, and honourable as he is true." Now I could help and advise, so that his truth and honour might not be put to shame, now I would be able to work at his happiness with every chance of success; with this distinction, that it was not he who was being taken in hand, but she.

And really, when I came to consider her more carefully, she was not so bad after all.

How happy this letter made me. Certainly an unknown Frau Schulz had written it, and the postman had brought it, but I won't be turned from my belief that it came from Providence, even if Frau Krause were six times as enlightened as she is.

I sent a commissionaire off at once with an urgent message to Herr Max, I was in such a state of mind; and besides, think of the excitement and fear: "Supposing that she should refuse! Then it is all done for."

It was not long before he came. I had him shown into the best room, and as soon as he sat down, I addressed him seriously without further circumlocution:

" This is not the first time that we have discussed very important matters between ourselves in this place ; they bore reference to your friend Felix before. Sponge that out. To-day it is your turn."

" I did not know that——" he stammered.

" Keep yourself cool and listen quietly. First of all, I must tell you that I never met with a bigger lump of frivolity than yourself."—" I am of age," he interrupted.—" Worse luck !" I answered. " You can both do and leave undone what you like, without having to give account to any one—you are your own master. And secondly, I must remind you that you knew me : why did you not come and confide to me that you were going to get engaged ? I would have given you good advice."

" Good advice ?" he asked. " I do not understand you."

" Don't be a hypocrite ; you know what I mean. Therefore answer me honestly, do you believe that you will be happy with your Frieda ? "

He was silent for a space. " I hope so," he then said low and nervously.

" We all hope the same," I continued impressively : " all of us who have learnt to know you and care about you. We do not reproach you because you have become engaged, quite the contrary ; all young men ought to follow your example as speedily as possible ; but why did you not wait for a little ? We might have found some one more suitable for you."

He shook his head slowly and repellantly, then he turned his fine, candid eyes upon me with such a good, truthful look in them that I was greatly moved. " I love my future wife," he said, and his features took a joyful expression.

" And she ?" I asked expectantly.

"She loves me too!"

"But with a very poor kind of love. Don't be vexed with me for saying so," I hurried out. But who could have helped it? When a pistol is loaded, it is apt to go off. That is one of Nature's laws.

"Let that be as it may," he answered with great self-control, biting his mustachios as he spoke; "she is my future wife."

He got up, and said as he bowed stiffly and icily, "I suppose that I may venture to withdraw? I can scarcely think that you have anything further to communicate to me."

And he really did mean to go.

It was made clear to me without much subtle thought, that every sausage has got two ends, and that I had seized hold of the wrong one this time.

"Are you angry with me?" I asked, and laid my hand gently on his shoulder. "If I have seen wrongly I shall be delighted, but it did seem to me as if your *fiancée* often displeased you."

"We do not quite agree on many subjects," he answered with hesitation, "but reasons for that may be found in the surroundings in which she grew up. She is wanting in the forms of social intercourse, I acknowledge; but then she is pretty—she looks as beautiful as a picture sometimes. Don't you think so too?"

Had he lent me his lover's spectacles, through which he regards the world, I might perhaps have said that the Venus di Medici was simply nowhere in comparison to her; but as this most certainly was not the case, I contented myself with nodding my head, which he could translate into as high an expression of praise as seemed good to him.

Encouraged by the nod, he continued: "She is perhaps somewhat spoiled. She was still a child when her mother died, and her father let her do just as she pleased. Her relations flattered her, especially some elderly cousins who speculated on becoming Frieda's stepmother. That has probably made her rather obstinate. But the little piece of perversity pleased me more than enough ; the colder and more unmanageable she showed herself towards me, the more zealously I endeavoured to please her."

"That is to say that you got obstinate too, and made up your mind to have the girl at all costs. Was that the case or not ? "—" It was."

"How is it possible to become engaged through mutual dislike ? What mischief it may lead to ! "

He smiled. "We loved each other. When I asked her very seriously if she would be my wife, the little fights that we used to have up to then came to an end. She confessed that she had liked me too from the very first moment, but that her father and relations had tried to persuade her, and she would not allow herself to be dictated to—no, not by any one in the world— and that pleased me still more."

"I cannot say that she was altogether wrong there. Made-up matches have no backbone."

"How happy it made me ! " he went on rapidly. "I had no one who loved me for myself except Felix, my friend ; but he was away, and I was solitary and alone in big Berlin."—"You forgot Frau Buchholz," I exclaimed.—" Felix avoided your house, and I had to remain away too until there was good news to be brought."—"For which you have won our eternal gratitude," I interrupted him. "You were your friend's advocate, and my Betti's happiness was the immediate result of it. I can well understand how it came to pass that you felt yourself deserted, and sought somebody that you could love. Nobody can live without love—nobody. And so you were in the so-called seventh heaven ?"

" I was."

" And now ?"

He drew a deep breath. " A blighting frost has set-tled on the hopes that filled my heart and made it beat so joyfully. You wish for my confidence, Frau Buchholz. May I speak plainly ?"

" Say whatever you like," I encouraged him.

" And will you not be angry, should I—accuse you ?"

" Me ? What nonsense ! "

" Yes," he answered, and became very pale. " No-body pleased me better than Frieda. I was proud of her. I found her charming ; she seemed perfection to me just as she was. I paid no heed to her little foibles, I did not wish her to be different in any way. You then permitted me to introduce my future wife to you ; and how I looked forward to the moment when you would approve of my choice, welcome Frieda, and learn to love her ! However, I saw at the very first meeting that she did not please you. I felt that your dislike increased instead of vanishing. That disquieted me. From that moment I began to observe my *fiancée* more attentively, and saw that in the family circle of the Buchholzes she differed from those around her in manner as well as in all her ways. Her ob-stinacy produced a painful impression on me, her de-ficiencies of education were made apparent ; and the more she saw that she was not adapted to those whose friendship was an inestimable boon to me, the more Frieda withdrew within herself. She felt hurt."

" I am not aware that I ever said anything to her prejudice by so much as a word."

"And yet the icy coldness proceeded from you. The silent neglect, the unexpressed reproaches, the forced politeness,—those were the things, those composed the frost that settled on our budding happiness. We were despised on account of our love. You have wounded us cruelly, Frau Buchholz. Can you take it amiss of Frieda if she has become more silent and repellant than formerly ?"

I was silent. We certainly do let our fellow-creatures feel sometimes that they are hateful to us ; but who thinks hard thoughts on that account ? I wonder whether my Carl would think the young man had right on his side were he to hear his accusations?

"But it was not you alone," Max continued, "who reproached me with my choice. He, the brother of my heart, my friend Felix, who was satisfied at first, had words of pity—nay, even words of blame—for me later. Who occasioned him to use them—who ?"

I made a sign of denial.

After a pause,—I felt how hard it was for him,—he went on : " I have already faced the fact that I am to lose my friend, although I believed that nothing but death would divide us, nor shall I trouble you further with the presence of my wife that is to be. Frieda and I will return to the old solitude."

" No," I exclaimed, "you shall not. Do listen first to the reason why I asked you to come and see me. I wanted to speak to you about Frieda. I have seen that she is wanting in many things, but that may be rectified. I want to have her here with me in the house. I will treat her with kindness or with strictness, according as it may be required. She is such a pretty, good-looking girl, and things must go very crookedly if she does not become a charming one as well."

" You will do that ? " he exclaimed. " How beautiful, how noble ! She has really never had a proper
stay. You——"

" Well ? " I asked.

" I am afraid that Frieda will not consent to it."

" That would be still grander. Surely you have
sufficient power over her to make her see what is reasonable ? "

" If she notices that she is being disposed of, she is
sure to refuse. Besides, she is not particularly well
disposed towards you."

" That will come with the sweeping out of the rooms."

I considered ; nothing came. I had to think a bit
longer.

" That will do," I said at last. " When Betti is married, I shall need assistance : I intend anyway to take
a young girl into the house—here is the letter in which
negotiations have been begun—and that being so, I
prefer two to one. Frieda will do me a kindness—tell
her so—a great kindness by coming. Explain to her
that she really must learn housekeeping, if there is a
spark of love in her breast."

" I cannot accept your kindness," he said. " Neither
of us can."

" My dear young friend," I answered, " think that a
mother is speaking to you, and so I repeat it : bring
your *fiancée*, that I may teach her so far as in my power
lies. God will give His blessing to the work."

" A mother," he whispered to himself ; " I have never
known mine ! "

" Adopt me," I exclaimed, " then everything will
come right ! " and I offered him my hand. He seized
it, and raised it to his lips, and hot tears fell upon it.

" That is right," I said ; " but sons must be obedient.
Go and win Frieda over to me."

I remained alone, and again began to think. But everything that I had thought out for myself resolved itself into one and the same reflection : What will your Carl say ? How will you manage to put it to him gently without astonishing him too much ? You have lost your wager.

But after all, what is a tour ?

A terribly fatiguing affair.

AT THE HASENHAIDE.

About week-days—The mustard uncle and the new bonnet-trimming—About faithful attachment and the finest time of year—What happens at the Hasenhaide—About kites and tyrants—Why Wilhelmine is a ruin and Herr Briese a Jesuit.

It always goes against the grain to tell my Doris that she must give up her afternoon out because I want the Sunday for myself, but it could not be helped. Contrary to my expectations, Doris was quite obliging on this occasion, for she generally insists on her rightful privileges, and she said : " If Madame is absolutely obliged to go out, such as I will remain at home."—"You may have your Wednesday free instead, Doris."—"Oh, no," she answered; "a week-day is no good to me ! You think to get roast meat, and after all you don't even get boiled."

"I get a fit of the horrors when I only think of the Sunday's tumult," I answered, in order to hint that her afternoon was not desired for purposes of amusement. "If the weather is tolerably fine, one-half of Berlin wanders off towards the meadows ; and if it is very fine, the whole of it goes ; and then the places in the neighbourhood are crowded beyond what police regulations permit."

"Where does Madame wish to go?" asked Doris.— "I do not wish, Doris; I must."—"Nobody ought to *must*. If I had a longing to stay at home, not half a score of horses should drag me outside the door."— "Doris, in the higher grades of life there are occasions when one would like and yet may not. The rules of society impose obligations on us, and according as we behave so is our reputation."—"Oh, then, it is tip-top company!"—"Oh, dear no, Doris; just a little excursion into the country, so to speak. A friend of your master's, or rather a former acquaintance, a certain Herr Briese, who used to come a good deal to my father's house, has announced his intention of calling on us, and we must take him somewhere. I had totally forgotten him, as he has been living for many years in Rawitsch, where he is well-to-do, as he says, and still leads a bachelor's life, although he could surround a wife with comforts." — "Then why doesn't he get one?"—"Who can fathom his fellow-creatures? Perhaps his pretensions are too great, or else, she may not have wanted him—although he was said to be a very good match in those days, with which many a girl might well have been satisfied. But, no doubt, a good many may not have cared about him, for he had left his first youth behind him, and his forehead already went back to his neck. That does not incline one towards matrimony, though he really could look very languishing. No, it was certainly better for him to settle down in Rawitsch, than to rush about here in Berlin with a broken heart."

"That must be dreadful," said Doris.

"He had some distant sort of a great-uncle, on the strength of which he wanted to enter on an engagement; but when the year was out the old man was still alive, and I must confess that my feelings are quite opposed to the erection of a household on the dead bones of relations."

" Uhu !" shuddered Doris.

" The old gentleman died afterwards, leaving a fine will behind him, according to which he made Herr Briese his sole heir, conditionally on his carrying on the business himself and keeping the mustard-mill, which had been the old man's greatest pride, at work on the different qualities. He has sent us samples, too, especially of a herb mustard, which was splendid. And now he has happened to come to Berlin, and it is impossible to do otherwise than receive him well, were it only for the sake of old memories."—" Has he brought some with him this time? Ours is just out."— " People must never be rated according to what they bring with them, but rather according to their inner worth. I am pleased to be able to talk to him about old times, and to amuse myself by finding out how he likes Berlin now, for he has been going about a good deal on his own account before coming to us, but has not yet been outside the gates. That is the reason we are going together to the Hasenhaide on Sunday."

" To the Haide ?" asked Doris in astonishment, as if she had heard wrongly. " But isn't that too mixed for Madame and the mustard gentleman ?"

" Doris," I admonished her, with a touch of superiority in my manner, " mixture ceases where cultivated people are to be found. To prevent the time seeming long to you on Sunday, I will make you a present of the flowers on my second-best bonnet, and you can put them on yours."

She was very pleased with this, and I as well, for she deserved a reward for so readily waiving her rights,

and by this means I secured a new bonnet-trimming
without Carl being able to accuse me of wasteful
vanity.

The lucky idea of the Haide originated with Uncle
Fritz. Since he set up housekeeping with Erica, everything has been going on well; still, she is not suited
for a big town. The streets are too long for her, the
noise upsets her, she would not venture to cross the
road at a slant for fear of finding herself under the
wheels, and shopping presents insuperable difficulties.
It is one thing for the parental garden to deliver
vegetables straight to the kitchen, and quite another
to have to bargain with Spandau cabbage-women and
the Werder folk, who take advantage of every kind of
inexperience and palm off their bad wares upon it.—
"When she has plucked up a little more courage, she
will get on well enough," said Uncle Fritz a couple of
days ago. "She must be forced to mix frequently
with people, then she will acquire a feeling of safety
and know that nothing is going to happen to her."
—"Didn't I tell you from the very first that a Berlin girl would have been more suited to you?"—
"If I had to make my choice over again, I would not
have anybody else. If you want to give me a pleasure,
Wilhelm, you will accompany us on Sunday to the
Hasenhaide. Don't make a fuss, but come along."

Herr Briese's advent interrupted a direct refusal.
At first sight I could not find a place for him in my
memory; but as his loaf-like pate was still the same,
the intervening years vanished like window-shutters,
and I remembered with dreadful exactitude the day
upon which he flattered himself that I was going to
make him happy. He sent a letter like copper-plate,
and got a carefully-worded refusal from my father by
return, in which no objection was made to himself

personally, stress being rather laid on the very un-grown-up juvenility of the desired one. He wrote again, but his second epistle profited him as little.

I left him alone with Uncle Fritz while I went to fetch my Carl, and inform him that this Herr Briese was the very same who had paid his court to me with-out winning my love in return. "Wilhelmine," said my husband, "I trust that this Herr Briese will give me no occasion for jealousy!"

"Carl, look at yourself in the glass, and then let him have a look. Why, there is no question of a com-parison!"—"Faithful devotion ends by touching a woman's heart."—"He was refused twice, and after getting the mustard he never made a third move; you know that as well as I."—"Don't be tragic, Wilhelmine. I am prepared to welcome Herr Briese."

We returned and found Uncle Fritz deep in conver-sation with Herr Briese. My Carl showed himself well-disposed towards him, and asked how he liked Ber-lin now that he saw it after so long an absence. "Not at all!" exclaimed Uncle Fritz.—"I can no longer find my way about," complained Herr Briese. "The old streets do not look like their former selves. A palace stands now where a tiny house used to be. Where open fields were, streets are now built, each one more magnificent than the other. Kranzler's has no longer rails enough for us to rest our feet against, when we want to see Berlin parading past us. They have pulled down the old simple familiar taverns and built new ones, with coloured glass windows outside like churches, and inside architecture like feudal castles. One hardly dares settle oneself comfortably amid all the grandeur."
—"But surely the beer is excellent?" asked Uncle Fritz.—"We have just as good, not to say better, in Rawitsch," answered Herr Briese with self-compla-

cency, " and not nearly so dear. You pay just half as much for a pint with us."—"A place for good fellows, according to that," remarked Uncle Fritz.—" It has its drawbacks, but also its advantages. For instance, one of its drawbacks is, that it is so far away from Berlin ; and one of its advantages, that one cannot go there too often—one might not be quite so well pleased with Rawitsch afterwards."—" So you *are* enthusiastic about Berlin in comparison !" I interrupted. " If you carry your thoughts back, you will see that it could not be otherwise. Youth is the most beautiful time of our life."—He gave me a melancholy look. " I no longer know it. I have been away too long. My friends and acquaintances are gone, as well as the old spots where we used to be young and merry together. We strolled arm-in-arm along the footway ; now you can scarcely push your way through singly. I have not learned how to elbow my way along, and feel uncomfortable in a crowd. I shall return thanks to my Creator when I find myself once again in quiet, peaceful Rawitsch. The Hasenhaide is the only other place I am going to. My pleasantest Sunday afternoon memories are connected with it. I smoked my first secret cigar there. How delicious it was to lie full length on the grass ! I felt as if I were in the country. And if I felt inclined for a little dance, what charming opportunities there were for indulging in it in one saloon or the other! It was idyllic ! "

"We will make an excursion to it together," exclaimed Uncle Fritz, and trod persuasively on my foot ; " won't we, Wilhelmine?" I consented, having the prospect of seeing what sort of face Herr Briese would make when he beheld the Haide again after a lapse of years ; and my Carl had not one of those parliamentary fits that first lead to an uncompromising refusal and then give way after all.

We discussed the arrangements. I made up my mind to negotiate with Doris concerning her afternoon out, and Herr Briese remained with us for supper.

When Sunday came the barometer had done its duty and clambered up above "fine" without telling a lie, for it often points to "dry" and there are continuous downpours, science notwithstanding. We started off in the very nick of time, and walked till we found the right tram, which took us as far as the Halle gate, where we joined the stream of people turning towards the left—for Uncle Fritz thought that we should see more and not be so knocked about as if we kept along the carriage road.

"We seem to have come to the wrong place," said Herr Briese.—"Why?"—"Because there is no country yet."—"That comes later," said Uncle Fritz.— Herr Briese shook his head and complained, "I can't recognise it at all. The town never seems to come to an end."

We proceeded on our way past the new church which is being built on the Johannistisch, and immediately behind which the pleasure grounds extend. It is astonishing to see the number of curiosities that the people have in the booths on either side of the road, and the noise they make to induce passers-by to go in. Every one shouts that nothing like his wonder has ever been seen since the world was made. They have giants and dwarfs, panoramas with the most horrible accidents, learned horses who know precisely how old everybody is, as well as wolves and trained goats, savages and Herculeses, and many other objects which art and science can produce at a trifle, for the best place only costs twopence.

My Carl suggested that we should go into a booth in front of which a female giant, who was painted on a huge picture, was cried up as being ever so many hundredweight, and possessing enormously big arms and legs. However, I signified to him that this was no sight for him. Nor was it.

Swings and merry-go-rounds fly along amongst the booths. A whole fire-engine was fixed on one of them, with hose, water-tanks, and vehicles for the men, and the blessed children sat on the horses and tore at the bells so lustily that one imagined the Wild Hunt itself was coursing round and round. Add to this the noise of the hurdygurdies and the bands of the tea-gardens, where thousands of people are sitting, and every garden, big or little, chokeful, for beer-drinking meanwhile has become a natural characteristic of man. Then for a change there are gambling-booths and shooting-galleries, flower-stands, where one may venture money and win pretty plants for pots, as well as marketable rubbish of every description. Some expose sandwiches of garlic sausages for sale, and one woman baked real potato-puffs on a portable stove, which sold most rapidly. A stranger may carry away with him a correct idea of the migration of a race from this place. The road was black with old and young, but there was a good deal of colour introduced by the smart defenders of the Fatherland, who either kept together in herds, or took their young women out walking singly. Every species of official was represented—dark blue, light blue, and even the quite red from Potsdam. As the broad pathways were insufficient, hundreds walked along the lines, making the dust rise in clouds, and heavily-laden trams and other vehicles had to take heed that no bones were broken. We progressed but slowly.

Before coming to the military shooting - galleries
there is a small strip of heath on the right-hand side,
where the public may lie down under the trees. Here,
too, every spot was taken. The people had established
themselves in family groups on the grass, and were
enjoying the dainties they had brought with them.
Vendors of cakes and hot sausages strolled about
offering their wares, while portable *bodigas* supplied
the necessary drink. And all went on in a peaceable
and orderly manner.

My Carl said, " One can get to know the Berlin people here as they really are. Being easily satisfied, they
amuse themselves with a nothing ; being quick at a
pertinent witticism, they are never at a loss for conversation. Being sociable, they do not begrudge their
neighbour getting a good place too, and noisy bluster
is displeasing to them. You may look in vain for
drunken people. The forty or fifty thousand people
who visit the Hasenhaide on Sundays govern themselves by means of a strongly developed sense of
order, without which sociability on such a scale would
be impossible."

Herr Briese could not get over the fact that the
Hasenhaide had changed itself, so to speak, into a
colossal fair. " It was much more romantic here formerly," he sighed in pain ; " but that was long ago."
—" When Old Nick was quite a boy, I suppose," remarked Uncle Fritz.—" And had to fetch spice-brandy
for his grandmother," continued my husband in the
same popular phraseology.—" Carl," I said reproachfully, " what will Herr Briese think of you? Such
phrases are not used in Rawitsch."—" It is all very
well for you to jeer at me," returned Herr Briese ;
" but you try living for thirty years in Rawitsch, and
you will be just as horrified to see the way Berlin in-

creases in length and breadth."—"It can hardly circumscribe its limits to please you!" laughed Fritz.—
"It would be unreasonable to wish it," said Herr
Briese testily. "Do not take it amiss if I grieve that
good old customs have to make way for modern ones.
Everything is gone to which my heart clung; but that
was always my luck! Nothing favours me in Berlin."
With these words he looked sorrowfully towards me,
as if he wanted to burden me with the responsibility
of his having vegetated meanwhile. But how could I
help not taking a fancy to him?

Uncle Fritz clapped him good-naturedly on the
shoulder and said: "Don't let us quarrel about it.
Every one gets his dose of physic—the only question
is as to how he will take it. And now let us go into
the New World'—the entrance is my affair."—He
got the tickets, taking them grandly for the best
places, and we passed through the portals.

The impression made by this smaller Hasenhaide in
the big one, is very pleasant. Green trees, with numberless chairs and tables beneath them; in the background the broad Indian pavilion on the hill, with the
pond and its fountains in front of it; to the left, booths
and their curiosities; to the right, a *bal champêtre*,
merry-go-rounds, the pony race-course; on one side
the stage and the big orchestra, and whatever else is
requisite for the amusement of some ten thousand
people. It has a most prepossessing effect.

We got a table close to the balloon, which was just
being filled; a number of soldiers were busy helping
to hold the monster. "Any one can go up in it on
payment of fifty marks," said Uncle Fritz to my Carl;
"don't you feel inclined to let your *kite* * have a fly for

* The German for kite is Drachen (dragon), which Frau Buchholz
regards as an allusion to herself.

once?"—"I forbid the use of such personalities!" I exclaimed. "You will keep your insults to yourself, unless you wish me to take a seat elsewhere!" Whereupon I got up, and looked as if my threat had been made in earnest. At this moment one of the balloon people came up to us with the warning, "Please do not tread on the pipe, or there might be an accident." I now noticed on the ground behind me a thick roll of oil-skin, through which the gas was conducted into the balloon, and this scarcely contributed to my pleasure. Should such a thing explode, one would be expedited into the blessed hereafter in less than no time.

"Carl," I admonished him, "we will get away."—"Don't be ridiculous," said Uncle Fritz.—"You, perhaps, have had your life insured! Mine is not. Erica, let us go!"—"I shall remain with my husband," she piped.—"Wilhelmine, nothing in the world will happen to us," said my husband persuasively. "You cannot get a better view anywhere."—"Herr Briese, will you give me your arm? One expects respect even though one may be in the Haide!"

He did not feel quite happy, either, in the neighbourhood of the gas-pipe, so he placed himself at my disposal with great alacrity. We forced a way for ourselves through the crowd and vanished.

We walked silently beside each other for a space, I being still so full of my first anger. And could I be gentle? Instead of Herr Briese feeling himself to some extent overcome, he prosed away as equably as if Berlin were a suburb of Rawitsch. Then my Carl would take an interest in the fat woman with the weights, in comparison with which his wife's life is indifferent to him. And lastly, Uncle Fritz puts me down as a dragon in the presence of the travelled gen-

tleman! It would be a new fashion to put up with
things like that.

But there was still worse to come. " I pity you sin-
cerely," began Herr Briese, "for not being understood as you deserve to be."—"What do you mean by
that?"—"Another would have fulfilled your every
wish—nay, he still would do so—day by day. Oh,
how unhappy you must be beside such a tyrant!"—
"What tyrant do you mean?"—"Whom can I mean
but your husband?"—" Now it's beginning to dawn on
me," I interrupted him. " Do you wish to breed discord between me and my Carl? to paint my husband
black and insinuate yourself into my good graces '
That really does go beyond bounds. What are you
thinking about? No, no, most worthy sir, I will none
of you ; no, not even if you anoint yourself with oiled
butter. Good-bye to you!" I looked him piercingly
through and through, and left him standing there in
all his worthlessness. Such an old serpent!

Meanwhile there was the roar of a cannon-shot, the
music struck in with its big drums, and the balloon
began its ascent.

This was a marvellous spectacle for the thousands
assembled there, but for me it was a mere detail, however high it might fly. What did this man Briese take
me for, that he dared so to insult me? I hardly ventured to near our table again.

I approached it downcast and deeply wounded.
Had I derogated from my own dignity that this un-
scrupulous sinner dared to become my tempter? Oh,
no ; my course of life lay bare to view, white and vir-
tuous as a freshly-shorn lamb! No blemishes were
to be found there which I needed to conceal from my
Carl, and still I seemed unpleasant to myself—de-
graded in my own eyes.

"Where is the strange gentleman from Kottbus?"
asked Uncle Fritz.—"He has taken his legs in his
hands and is running on his elbows to Rawitsch," I
answered with bitter scorn.—"Have you treated him
badly?" asked my husband.—"Him? Oh, Carl, if
you only knew! But no, never shall you discover
what a generation of vipers out of Paradise this same
Briese is. He has so completely spoiled the entire
evening for me that neither music, nor whatever else
they may give us, can please me. If I were asked
what we should do, I would suggest going home,
more especially as Erica is afraid of a crowd."—"If
Fritz is with me, I am not at all afraid."—"We will
wait for the illuminations," said Uncle Fritz, in opposition as usual.—However, my Carl yielded, partly
because he saw that I really was suffering, and partly
also, no doubt, because he wanted to know what had
happened.

It was not until we had left the Hasenhaide and the
crowds of homeward-waltzing pleasure-seekers far
behind us that I was able to clothe the unheard-of in
words.—"What do you think can have happened?"
I asked suggestively.—"I have not learned thought-
reading."—"So you do not know what Herr Briese
wanted?"—"Oh, yes; to go in quest of the ruins
of his youthful reminiscences!" — "Carl, am I a
ruin?"—"Who says so?"—"You! It was for my
sake he came. While making little of you, he had
the audacity to attempt a sort of love-making, Carl."
—"But really——"—"Don't be disturbed; he got his
deserts."—"If only I had him here, I should belabour
him as he deserved."—"Carl, do leave bodily prowess
out of the affair; culture must turn the scale here.
And I can tell you that he will make no second attempt. But I should like to request rather more con-

sideration from you ; such a thing could simply not occur then ! "

" Minchen——"

" Carl, be silent. I shall need a long time to recover from my experiences of to-day."

When I went into the kitchen next morning, Doris asked me how the pleasure party had gone off. " So-so," I answered.—" Yes, yes ; too many boors go there."

" There is not the least complaint to be made about the people, Doris, but the worst Jesuits hide themselves under the cloak of education."

Doris looked at me very inquisitively, but I dared not make myself more intelligible. One discusses many subjects with a servant who behaves well and has proved herself attached to the family, but if one goes too far she may make use of it later in an outburst of anger, and the town get something to talk about, though it may be utterly false.

FRITZ AND FRANZ.

About perambulators and lady-shows — Suspicious reports and turned-back carpets—Why marbles are dangerous and Franz is vastly amused—Why human feelings are hurt, and a commissionaire is sent off—Why Herr Kleines departs.

THERE are people who use up one day after another without ever arriving at the conviction that no return tickets are issued for their life's journey,—who will not be taught that joys and sorrows are stations where apparent stoppages are made, though the journey goes on without break, while the grey of age settles on them by degrees, like the dust of the railroad and the ashes of the burnt-out coals. It is hard to see, either by oneself or one's fellow-passengers, how one is getting along, and just as little can we see the slow changes in our own faces, for we accustom ourselves to the picture that the looking-glass shows us daily ; but when fresh passengers get in, they make known to us how long we have already been on the road.

The weather gradually became very autumnal. For weeks already the trees in the town had been looking like brooms, and the remaining foliage on the branches in the Friedrichshain could be counted by leaves. How short the time is which separates the green of May and the breezes of spring from autumnal browns and from winter, with its longing for returning life ! Is it true that with increasing age, years, like winter days, become shorter—those self-same years which seemed so boundless to us in our childhood ? The compilers of calendars have calculated them to be the same, but when we measure them by our wishes and hopes, we notice that they have become smaller, and we see by the young plants that spring up around us, how rapidly they range themselves in rows. How long ago is it since Emmi crept about the carpet at my feet, and now she sits there just as I used to do, and has her two little ones whose play she watches over. Did I meditate upon my grandmotherhood in those days ? How should I have done so ?—the years were still too long.

It cannot be denied that scarcely anything could be sweeter than the twins when they are being put to bed, the pure, tiny Raphaels, with their sweet fat little arms and legs, and dimples on their necks that one longs to bite into. It is impossible to kiss them enough, and Amanda Kulecke, who is so fond of seeing them in nature's garb, says that they are real little Cupids. And they know very well that people are fond of them, and shriek with delight when Granny takes them and hugs them one at a time, which is the only way to manage when there are a pair of brothers.

But for all that, I prophesied from the very beginning that twins, however charming, would entail a good deal of trouble, were it only for the bother with the perambulator, in which there is room for half a squadron, and which the strength of one person is insufficient to get down-stairs. But it was he who gave such a clumsy order, and we ladies might slave away at it, for the nurse was far too high and mighty to help with it. Oh, dear no! she had to be attended to all round like a sea-monster; no dinner was good enough for her—she demanded a double portion of butter and sandwiches for her lunch! Emmi and I sang a Te Deum for joy when she evaporated back to the Spreewald to recruit for her next situation. One really felt free again in one's own house.

The Doctor had, as usual, opposed a deaf ear to all my complaints, though the woman grew more presuming day by day. He even forbade our taking any measures against her, for fear of her anger taking effect on the children. But had *he* to put up with her the livelong day? He goes off to his patients, and does not enjoy the domestic worries with us. Under such circumstances, there is no art in playing the father.

Since the children made their appearance in this life, he has become very sparing in the matter of large parties, with the exception naturally of the christening, for which I composed the *menu*, on this occasion only; but I fear that it was too grand for him, and he now wishes to return to simplicity in the matter of expenses, for indeed he generally gets enthusiastic about what is beautiful and costs little. It can hardly be considered a sign of culture when he says that large parties are nothing but lady-shows. But doctors do allow themselves to have prejudices sometimes. If one has acquired a family, outside circles ought not to be neglected. Some festivities should take place from time to time. What are the neighbours likely to say if they never notice illuminated windows? Why, surely, " Poverty and pride rule on the Doctor's floor !"

And further, ought *we* not to have a care that family circles are provided for the growing children, where they will be invited and find companions such as young ladies when they have arrived at the age of adolescence ?

Herr Kleines has the habit of paying his formal calls on Sunday afternoons, and playing with the children, in order to tighten his hold on the mother's esteem, on which occasions he is given to hopping about like a crow, and making faces in his endeavours to amuse them. However, his success is mostly doubtful ; indeed, energetically as he moves his scalp up and down and waggles his ears, we have experienced the fact that Franz has yelled till he had to be taken away, and was only restored to equanimity by laborious patting on his back. This is a particularly rare gift of nature ; but of what avail is such a gift, when it appears to the children in their nightly dreams, causes them to shriek horribly, and was only given up after he had been forbidden to wear out his powers ? Also when he first came, he used to bring a number of toys as presents, which led him into unnecessary expense, as there always had to be duplicates. My son-in-law's hospitality does not afford a sufficient return for such

extravagance, and one does not care about taking
presents from a person whose salary, though fixed, is
by no means too ample. Notwithstanding the toys,
the children displayed an invincible dislike to him
which may have arisen from the fact that they had
not developed sufficient intelligence to appreciate the
hygienic objects warranted proof against licking, and
manufactured according to the dictates of the Imperial
Office of Hygiene ; and when he made them a present
of marbles painted with a colour free of arsenic, let
us hope that he himself had no idea of how dangerous
marbles themselves are, nor how sternly they should
be forbidden as opposed to the laws of sanitation.

The following is what happened.

Herr Kleines brings his marbles with him, and being a cheap luxury, he is allowed to bestow them on
the children. He proceeds to count them over himself : six for Franz, and six for Fritz, and everything
is in the most splendid order as he gives them to
them. The little folk amuse themselves capitally with
the rolling balls, and Franz abstains from screaming,
and Fritz from scratching and biting Herr Kleines, as
usual, and there is nothing but laughter and jubilation.

While the children are busy playing, Herr Kleines
tells us—I happened accidentally to be at Emmi's—
what is going on elsewhere: what takes place in families that we mutually know, where he too visits : how
thoughtless Mrs. So-and-so is, where he has just been
calling: how badly Mrs. X. dresses herself, though she
gets her gowns from Paris (N. B.—which I doubt):
and what such a one has said about her, and what she
has said about him; and all the rest of it; which is
very entertaining to listen to when it concerns people
with whom one is not connected, but which may lead
to a good deal of mischief should they hear about it.

Then when I interrupt him in extremely question
able details: "Herr Kleines, let us hope that they are
imaginings of your own manufacture," he flies into a
rage directly, swears that both eyes and ears have been
witnesses of what passed behind closed doors, and
that silence is kept because a challenge to a duel
would be the only possible result. But neither Emmi
nor I quite believe all that he says. One must consider that when paying a visit, people merely want
something to tell; and that being so, a little more or
less is not of much consequence.

After Herr Kleines had left, and the children did
not want to play at marbles any longer, I gathered the
things up. "I say, Emmi, were there not twelve marbles?" I asked.—"Yes," she answered; "he gave six
to Franz, and six to Fritz—that makes twelve together."—"But there are only eleven here."—"Quite
enough too," said Emmi.—"I am not thinking about
that," I answered; "but where is the one marble?"—
"Lost," laughed Emmi at my anxiety.—"I know that,
but the question is, where is it? I only hope that no
one has swallowed it."

"Good gracious!" exclaimed Emmi, in a desperate
state of fright. "That ball must be found. Let us
look for it, mamma."—"Where is the nurse?"—"Gone
out."—"Then we must set to work."

So the two of us began the search; on the carpet,
under the carpet, under the furniture, upon the furniture, in the ante-room, on the window-sill, we lifted
the children up, put them down again, turned back
the carpet again, lifted the children once more, search-
ed once more in every corner, turned up the carpet
once more. No marble was to be found. ·

"One of them has swallowed it," said Emmi, in
fearful conviction.

"But which?" I asked. "Franz or Fritz?"

"How am I to know? If only my husband were here; and it may be a full hour before he comes! What are we to do until then? Shall we give the child a hot drink?"

"Which of them?" I asked energetically, the better to recall her to presence of mind, for her composure was visibly failing. "Do you know which? I imagine it is Franz."

"Fritz, beyond doubt. He puts everything into his mouth."

"Excuse me, Fritz takes more after us Buchholzes, and I am not aware that, even in our earliest youth, any one of our family was distinguished by greediness and gluttony; no, if either of them has swallowed it, it must be Franz."

Emmi examined the children with anxious scrutiny: "Don't you find too that Franz is looking quite pale already? Oh, Heavens, if he should die! Where can my husband be?" She put her forefinger into the child's mouth and rummaged round and round it, as if the ball were likely to be sticking there still; but without any result, except the natural one that the boy yelled lustily.

"How awfully he must be suffering! That abominable Herr Kleines! What business had he to bring the children those stupid marbles? He must know that they are just the sort of things for them to put into their mouths. He shall have the pleasure of hearing a piece of my mind! Try to be quiet, my precious Franz; you will soon be better; papa will cure his little boy; he will find out directly where the marble has gone. Oh, dear, I hope he won't have to use the knife!"

"Emmi," I said, "don't talk yourself into an unnecessary state of grief and excitement. Do wait till you know more, so that, should it be required, you may have strength to keep your head clear in the event of the worse. Imaginary dangers are no dangers—they are merely a form of self-torture——"

"Really?" she interrupted me; "then perhaps the marble does not constitute a danger? According to that, I suppose the child would need to have swallowed a nine-pin in order to arouse your sympathy!"

"Emmi!"

"Well, yes," she remarked, with symptoms of yielding. "Here I sit in terrible trouble, and you worry me with your moral lessons! Oh, mamma, where can Franz be stopping? Don't you see that the child is getting weaker from minute to minute?"

"That is the result of his bellowing."

"Oh, my precious child, my sweet little Franz, don't cry like that!" she now began. "Do be a good boy again!" and she rocked him backwards and forwards in her arms. According to my ideas, the child was simply made unmanageable by this exceptionable overflow of tenderness, and determined not to give in.

"Emmi," I remarked, as dispassionately as possible, "under existing circumstances I should not rock the child so violently, if I were in your place. The marble might easily be jerked lower down, and harden there afterwards."

She stared at me in horror, just as I have seen a girl do, who was acting Ophelia at the play-house, when she went mad.

"Do you think so?" she shrieked. "Then there is no longer hope? Franz had a similar case the other day, where a lead soldier had been swallowed. The boy had to die. Oh, my Franz, my precious Franz!"

The Doctor arrived now, and relieved the tension of

the situation. Emmi screamed at him like a lunatic:
" Save your son ! " and sent a perceptible thrill through
him. It was not until after I had explained to him
how the marbles had come into the house, and what a
fool Herr Kleines was, that the doctor took the upper
hand of the father, and he began to examine Franz,
which amused the little scamp vastly. After a pause,
he said : "The boy is as well as ever ; what are you
making such a fuss about ? "—" Possibly Fritz has got
it," sobbed Emmi.

" Or neither of them," said the Doctor.

" One of them must have swallowed it," I answered ;
"for the ball has vanished from the earth without
leaving a trace."—"If it is only properly looked for,
it is sure to be found," spoke the Doctor.—"We have
turned everything topsy-turvy already."—"Women
are never thorough," he grumbled, and set to work to
unearth the marble.

I had no time to answer him with the want of consideration that he deserved, as the rolling back of the
carpet, frantic grabs behind the furniture, and turning
out of corners began afresh—in a word, the whole
bother over again. At last he counted the marbles
over once more; but the full dozen could not be made
up for all his endeavours.—"Eleven remain eleven," I
said angrily.

The Doctor scratched the back of his head : "The
marble has disappeared."

" We knew as much as that long ago," I gave him
to understand, "although we ' women ' do not possess
thoroughness. No, positively not a scrap."

" Can Pitti have carried it off ? " he asked.—" The
dog never showed his nose in the room." — " Then
something must be done," he said ; " but keep quiet,
Emmi ; it is a matter of no importance. Franz must

be given a tablespoonful of salad oil, to be followed by a prescription which I will write out."

"And how about Fritz?" I interposed.

"What is the matter with Fritz?"

"Are you so certain as to which has swallowed the marble?"

"Both boys to have the same treatment," decided the Doctor shortly. "The marble must be found."

"Now one innocent creature is obliged to suffer for the sake of the other," I remarked, my humanitarian proclivities being somewhat hurt. "I consider that it is simply inexcusable!"

"It is inexcusable that the children were not better looked after!" he scolded. "If they had been with the nurse, it would certainly not have happened."

This reproach roused my ire. "My worthy son-in-law," I therefore answered in measured tones, "the nurse was a horror. The responsibility does not rest upon us. I said at once that there would be terrible confusion; and matters can hardly be worse than they are at present. If the blame is to rest upon any one, it must be upon you, for there have never been twins in our family."

And what was the answer he made to this with jeering laughter, instead of being reduced to abject silence? "I am sorry for that—the race is good."

The only possible answer to this was to turn away in wounded disgust.

After he had endeavoured to pacify Emmi by assuring her that so far there were no grounds for alarm, he went off to write his prescription. The little ones got their oil, which did not increase the charm of life, and when the girl brought the medicine later, they seemed still more out of love with existence; at least, if one might judge from the expression of their little faces, which were drawn into heart-rending grimaces. But must not every one from earliest youth find out by experience that this earth of ours is occasionally a vale of tears whose paths are not paved with pancakes?

After the oil and medicine had been administered to them, they were put to bed. But such a fuss as they made! The bare recollection is enough.

First of all, it never struck them to feel tired, for it was not going-to-bed time, and then Franz is such a fidget that he never can lie still under any circumstances. As, however, bed is the place for sick folk, and marbles taken internally may be counted among the most threatening symptoms, we transferred this at-home day to the bed-room, Emmi sitting beside Franz, and I by Fritz, who utterly belied his Buchholz nature from sheer perversity, and behaved just as naughtily as Franz, although he is usually a thoughtful child given to amuse himself quietly. Did we hug ourselves in the belief that they had settled down, up jumped the brothers; and if we had just taken them up, back into bed they wanted to go. The Doctor must have prescribed something of a velocipedic nature for them, otherwise they never could have carried on as they did.

Emmi was getting visibly worn out. "Child," I said, "do me the favour of taking a proper dinner with your husband—the girl and I will do sick-nursing meanwhile; I can get mine later on. We will send a commissionaire to the Landsberger-strasse to tell them that I am remaining here and will return home towards evening."

"Do you think I am one of those unnatural mothers who desert their angels when they are tottering on the brink of the grave?"

"Rubbish!" I said; "when only one of them can be in danger, and even your husband does not know which it is! And if there really were danger, he would tell us of it. Go, Emmi; he does not like dining alone, and I shall have you ill on my hands too."— She allowed herself to be persuaded, and as the Doctor came in again to see how matters were progressing, she plucked up some courage when he was unable to discover further cause for anxiety.

He understands his profession thoroughly, I must acknowledge that, but yet he was unable to bring the marble to light; and Emmi grew more and more excited the oftener our hopes were deceived.

This being so, it would have been my duty to remain overnight and assist my daughter; but the Doctor advised my going home, more especially as there was no fever, and the children were slumbering peacefully. The only thing that ailed them was that they were a little pulled down from the effects of the medicine.

When I got home I found my good Carl in the middle of a pleasant game of skat, the players being himself, Herr Felix, and Herr Kleines, whom he had met out walking and taken back home for this purpose.

"Was there anything wrong at the Doctor's, that you had to send a messenger?" he asked.

"Oh, yes," I exclaimed, and, letting fly at Herr Kleines, "you are the cause! How could you be so unreasonable as to bring toys to the children which may cause them to lose their health?"—"I do not understand you," he answered, trying to smile down my indignation.—"You never do seem to comprehend when you do mischief, and consider yourself diabolically clever into the bargain to practise such sleight-of-hand as you did with the marbles."—"But, excuse me,

surely the children are not able to count as yet."—
"How so? What do you mean by that?"—"Well,
two into eleven won't go."—"Do you mean to jeer at
me?"—"Certainly not. I only had eleven marbles,
and in order not to spoil the symmetry of the thing, I
said to Franz, 'Here are six,' and just the same to
Fritz."—"Then Fritz only had five?"—"That's it! I
did a bit of conjuring."—"Thank God!" I exclaimed;
"and we thought that he had swallowed one."—
"Which of them?" asked my husband; "Fritz?"—
"No, Franz."—"You said Fritz just now!"—"Don't
make me mix up the twins more completely than I
have been doing all the afternoon, Carl; at last we
really did not know which was which. And as for
you, Herr Kleines, make your way as quickly as may
be to the Doctor's, so that my daughter may be relieved of her cares. It is all through you that the poor
little souls have had to take such horrid stuff."—"But
surely it was only Fritz?" said my husband.—"Carl,
how can you talk such nonsense? it was Franz who
swallowed the ball!"—"Oh, it's Franz now, is it?"—
"No, neither of them."—"Then why had they to take
horrid stuff?"

Words failed me. My brain was all in a whirl with
this questioning. I sat down and fanned myself with
my handkerchief. The only sign of life I gave was by
my breathing.

Herr Kleines showed himself from his most agreeable
side, which on this occasion was the invisible one; indeed he probably recognised that a messenger of peace
could never arrive too early.

Betti made me a cup of tea and a sandwich, of which
I stood in need, and did all in her power to quiet my
nerves again, so that I gradually found myself capable
of relating the events. They were all glad that it had

been a false alarm, and now that all was quiet again,
I felt with absolute clearness how completely the two
little ones had grown into one's heart ; for while I was
at Emmi's, I had to take the matter with apparent
ease, as a kind of set-off to her despondency. No ;
rather let us have a pair of twins than lose one of
them, even though Grandmamma Buchholz must work
till she drops.

"Well," I said, "a few more rounds will be a good
antidote for our fright. I can tell you that it is no
easy matter to nurse one child through such an ill-
ness, let alone two. But I do feel confidence in our
doctor—he knows what he is about."

My husband declared a solo in clubs straight off,
but as I held two knaves and five trumps against.him,
he was bound to lose. That was a bright spot of light
after the troubles of the day.

A BAD TIME.

Why silence is golden—About overweight and playing at hide-and-
seek—Why Max wishes to marry and Wilhelmine is without a
sign—About protection from draught and the law relating to
accidents—Why the Aunt from Bützow "walks," and " E " is
pronounced like "I"—Renz is announced and the auction has
taken place—About genealogical trees in Zehlendorf, and the
millions who are to be embraced.

I WONDER who can have invented that stupid phrase,
"Silence is golden "? Of course it is pretty much the
same to me, whoever it may have been, for generally
speaking it is in a very few cases that people know
where a thing is derived from, and continually make
guesses that are invariably wrong, at Schiller or Faust,

when later researches reveal that it comes from Uhland or some book that is close at hand ; but if I did meet him, I should like to ask him : "Sir, have you ever held your tongue for a considerable space ?" and when he speechlessly retorts, "What do you mean ?" I would answer, "Because, if so, you never would have dared to give utterance to such rubbish. For the rest, pray sit you quietly down, and I will put the matter in a nutshell for you.

"Supposing a person has some anxiety and can thoroughly talk it over, she feels as if she had just come out of a bath or put on her Sunday clothes, even though her listener should be nothing but a neighbour with whom she is not even on bowing terms ; under such circumstances, one comprehends the meaning of freedom of speech for which all the world is clamouring. But should circumstances ordain that you are obliged to hold your tongue, you move about as if a weight were keeping you down."

During the many years we had been together I had not had one single secret from my husband with the exception of Christmas and birthday presents, and to these may be added broken kitchen utensils, or short-lived glass, which puts in a fresh appearance unperceived, for he waves such things aside as trivialities when I bring them under his notice ; and now I was bound, with respect to Max, to take Frieda into my house, and the other girl as well, without my Carl dreaming anything about it. Of course he must hear of it some time, but I was in a deadly fright of this some time. For, firstly, should I not be obliged to acknowledge that I had lost my wager? And secondly, he had an undisputed right to build, which would cause him, thirdly, to laugh at me ; and fourthly, he would obtain Uncle Fritz's help in doing so.

Fifthly, I should be compromised in Max's eyes in the event of my husband withholding his consent, and therefore, sixthly, I should come to grief all round. I was sitting, as it is allegorically expressed, in the mire between two chairs.

In hours of deepest despondency the thought sometimes crossed my mind that I would explain to Max that my Carl would none of it. But to go to Switzerland by means of lies! No; the consciousness of it would have become an unbearable extra-charge, which would have murdered every pleasure of the journey. Fancy sitting in the train like Cain, and being unable to rise to enthusiasm over the picturesque charms of Nature! Far better relinquish the idea.

At last I devised some sort of a scheme by concerting with Max that the business should not be made known for the present, until Betti's marriage, or until I judged expedient to speak about it. Meanwhile, I hoped for a suitable moment that chance might afford for my better assistance. Frieda had only consented to the proposition after having declined it peremptorily at first. Max has not informed me again as to what she said about me, but I am convinced that cross-patch was quite the most complimentary term.

When she learnt further that I had a general idea of taking in some young girls, and that she would find a companion, she became more reasonable, and was disabused of the idea that the Buchholzes' house had been turned into a den for the taming of neglected creatures, expressly on her account. If she had got wind of it, were it only as much as gets through a shut stove-door, then it would be all up with us.

Besides this, I treated her with greater sympathy when I met her, and closed my eyes internally in order not to see her faults; for looked at by the light of clear intelligence, she was a very undesirable girl. I will not absolutely say that Love was as blind as a bat in Max's case, but certainly he had a film over his eyes, or was short-sighted, to say the least of it.

Frieda too drew rather nearer to me, but unfortunately I was obliged to turn the conversation when she hinted at her approaching appearance as a pillar of the house. My being condemned to silence unquestionably did not cause my couch to be spread with gold, and the longer I put off the period for a general confession, the more completely my courage was reduced to a state of unconquerable flabbiness, in consequence of which my health also went overboard. The Doctor therefore was quite right in his diagnosis when he explained that my occasional increased difficulty in breathing was due to asthma on the nerves, and advised me to take valerian ; which, however, was useless beyond spreading disagreeable odours, for it was not a proper prescription, but merely a recommendation. How can that be of any use ?

My kind Carl even stinted himself in tobacco while in my company, as the smoke irritated my throat ; but even that was in vain, as I could not put aside my cares and endless games of hide-and-seek ; for was not the other girl still weighing me down ?

I had conveyed my consent by letter ; Frau Schulz had got a faithful promise that her daughter would be received by me for her further education, and I had about three letters a fortnight, demanding the carrying out of her offer.

"Wilhelmine," remarked my Carl, "your foreign correspondence has been unusually lively for some time. What have you in view ? "

" Nothing ; it is all about the geese."

'What, now that we have the covered markets ?"

he interposed. "I should think that you would find choice enough there. Don't bother yourself on my account, Wilhelmine. I can eat them, even though they may not be so well fed."

"Oh, Carl," I longed to exclaim, "this sort of goose would turn away your appetite !" but his undeserved kindness covered me with confusion and rendered me incapable of telling the truth. Could I abuse this moment of sincere affection, by making a murderous onslaught on my unsuspecting husband with two sudden housewife's helps? No, I could not do it.

Nor could a suitable occasion be found during the next few days ; the record of my sins and secrets had grown too big a one for me to begin on it of my own accord. After a few more days Herr Max came round to beg that his Frieda might be taken in at once, as her father was on the point of making a marriage which was lowering to Frieda. There certainly would be some misfortune when the new wife was brought home ; the only thing left for him to do was to marry Frieda, in the event of my not being able to give her shelter.

"Max," I exclaimed, "has everything entered into a conspiracy against me?"

He allowed me some little time for reflection. That gave me a trace of relief, which, however, was not to be of long duration, for in her next *billet-doux* Frau Schulz opened out before me the pleasant prospect of taking me unawares shortly with her daughter in the midst of my daily avocations, without ceremony or preparation, so that she might be able to see at a glance what our habits were. Would not that be charming ? Oh, certainly ; charming with a vengeance !

Now I had to devise further subterfuges. How

painfu! it is when one has recourse to concealments and untruths! It was nothing but a tiny, tiny necessary reserve to start with, and now I have floundered into the midst of embarrassments, and am obliged to prevaricate until I hardly know myself whether I am telling the truth or not. But I have vowed that as soor as everything is once set straight, there shall not be the slightest veiling of events in future. The truth, the whole truth, and nothing but the truth.

What pretext had I better impose on Frau Schulz to prevent her making her invasion? Should I write that we had upholsterers in the house? That would come out later. Or that we had small-pox? That would be simply wicked. Or spring cleaning? That might be just what she wanted to see. At last I hit on the idea of having visitors in the house. She would feel in their way, and they would feel in her way; besides, we could not know whether we might not be making an excursion; enough, did she wish for anything, she must specify accurately both date and hour, and we could arrange a meeting in the "Franciscan." I could make no other arrangement. Selah!

However, she did what such an individual would be likely to do : chose the exact hour when we would be at dinner and announced herself for the following day, so that escape on my side was an impossibility, and a plausible excuse for my absence from the dinner-table had to be invented. But what an arduous piece of work it was! After I had been nearly reduced to despair and my brain was well-nigh reeling, I discovered the advertisement of a sale of furniture by auction at Leppeke's, where, as I made my Carl believe, I might perhaps acquire some old pieces suitable for Betti's establishment.

He certainly thought that the antiques were made much better new in Berlin ; but although he was right seven times over, I was forced to hide my opinion from him on this occasion. Frau Schulz was in sight.

Just as I am about entering the "Franciscan," and soliloquising, " She is sure to be near the entrance on the right-hand side, so that you will meet her straight away," I remember with the utmost horror that I don't know Frau Schulz at all, and that Frau Schulz does not know me, and that no single symbol of meeting, such as a rose or a handkerchief, has been agreed upon. "Never mind," I continue to myself ; "a mother with a daughter cannot well be missed, and after all one has an eye for country cousins." So into the Dardanelles I plunged.

After searching through the first room without discovering her, I inspect the second ; and as there are nothing but men seated there, I pursue my devious way through the third and fourth rooms, without finding any one among the many guests bearing the least resemblance to a mother and her daughter. The same perspective meets me everywhere ; not a sign of Frau Schulz. Such waiters as I interviewed declared that they had seen nothing resembling her—no, not even with the promise of a *douceur*.

" Probably Zehlendorf time is slow," I consoled myself, like Columbus, who had, as we know, to make many fruitless attempts at discovery before he at last saw New York lying before him, "and she will be the next to enter the building." That being so, you must take up a position at the entrance ; she will not be able to slip past you there. As there were only a gentleman and lady sitting at the table in closest proximity to the door, I was kind enough to sit down beside them, which they very good-naturedly permit-

ted, for, as I shall explain in a minute, I provided them
with some protection against the draught, which the
portière alone was insufficient to keep off.

"How touchingly egoistical they both are," I
thought, and determined to favour them with never a
word ; for if one meddles with selfishness, one is invariably the loser. As it was Wednesday, and they
seemed greatly to enjoy the broad beans and bacon
which formed one item of the bill of fare, I ordered
a portion for myself, together with a pint of ale, and
became absorbed in the enjoyment of this nourishing
dinner, which my husband also appreciated greatly in
former times, but has somewhat neglected of late
years on account of the husks. "What may he be
doing now, my good Carl? is he enjoying his dinner
without my presence?" I was on the point of beginning a train of thought directed homewards, when
suddenly, with the rapidity of a telegraph wire,
the thought flashed through me : "Can Frau Schulz
perhaps have stormed the Landsberger-strasse and be
cheerfully making her revelations there while I am sitting down to my broad beans here?"

My first impulse was to spring from my place and
pursue her, but reason kept me in my seat ; the woman
might come in at any moment, and if she were not to
find me, matters would be just as critical as they are
now. Of what avail was the parsley on the beans, the
well-fed bacon, the foaming beer direct from the barrel? The last meal of a culprit sentenced to death
cannot well be cooked without the feeling,—in half-
an-hour more your time will have come. I consumed
the remainder under difficulties—but then, it had to
be paid for !

Whenever the door opened I watched it like a
pointer, but nothing appeared which could be ex-

plained into Frau Schulz with her daughter. Fat and thin people came, gentlemen and ladies, old and young of every description ; the entire red book was represented, the expected one alone came not.

What could the waiters think of me, peering hither and thither without rhyme or reason, more especially as I could not hide behind a newspaper owing to my watch on the door? In sheer despair I finished my pint and ordered another. "There," I scoffed furiously, "the downward path is now complete! Wilhelmine, you are beginning to drink now." And then I wished that I had a big, big newspaper to bury myself behind, for he who was now entering the restaurant was Uncle Fritz. This was the only thing wanting.

"Is it you or is it not?" he asked, after he had got over his first surprise.—"Certainly!" I answered testily ; "it is I. Do you object?"—"Certainly not ; but how do you come into this part of the world?"— "I might ask you the same question."—"I am delivering chandeliers close by, and have to superintend the workmen. If a stupid servant-girl with two left hands drags one of them down upon herself later, the law comes upon me for compensation. Have you had a quarrel with your Carl, or are you travelling beer on your own account?"

"Neither the one nor the other!" I burst out angrily. "I am sitting here and waiting for an old woman from Zehlendorf."

"You are expecting some one from Zehlendorf?" my female neighbour suddenly interrupted our conversation. "Are you, perhaps, Frau Wilhelmine Buchholz, of the Landsberger-strasse?"

"Who else should I be?"

"I am Frau Schulz, of Zehlendorf."

" You don't say so ! " I screamed at her ; " and you only come out with it now, after letting me sit here like a fool, in the most deadly fear ! "

" In fear ? And on my account ? " she asked.—" In case you might have got mixed up among the carriages," I managed to say. " Where have you left your daughter ? "—" She is visiting a friend, and ought to be here every moment. She promised me faithfully to be punctual ; it is impossible for her to be long now. But young girls are all like that, are they not ? They have so much to tell each other when they have. not met for a long time, although I impressed upon her : ' Make haste, my child ; Frau Buchholz is sure to be pressed for time, as she has visitors staying with her.' "—" Visitors staying with you ? " asked Uncle Fritz, who was hesitating as to whether he should establish himself beside this idiot. " Who is staying with you ? "—" Our aunt from Bützow," I said, merely to mention some name, and made signs that he was to enter into my subterfuge ; but instead of helping me out of my dilemma, he played the innocent, and laughed, " She has been dead a long time ; or does she walk ? "

" Fritz," I exclaimed, boiling over with rage, " can you not see that you are one too many here ? " and, turning to Frau Schulz, I continued : " One of my aunts in Bützow certainly has died and left me a good deal. But this aunt about whom my brother seems to know nothing——"

" Is a very charming woman, with seven uneducated children and a tame parrot," Uncle Fritz interrupted my remarks ; " but as I only count those people from whom I am to inherit among my relations, I never thought about her. I must say good-bye now." He had understood me and retired.

As the long waiting had already turned my good-humour into a very sour one, I determined to dispose of Frau Schulz in the shortest possible space of time, and said, "I cannot wait here for a week. So you agree to the understanding that your daughter is not to refuse any kind of work?"—"Oh, certainly, certainly! Are you very much given to scouring?"

"It depends; for many things may be ruined by cleaning. I allow no misuse of water."

"Quite so. I say just the same. Edith cannot bear wet."

"Still, your daughter Ida will have to encounter it, in order to learn everything thoroughly."

"If matters cannot be otherwise arranged," she sighed. "The principal point is loving treatment. She has a wonderful spirit and great imagination. She would lay down her life for theatricals."

"We have no theatricals in our house."

"I merely mean that she ought to have an occasional amusement after her exertions. Is your cookery nourishing?"

"It is homely fare."

"Coarse food does not agree with my daughter."

"My friend, homely fare is quite distinct from fare for menials. I must beg of you to understand that. But it seems that your Ida has a vast amount of pretension."

"Ida? You call her Ida always, excuse me; but my daughter's name is Edith, with an English 'th' and the E pronounced like I."—"Could you not have found a name that was still more absurd?" I asked.—"Is it not exquisite!" she exclaimed. "Ah, German names are all so common!"—"My dear friend," I answered, "it does not matter what one's name is, so long as it is borne with honour, and has pleasant associations when used by other people. But pray tran-

quillize yourself. I will manage to expel these foreign
fads from your Ida's mind. I shall certainly not dislocate my tongue on her account, not even if she had
a dozen English 'th's' dangling after her. So now
you may either accept or refuse, just as you feel disposed, and take your sugar-plum of a daughter straight
back with you. I don't care about tropical plants."

"Oh, no, dearest Frau Buchholz," she turned to en-
treaty now; "you cannot be so cruel! Edith has her
faults—I acknowledge that freely—but her character
is so sweet, and under your guidance she will become
quite perfect. You keep to your promise, won't you?"

"On condition that she is obedient and submissive."

"You will find no cause for complaint."

"I will hope so. But we have now been waiting for
over an hour. There must be an end of it. Where
will my husband imagine that I have got to?"

"Put all the blame upon me. Surely your visitors
can do without you for a short time!"

I was silent. Just before I had virtuously mounted
my high horse and been speaking about "bearing with
honour," and my visitor dragged me suddenly off it.
That was painful.—"We all have our failings," I said,
"and should therefore not look for perfection in our
fellow-creatures. If your Idiss feels confidence in me,
we will be sure to get on together. But there is one
condition I must make. Idiss must be truthful and
sincere. I cannot bear untruths."

"I will impress that especially upon her. Of course
little fibs may occur now and then."—"They are the
worst, believe me; they can embitter one's life. Where
is your husband?"—"My husband?"—"Well, the gentleman who was sitting beside you."—"I do not know
him. I sat down at this table to make sure of not miss-
ing you."

The daughter arrived at last—a thin, lank creature, still requiring a deal of nourishment, before she would be able to develop a proper figure. She made her excuses to the effect that while with her friend she had never given a thought to the time, and that she was very pleased to come to Berlin. "What splendid streets there are," she said enthusiastically, "and magnificent shops, and performances at Renz's are already announced ! I wish I were going to stay now."

"My dear child," I answered, "amusements are the last things we are going to think about. It is not easy to learn housekeeping ; so much practice in numberless small details is necessary for that purpose, that one learns at last to be nothing but practical. Then only does one's knowledge begin to take form. Do you feel inclined to set to work at it ? "

"Yes," said her mother.

The daughter seemed to agree with this answer, for she nodded her head.

"My time has come to an end," I said, as I prepared to take my leave. "You will be told when I can receive you, but it will not be just at present. So far, my arrangements have not been made for it. You must wait until I write."

The farewell on both sides was a satisfactory one. "I shall be able to manage her," I thought, and Frau Schulz said : "Edith's one consideration will be how she can please you."

But what Frau Schulz's idea of pleasing a person was I only discovered later. Why is it that the future is closely barred against our gaze? In order that we should not see the vexation awaiting us in it.

Betti was too delighted that I had brought her nothing antique, because it goes out of fashior so easily, and is sure to have the worm in it—either the natural article, which cheerily bores its way onward, or the artificial, which vendors of furniture introduce into it, and which conduces more to the pleasure of the connoisseur than to the durability of the article. Besides, now that the Louis Quatorze style is coming in, one must be more than careful, if one wants to keep on a level with cultured folk. She went to tell my husband that I had returned, and he put in an appearance at once. "Have you convinced yourself that the purchase of antiquities has its *yets* and *buts*?" he asked.—"Carl, there was nothing there of a really good, durable style."—"Ay!"—"And frightfully dear."—"Oh!"—"I am certain we could buy new things to greater advantage."—"Ah!"—"Carl, why are you so monosyllabic?"—"You have been out, and have more to talk about than I, as it seems to me."— A crushing presentiment took possession of me. Could he know anything about it? "Has Uncle Fritz been here?" I asked.—"No."—"Anything unpleasant occurred in business?"—"No."—"Is anything the matter with you?"—"No."—"Carl, why are you like that?"—"Wilhelmine," he said quietly, "the auction took place last week," and put the newspaper before me in which I had read the advertisement. I was found out now, and by such a trifle too! It really was an old paper. What had I better do? "Then," I stammered, "I suppose that I must have made a mistake."—"Let us hope so."—"Carl," I wanted to break forth, "am I still a child to be catechized like this?" but at the moment I really was a child, and could no longer control myself. "Forgive me; forgive me!" I exclaimed. "I won't do it again!" and flung myself on him and hid my face against him.

How indulgent he was, how gently he spoke to me! So I began my confession and told him what had been worrying me during the past weeks, and how ashamed I had felt in his sight—a shame that grew day by day—and how I became more and more cowardly and unable to confess the truth.

"Old woman," he said, "have you learned to know me so little during all these years that you are still afraid of me, of your husband, who loves you above everything?"

"It is because you love me that I was silent. Could I help believing that I would be hateful to you, remembering all the deceit in which I had involved myself? My wish to prove myself in the right is to blame for it all; I wished to show you that I was perfectly able to be consistent; but, Carl, one can get over one's nature. I was so sorry for Max, and then I promised him to take his *fiancée* in here without having asked you first. I have lost my wager, and I give up the journey willingly, if only you will be friends with me and forgive me. What is building, with all its upsets, compared with the torments that I have been enduring recently? It was my conscience that caused me to suffer, and valerian is of no avail against that."

"But you really should take more care of yourself, Wilhelmine, or else your asthma will get bad. Betti and I were only saying to-day that you ought to have some help, and that the companionship of a young girl would be necessary for you when Betti married."— "Carl, did you hit on this idea quite by yourself?"— "The idea is not far to seek."— "You might have said something about it sooner."— "Would I have dared to?" laughed my Carl; "did you not expressly assert that you did not intend worrying yourself any more about anybody?"— "Carl, don't jeer at me; I cannot bear it now."

After a pause he began again : "It would be advisable to get the girl soon, to have her trained by the time Betti goes."

"Carl," I answered timidly, " there are *two* 'helps'—Max's *fiancée*, and another one. It could not be helped, my Carl. But I doubt whether you will be able to pronounce her. What you have to do is to bite a piece off your tongue, and then proceed as if you wished to spit it out, but keep it notwithstanding between your teeth. She writes herself down English, and is called Idiss Schulz."—"Idiss is good," said my Carl.—"Her genealogical tree is rooted in Zehlendorf."—"So she is merely Englishified !" retorted my husband. "That will have an end some time, like the horses' tails."—"Carl, my ears are not made to listen to such comparisons."—"Wilhelmine, you must take me as I am ; I expect I am too old for improvement. Besides, I think neither of us is going to reproach the other ; we will have patience with one another." He gave me his hand ; I took it in both of mine and carried it to my cheek. Now I had my support again, my Carl.

I felt lighter and better than ever I had done before, as if burdens and threats had been lifted off me ; a delicious feeling, soft and mild as the breath of evening, surrounded me. Peace returned once more to the heart which had so often beaten with the fright of not being able to exist in my husband's sight. Reproaches ceased, fear fled away, I was delivered from pain. I should like to have embraced the whole world, and bell-like voices resounded in and round me, "Seid umschlungen Millionen," just as I had once heard it sung at a concert, in which Niemann took part. In those days I thought it very beautiful, but it was not until now, when memory recalled it to me, that I

understood how poets and musicians have sung for us
dumb children of humanity.   Now it resounded again
from my inmost soul, and took all my troubles away
with it.

When Betti came in to announce Uncle Fritz, I
saw everything in such a rose-coloured light that I
was able to receive him.

"Where have you hidden your visitors away?" he
exclaimed; "I should like to make the acquaintance
of my new aunt. You can tell stories well, Wilhelmine;
the Zehlendorf lady was quite taken in by you!"

"Fritz, those are matters that do not concern you.
Is it not so, Carl?"

My Carl looked roguishly at me and smiled.   Then
he said to Uncle Fritz, "We have had a visitor staying here, certainly, but she left half an hour ago, and
never intends returning.   By the way, I can give you
quite the latest items of news; my wife consents to
my building, and we are going to have two assistants
in the housekeeping."

"Two?" queried Betti.

"For the one to finish the mischief that the other
would not be able to get through alone!" remarked
Uncle Fritz.

"Yes, if they were anything like you.   But it's no
use your trying; if you want to vex me, you must
seek out another day for the purpose."

I went off with Betti to have an undisturbed chat
over the arrangements for the young girls, and left
the two men to themselves; for even the greatest
patience may give way, if a person drags perpetually
at it.   And unfortunately Uncle Fritz is greatly given
to do so.

THE PILLARS OF THE HOUSE.

Why Frau Schulz departs and Wilhelmine discourses in Chaldee—
Why there is to be no quarrelling and Herr Buchholz is threatened with the Day of Judgment—Why handkerchiefs are to be
hemmed and the piano is tormented—Why it is difficult to please
and Doris forgets the stove cover—About prose, poetry, and
such-like matters—Why Wilhelmine has to preach and my Carl
escapes the guillotine—My Carl a member of the corps of stu-
dents and Wilhelmine in the arm-chair—Why there is no occasion for dead bodies and the newest fashion gets worn out—
Why Frieda changes her room.

WE had at last seen the last of Frau Schulz of
Zehlendorf. She brought her Idiss with bag and bag-
gage—including three bonnet-boxes—and developed
such a gift of narration that my Carl took French
leave and left me to listen to the remainder. But
when my heart misgave me that she would chatter
away till she missed the last train, I said simply,
" Frau Schulz, unless you hurry you will have to spend
the night in Berlin. It will be well for you, and for
us too, to get a little quiet. We cannot hang on to
each other's aprons for ever." I had vowed to exercise
the strictest candour, and was not at all disposed to be
sparing of it where she was concerned. Mankind
must have what it wants ; so says my son-in-law, the
Doctor.

" It is so hard for me to tear myself from your
home-like abode," she said loudly and pointedly; " it
is so comfortable here ! Ah, one is conscious at
once of the careful superintending spirit, everything
is so clean and well arranged; and not a vestige of a
spider's web anywhere ! I cannot endure spiders; and
as for mice, really I cannot describe to you the fright
I am in about mice. Is that not so, Idiss? You have

been here for a long time? I can imagine it. And do you like living here? Of course. Would you like to live anywhere but in Berlin? Berlin is too charming. Are you afraid of mice too? Ah, no, I am sure that you are courageous!" And so forth, as if she had been wound up.—"If you take a fly, you will just be able to catch it!" I interposed quickly, as she caught her breath in the rapidity of her utterance. And now she prepared for the journey in all haste, embraced her Idiss violently, and was off.

Betti looked at me, and I looked at Betti; it was a silent Thank Heaven, in order not to let Idiss notice how delighted we were that the visit had come to an end. I do not know the equal of this old chatterbox in wearisomeness.

"And," upon this I said to Idiss, "you will now go up to your room and settle your things in their places. Hang up your dresses in the left-hand side of the wardrobe— Fräulein Frieda will be using the other half later—and put away the rest of your things in the one chest of drawers. When you have finished doing that, you can help my daughter to get supper ready. Generally speaking we have cold things, and you will undertake the tea department."

Idiss made a face as if I had been talking to her in Chaldee, nor did she move from the spot.

" Well?"

" I have never put away my dresses myself," she said.

" Who has done it, then?"

" Mamma."

" Really! But you are going to learn to look after your own things. However, I will willingly give you a little help to start with. Come with me."

So I went off and up-stairs with her. The trunks were already awaiting us there.

" Unlock them."—" I do not know the keys."   Well, there was nothing for it but for me to open the trunks ; and as she pretended to know so little about it, I hung up all her dresses in the wardrobe as well. In this way I certainly find out what she has, but that is not much of an advantage, when she stands looking on with folded hands, to see how I manage as lady's maid.

" Keep your things nice and tidy, for there is nothing so hurtful as creases, and putting them away higgledy-piggledy.   Now we will go down-stairs again, and my daughter will show you what your duties are in the kitchen."   I thought to myself, " If Betti should give her a shake-up, it will do her no harm—she is too pomady."

When we sat down to supper, I saw by Betti's updrawn lip that something had gone wrong with her, and the daughter of Frau Schulz of Zehlendorf looked a good deal put out.   An infant could see that the two had had a squabble.   My Carl, who probably noticed something of the same kind, took his supper without giving any assistance to the conversation, and seemed as uncomfortable as if his coat were too tight for him, although he had his old one on.   Idiss groaned frequently, as if suffering internal martyrdom, a fact that did not in the least touch Betti, who sat there like a statue, though it caused my husband to look towards her each time she did it, whereby Idiss's sufferings were only increased.

This state of affairs could not be borne for long, and so I said jestingly, " Have you learned a little about housekeeping already, Idiss ? "

Instead of answering, Betti took the cream-jug and placed it roughly in front of me.   The spout of the jug had been freshly broken.   " What is the meaning of that ? " I asked.—"A specimen of Fräulein Schulz's love of art," answered Betti.—"Oh, no," said our guest; "it broke off of itself!"—"That is not its usual habit," Betti retorted shortly.—"Then the cook must have done it !" exclaimed Idiss.—"You had better let Doris hear you say that," answered Betti; "she would recall you to a sense of truth pretty sharply." —"Children," I placed myself in the breach, "let us have no quarrels. We will all suppose this time that the jug has been struck by lightning, but that won't do for a second occasion."

My Carl chose to go to his district club for a few minutes, and we soon sent Idiss to her room. When we were alone Betti said : "Mamma, I have never met such a clumsy, ill-trained girl."—"That is the reason we have her here. Be patient, Betti. You were only able to work yourself into housekeeping by degrees, but then you certainly had not a Frau Schulz for your mother. Just let me arrange matters. 'Helps' must be gently dealt with."

My hopes for improvement were not particularly lofty, but things went worse and worse during the following days with Idiss, whose favourite occupation seemed to be that of idling. The sudden change might possibly account for that. Until quite lately she had still been playing with her dolls; and now she was suddenly called upon to distinguish between ginger and nutmeg, naturally she stood before them and wondered.

Such, generally, is what I imagine the scientific explanation to be; for if a young thing like that be suddenly taken from its home, and transplanted to another neighbourhood, where different beds and customs obtain, it displays its general human disposition, by objecting to both food and drink, and by letting home-sickness peep forth from eyes red with tears. Does not a newly-moved plant let its leaves droop at first, until it begins to think better of it? while weeds, on the other hand, do not mind transplanting, but go on flourishing wherever they may happen to be thrown. This being so, it was not very astonishing that Idiss should get an attack of sentimentality, and be more given to moaning than to taking her breath quietly, although it ended by inspiring my Carl with the fear that her lungs were full of bacilli, and that she would soon have to take to her bed. "We have a double responsibility," he said, "for she is the child of strangers."—"Carl," I answered, "it is the new and the unaccustomed which causes her moans. As soon as she feels more at home, she will become tired of her grief. Besides, you see, she has affections. A bustling girl who has no heart and is always hankering after change, would sing and hop about in her new position like a water-wagtail; but this one moves about in tender melancholy over what she has lost. We may feel very thankful that we have not got a flibberty-jibbet."

"I should like her to be more lively, and not given to search for things on the floor when one looks at her," said my husband.

"Carl," I took him to task severely for this remark, "in the first place, it is not praiseworthy to make the fitting timidity of young girls a reproach to them; and in the second, it is unbecoming of you to let your glance follow them secretly. Once for all, I forbid you doing that. Remember, these are children of strange parents, for whose reputation we are just as responsible as for their bodily well-being. Carl, how will you be able to stand at the Day of Judgment if you look at them with other eyes than those of a foster-father?—to say nothing of the fact that I am on the patrol, so to speak, day and night!"

"Wilhelmine, do me the kindness to shut up; you have gone off on a wrong tack. You have taken a burden on yourself which I may be good enough to help you to carry. I don't like Ida from any point of view."—"Carl, Idiss; you must practise the proper movement of the tongue."—"Oh, bother! Ida or Idiss, she is odious to me."—"That is because you are wanting in knowledge of humanity. Young girls have to thaw. When I have once got her beyond the feeble stage, so that she will be able to bear a knock, I shall set about drilling her."

"Let us hope for the best," he answered. "You would do me an especial favour if you would give her to understand that I find her lachrymose whining unbearable."

"It shall be done, my Carl."

"And don't forget to oil the doors; they squeak just like your 'help.'"

After this I took advantage of the very first opportunity, and said: "Fräulein Schulz, what is really the matter with you? If you have any kind of weight lying on your mind, out with it; you may safely confide everything to me that troubles you."—"Ah, Frau Buchholz, the parting from home!" she stammered.—"My dear child, people cannot be tied to their mother's apron-strings till they reach the grave; they must leave her some time, and learn to walk alone. Why do you keep moaning so dreadfully?" She did not answer. "Set to work; that will drive away your vagaries. Your mother wishes that you should sew as much as possible for yourself, also knit and embroider; that is the reason that you have only been provided with the most necessary things to start with. Have you hemmed the handkerchiefs already?"—"I am just doing them, but——"—"But?"—"My eyes suffer from working so much."—"Oh, that is very sad!"—"Yes, I am very unhappy about it."—"Is there nothing you can do to dissipate your sorrow?"—"When I was at home, I used to sit down to the piano and breathe forth my grief in music. I do not know whether I might venture to do so here; I dare say Fräulein Betti would not allow me."—"Nonsense! The piano is in the drawing-room, but it has not been tuned for a long time; perhaps that will make it all the more suitable to your sorrow. Breathe away as much as you like, only you must not scratch the floor—we have just had it polished."—"Thank you," she said, and went.

I did feel to some extent curious as to how she would soothe her sorrow, and so I listened to her playing behind the door. And what did it amount to? That lovely song,

"Mutter, der Mann mit den Koks ist da!"*

And she did not even play it properly, but stumbled over it, and played wrong notes, with both feet on the pedal! It was a mercy that my Carl did not hear this kind of chamber music.

After I had gone off with manifold headshakings, I felt anxious to see what she had done in the way of hemming her handkerchiefs, and felt it to be my duty to investigate the contents of her work-basket. Its aspect was—indescribable! Everything was muddled up together, and about sixty stitches had been badly put into one handkerchief. That to give her cataract indeed!

* "Mother, the man with the coals is there!" A Berlin street song.—TRANS.

It was my turn to groan now. The thought flashed through me, "She is untruthful. Wilhelmine, you have been thoroughly taken in by her. She repudiated the cream-jug the very first evening."

Horrible! How are people in the same house to get on together, if one cannot put faith in the words of the other? And what mental tares one sows, when fresh deceptions have constantly to be thought out, an old untruth to be hidden behind a new one! Under such circumstances, suspicion effects a lodgment, people think badly of those who do not deserve it, the cheerfulness of one's disposition is lost, and life here below becomes gloomy, because everything seems to be as untrue as one's inner life. Period of childhood, why is it that you are so full of sunshine? Because the young soul is without guile.

I am no connoisseur, but still I do know enough about music to feel sure that her home-sickness and the newest street-song were just as closely connected as the name Idiss was with her appearance, and that she just used the piano as a kind of finger-rest to muddle away her time. But is not a girl almost bound to be deceitful, when her parents overload her with a foreign name, whereupon she imagines that she is half a foreigner, and rather grander than other people, though there is not a photograph of her in the world that could have the Schulz profile touched out of it?

It was my duty to call her to account. I went to her and said: "Pray, Ida, do not torment the man with the coals any longer. He is too heavy for our piano. If you really wish to practise, we will set apart a certain hour for you to do so."—"Oh, no, that would try me too much! Mamma always says that the piano should be a recreation."—"She is quite right, especially for the drums of the ears of the surroundings.

Just bring your work and come and sit with me ; we are not given to dawdling here."

While I looked through the linen that had come from the laundress, she did her hemming. We had a good deal of conversation, and I discovered by this means that so far she had only done what she chose, and what she chose was to do nothing. Even her shoes and stockings were put on by her mother. Papa had certainly often scolded, but then it had been easy to impose upon him.—"And papa allowed that ? "—"Oh, he had to, for mamma had the money." She suddenly came to a pause.—"Has she any now ?"—"I think that she lost some ; we were obliged to reduce our expenditure. That was horrid. It was not nearly so nice as formerly. Mamma was often very cross."

"It is a delightful thing to look on at extravagance, but vexatious when one comes to think over it later. Not only does it open the door to poverty, but quarrelling and strife follow in its steps. Many people think that their candles must be six to the pound to enable them to find their way to bed ; we use ten to the pound, and nobody has broken a leg here yet. The pound costs the same, but lasts longer. Pay attention to this, Ida : one can keep house with plenty of money, and one can manage on a little too."

"Mamma says that it is all the same so long as one is pleasing."

"To be pleasing is a difficult matter, child."

"Yes, if one cannot be in the fashion. Formerly I was always having new hats."

"It does not depend so much upon the hat as on the face that is below it. If a person looks as if she were in her own way, others gladly turn aside from her. An open, frank expression, a pleasant mouth, are more winning than the most fashionable toilettes,

but her spirit must be imbued with sincerity and amiability.   Nor should tidiness be forgotten.   The tie of
your shoe is undone, Ida ; a girl that does not respect
herself will pay no attention to the trifling duties she
owes her neighbours, and it is those which make life
pleasant or the reverse.   Settle that first, and then it
will be time for you to go to the kitchen.   Our clocks
are not regulated according to the soup ; they take
the time from my husband, and he is punctual.   And
another thing, Ida ; do not damage the plates and
dishes so much."

"This has been a lesson in morals as well as work,"
I said when I was alone, and felt astonished with myself.   My two girls would have been taken to task
more roundly, but then they were my own.

I must admit that nothing came of the admonitions
which I certainly supposed were soon to bear fruit,
for a dreadful noise was soon heard from the kitchen,
the cause of which I had to inquire into.   What I
found was Betti and Ida engaged in hot dispute.   Ida
screamed that she was not going to let herself be put
upon, while Betti was inveighing against her and saying that nothing could be done with such an idiot ;
one's life was not safe with her.   In addition to this,
the whole kitchen was strewed with rice and swimming in water.   Betti was so soaked from top to toe
that the water was trickling from her, and her hair too
was ornamented with grains of rice.—"Holy Brah-
ma !" I exclaimed, "what is the meaning of this?
Here is a pretty state of things !"

"I gave her the rice to wash," Betti explained ex-
citedly, "and Fräulein Schulz was silly enough to put
it under the cistern and turn on the tap so that the
whole of it flew out of the dish with the splash ; and
now that I tell her she must clean it up, she won't."

"Never did I see the like of that before," said Doris, who stood there petrified, and forgot in her astonishment to put on the stove-plate, which she was holding with the tongs, so that the smoke affected my vocal chords, and asthma, with cramp, and unavailing gasps for breath ensued.—"Afterwards," I gasped, "Doris will clean up. Ida, you are to come with me."

It was long before I recovered even partially. My long conversation, the vexation, and the smoke, had combined in very ūnfavourable effects. The result arrived at after careful consideration at last was : "Ida, for the present you will keep out of the kitchen, and as a beginning you will only concern yourself with the coffee, and the tea with the cold supper; you will be, so to speak, the cold mistress. You are not to meddle with cooking for the present."

"I could not help it," she answered ; "the rice did it of its own accord."—"Extraordinary rice !"—"But it really did."

"Fräulein Schulz, I do not approve of unseasonable contradiction ; and besides, you are to do as you are bid without opposition. You have not yet tied your shoe."—"Yes, I have."—"It is not tied."—"Then it must be the other one that has come undone."—"No, it is the same one, and is just as slatternly as before, when I drew your attention to it."—"Really ?"—"Yes, certainly. And when I tell you anything another time, you will be good enough not to sit on your ears to impede your better hearing. Fräulein Schulz, either you must change tremendously or we must part. I have not the remotest intention of worrying myself into the tomb on your account."

One ought not to fling away one's weapons at once even when met by opposition. What trouble and difficulty I had with Betti, who now attends to the house-keeping in a most experienced manner, and deserves great praise! Of course she looks forward to her own house, and is as unwearied at her work as if she were already responsible to her dear ones for everything, although of course they can only make claims upon her after the wedding. Expectation is a powerful incentive. People break their necks gladly along steep mountain-walls in expectation of a beautiful view, a thing that they certainly would not do for money. How people can overwork themselves without getting faint when a dress has to be provided for an unexpected ball; how carefully the visitor's room is prepared for a guest; and how his coming is listened for for hours, although it is impossible for him to arrive so soon! And yet, what is the most incomparable panorama from the highest summit, when compared with the breadth of life that expands with so much promise before the eyes of a bride? what are the most intoxicating waltzes when compared with those strains of gladness which, after the first kiss, are wafted towards us out of the happiness to come? what is the visitor's room compared with one's home, where careful hands will surround the beloved one with perfect and complete comfort?

I admit that many turn up their noses at the bare mention of such words as housekeeping, domestic economy, the kitchen, knitting and the like, and ask with fine contempt: "Where does the poetry come in?"—"My good friend," I suggest to such a one, "flowers must be cherished if they are to blossom; their roots need earth and moisture; obnoxious plants must be weeded out to preserve them from suffocation; and they only open out in the sunlight. Domestic comfort is the soil whence spring those hours during which one's thoughts may wander towards the beautiful, rather than the commonplace, and wonder what happiness looks like, how it could be represented, and the like, and during which we feel with those who were the beloved of song. Such times are at once hours of idleness and of delight, *flowers on our life's path*, no made-up rubbish of material and wire, without odour and without refreshment. My best of friends, you cannot wipe away dust with your Goethe, and Nathan the Wise himself will be unable to help you when the dinner has been spoilt. And yet another thing, my dear; time is wasted in discussions about poetry, during which you might have been doing something useful, such as making your husband's life pleasant to him."—" To pine away in domesticity as cook and laundress is not compatible with our dignity as human beings," suggests another, "and I am too well educated for mending and darning"; to which I answer: "One can never have enough education, as it consumes nothing; but it is possible to have too much. Moderation in everything, my good friend. If a person murders the hours of mental enjoyment with a scrubbing-brush or drowns them in soap and water, she does just as wrongly as one who neglects the practical aspects of life, because it seems prosaic to her to put her hands valiantly to work. But very frequently, most honoured lady, it is idleness pure and simple which lurks behind an idea like that. Negligence is not poetry, not at least for the relations, who prefer a pleasant hotel to uncomfortable domestic life. Then comes dissatisfaction, for life does not accommodate itself to novels and lectures on culture; and when later the nerves of the tender soul get unstrung like the strings of a cracked guitar, she complains in addition of being misjudged and misunderstood If that be not the result, my friend, I shall be very pleased, for your sake."

Ida had not a glimmering of such-like things, but Frieda was a bride-elect, so she had reasons sufficient for arriving at a proper understanding ; still she seemed wanting in real liking for all that she did.

About a week after Ida had become our household companion, she too joined us, in order that she might share the same room and the same wardrobe with the former. Of course the first bickering was caused by this unfortunate piece of furniture, as it was only provided with one key, which Ida had invariably mislaid or hidden away in her pocket when Frieda wanted it. When, later on, it was confided to Frieda's care, she would not produce it if Ida required it. At last, for peace' sake, Betti broke the lock with the kitchen chopper—my beautiful wardrobe !

Besides this, Fräulein Schulz insisted that Frieda was to call her Idiss, although every one of us had re-christened her Ida, to try and break her of her affectation, upon which Frieda retorted : " I suppose Idiss is a dog's name ? " The consequence of this was, extraordinary to relate, not a pitched battle, but a mutual sending to Coventry, which certainly was noticeable to my husband, but did not cause him further trouble. But so far as Betti and I were concerned, we lived in perpetual fear that some fine morning we should find the one in her bed strangled by the other, and I made the suggestion that Betti should share the room with Idiss. However, she only said, " Mamma ! " There was nothing left but to get hold of Frieda and speak seriously to her. " Betti," I said, " I wish I had learned to preach a sermon twice a day ; I should find it easier work."

The opportunity for calling her to me alone, was a

splendid one, viewed as such, though otherwise it was rather unsatisfactory.

It might have been about seven o'clock one morning when Ida came flinging into my room without knocking, like a young fury, with her hair down and in most absolute night costume, and screamed : " She is teasing me ; she is teasing me ! I won't stand it ! "

My Carl, who was just shaving in the adjoining bedroom, had nothing better to do than to cut himself in his fright, and he rushed in before I could close the door, as he was as little a sight for her as she was for him. I had forbidden both my " helps " to appear in any sort of half-dressed condition, as that is the broad path leading to untidiness, and now she showed herself in this guise. " Carl," I said, " you look as if you were fresh from the guillotine, and the least that you might have thrown over you would have been your dressing-gown. As for you, Fräulein Schulz, what is the matter with you ? It is your week ; why are you not dressed yet ? Who is attending to the coffee ? "— " Fräulein Frieda won't let me look in the glass," she complained. " She has been standing before it for half-an-hour, simply to prevent me dressing myself, and to ensure my being scolded because the coffee is not ready."—" I suppose you have not been able to drag yourself out of bed again ! "—" Yes, I have ! "— " I shall ask Frieda."—" Ask her ? Surely you don't believe her ? Why, she does not speak one word of truth ! "—" Fräulein Schulz, you had better not see a beam in other people's eyes, when you have a perfect timber-yard of them in your own. See to it that you go up-stairs and dress yourself. I will speak to Frieda." —" She will tell you a lot of stories."—" Go away ! "

This conversation had passed as rapidly as an express train, but it furnished me with enough " help " annoyance for the whole day, and on the far side of yonder threshold was my Carl, the bloody sacrifice of that excitable person.

In I went to him. The towel was quite red already. "Carl, surely it is not an artery?"—He did not answer.—"Why do you not speak to me, Carl?"—"I wish the devil would fly away with the 'helps,'" he thundered; "it is a breed that's enough to drive a man mad! In the evening they sit and sulk till they turn the butter on one's bread rancid, and in the morning one nearly cuts one's throat for their sake! I shall live out."—"Carl, that would give rise to scandal."—"To more scandal than there is here? I really shall go to the hotel till they have been cleared out of this. And there's an end to it."

My husband had not been as furious as this for a long time; indeed, I do not think he ever had been, so far as I could remember. That upset me. "Do not be over-hasty, my Carl," I endeavoured to pacify him. "You don't usually burst out like this; why have you done so to-day? Let us put some sticking-plaster on it; it is so comforting, and will be sure to do you good, my Carl. You were anxious yourself that I should have assistance; now you must be patient as well. I exercise indulgence myself whenever I possibly can, and as soon as they have made some progress, they will provide us with a good deal of comfort, when my sufferings get worse, or they will thread needles—I have begun to think of spectacles when doing fine work, my Carl,—or they will pick up stitches. And there is one thing you cannot deny, since the young girls have been here there has been much more life in the house."

"Oh, yes; there has been life enough to drive one out of it!"

"Carl, it only seems so to you ; you must not begin to exaggerate. And why do you shave yourself? Doctor Wrenzchen has arranged for the barber to come' in every morning ; if he can afford it, it is seemly that you should have him too ; and besides, it is the proper thing to do. Your reputation will certainly not be injured by considering the outside world a little more."

"There would be still less harm in your considering your husband a little more."

"Carl, do you wish to quarrel?"

"I wish for air. I wish for peace. I wish to have my former comfort."

"And so you shall, my Carl. Just say straight out that I am indifferent to you. Why am I getting old and worn out, and why is help of such necessity to me?"   •

"Wilhelmine, you surely don't want to pretend to me that the nuisance which you laid upon yourself is an assistance? They are not a bit like 'helps.' What is the reason, do you think? Because you don't un derstand taking the two of them the right way."

"Carl, I don't suppose that you have had the slightest experience of 'helps.' But if you really think it wise, I will give them such a punishment as they never had before."

"Don't be too violent, Wilhelmine."

"Carl, young girls have elastic natures. Just ask them till what hour of the morning they could dance ? It is impossible to harm them, I can tell you. They to worry you ! They shall have a taste of what I am like."

Meanwhile, he had finished dressing, brushing, and settling himself ; and when men are once brushed up, and the set of their cravat perfect, they adopt gentler manners. The wound had been doctored with a strip

of black plaster, so that I could not help expressing
myself to the effect : "Now, Carl, you might pose as
a student of one of the corps ; the gaudy cap is all
that is wanting.   We will breakfast alone together,
without the stumbling-blocks."

Well, I had got him fairly satisfied, and all would
have gone well, had the coffee only been drinkable ;
but it looked so attenuated when I was pouring it out,
that I wanted to have it taken away at once.   "Don't
trouble," said my husband ; "I must go to the office
directly,"—as if I had defrauded him of time to sit
down.   He had scarcely tasted it, however, before he
exclaimed : "Ugh !" and pushed aside his cup in dis ·
gust.   "That is simple slops !"—"It is clean-tasted,
but a little weak."—"It's too bad to be given to an old
cow ! "—"Carl, you forget yourself !"—"I won't hear
anything more about it.   If I am asked for I shall be
found in the 'Prelate,' and I invite the inquirer to join
me there in a pint of beer."—"You are surely coming
home to dinner ?"—He was gone.

"Well, this has been a nice piece of work !" was my
first thought ; my second, "What am I to do now?"

Should I send to the Parcels Delivery Company, and
have the two girls prepaid to their parental homes?
That would mean eating humble-pie, and confessing
that they had conquered me.   Frau Schulz would be
rushing everywhere open-mouthed, and Frau Krause
trotting about with her cutting remarks : " Of course
it did not do ! Just as we all expected."—I could hear
their gossip already, and the principal person, Max,
would be just as badly off as before.   I never have
bothered myself much about women, but to explain to
the kindly young fellow, "I promised you more than
I am able to perform ; you must accommodate yourself to your future misery !"   No, it was too dreadful ;

I could not possibly do it. On the other hand, my Carl was more to me than the whole universe besides. He does not like restaurant sauces for a continuance. Nor shall he be forced to like them. He shall have what he asks for—peace in the house.

It is easy to say, peace in the house. How splendidly one can imagine it to oneself while sitting in an arm-chair! How well people can talk about it; what wise advice they can give on the subject! But to have it, and keep it, is a difficult matter. I almost think that when people know to some extent what ought to be done in order to keep it, there is not much time left wherein to make use of the knowledge. To have exhausted knowledge means to have exhausted life.

In my younger days there would have been a scene, but grandmother Wilhelmine first let her anger cool down before calling Frieda in for a scolding.

" Matters cannot go on as they are going," I began. " The looking-glass is there for both of you."—"What do you mean?" asked Frieda naturally.—" Let us have no pretence. Fräulein Schulz complains that she could not get at it because you put yourself in the way."— "The stupid creature only needed to have got up earlier; no one would have been in her way then."— "Such expressions ought not to be applied to one's fellow ' help.' "—" I did not choose her for myself."

"You should bear with the frailties of your colleagues."—" Even when they imitate your every movement and every turn behind your back, and laugh sneeringly, so that you cannot help seeing their ugly faces in the glass, and pretend that they have not done it at all when you turn round? And then, when I seize my hair-brush——"—"You were not going to——" —" She is not half good enough for that. She rushed off just as she was."--" That is the whole story?"—

"Certainly, Frau Buchholz." And my Carl and I had quarrelled murderously with one another owing to that rubbish! A piece of stupidity like that was to blame for my angel of a husband being located behind a foaming tankard, though beer always disagrees with him in the morning! However, I controlled myself so that there should be no broken bones, and said: "I have more confidence in you than in the other girl, Frieda, but that does not make you quite blameless. Confess honestly that you planted yourself intentionally in front of the looking-glass!"—"I was not going to move for a thing like that."—"You have a very good opinion of yourself, Frieda; still, reflect that you are not the axis of the world round which everything revolves. You take the smallest trifle amiss, you sulk on the slightest provocation; you will never get through life like that."—She smiled disdainfully.— "Do you expect to be stroked when you scratch?"— "Your remarks are quite beside the point," she answered, "for I am already engaged."

"But not married, by any manner of means!" I exclaimed.

"If you do not frustrate it, the marriage will take place next year."

"Frieda!" I exclaimed. "Is it possible? And you fling it in my face like that!"

"I am just as nature made me. If Max has acknowledged me openly as his *fiancée*, he must marry me; and when I am married I shall have nothing to do with the whole affair."

"And supposing you repulse him by your selfish love of ease?"

"He will come back again."

She looked at me triumphantly while saying this, and was really so pretty, so well formed, so bright

with the consciousness of victory, that I was fairly astonished to see how handsome she could be. Had I
been a young man I should have thought her lovable
at this moment. In this self-same moment, too, it became clear to me that Max had fallen in love through
his eyes, not with his heart. Where was the good of
teaching her some sort of manners, some amount of
cleverness in housekeeping? Her soul was dead, and
Max condemned to live beside it.

" Listen to a candid word from me, Frieda. My intention was to get you to unlearn all that made you
unamiable ; for you are as little ground into form as
a wooden knife. Your figure is good, but your movements are awkward ; it is no wonder that Ida made
game of you. Your face is pretty, but its expression,
generally speaking, is unpleasant, ill-tempered, and
sulky. What have you to boast of ? You are not rich,
nor are you of noble birth. You positively struggle
against being amiable. Supposing you were to get
small-pox, and your face to be covered with scars ;
what would there be left of you to fall in love with?
At the most, your newest dress, and that gets worn
out."

She got pale and red alternately. " No one has ever
told me that before."—" Because you are blindly in-
fatuated with yourself, and pay no attention to what
people may think of you," I interrupted her.

" I shall leave this house."

" I have nothing against it. You can return to your
father's house to-day."

She drew a deep breath and struggled with herself.

" No, not to my father. She—the person he is going to marry—is already there. Oh, Heavens, poor
unhappy girl that I am !" She broke into a flood
of tears.—" Frieda," I exclaimed, " Frieda, calm your-

self ! I did not mean that. Stay here as long as you like."

She did not hear, she did not answer ; she seemed utterly crushed. Now I really had been too hard.

It was ever so long before she recovered herself, and even then she could not speak. She peered about as if she had been a prisoner, and could find no way for flight, and she kept her hands in her lap wringing one another. I felt icy all over.

Then it seemed as if some invisible person opened my arm and drew it towards her. And as I embraced her and my lips rested in mute apology on her forehead, she buried her head on my heart and broke once more into a passion of tears.　.

Then she looked at me : "Am I really so horrid ? "

" Everything will come right, Frieda ; everything, everything, my child. Tell me, can you love me a little ? "

She nodded and smiled amid her tears.　　·

"I shall call you '*Du*.' Would you like me to, Frieda ? "—She kissed me.

"And do you know who we shall always be thinking about ; for whom we shall give ourselves trouble? Do you know who it is? Your Max ! "

"He will forsake me."

"We will bind him to us with cords of love. He deserves to be loved." — Her features were transfigured.

" As you and Ida do not get on together anyhow, it is better for you to share a room with Betti. Call her, child."

Betti came and agreed to it ; she would have done so solely on her father's account. — "Yes," I said, " papa cannot bear such goings on. The coffee was nothing but dirty water."

"No wonder, when Fräulein Schulz eats half of the beans while she is grinding them."—"Have you seen that, Betti?"—"No, but she does it."—"We shall see to that another time; I am too tired out now; I will go and lie down for a little."—"I hope you are not ill, mamma?"—"Go, children."

I needed quiet. Had the excitement been too much for me, or could I not do as much as in former years?

When I woke up from a refreshing sleep, Frieda was sitting beside my bed, to mind me.—"Are you feeling well again?" she asked sympathetically.

"Quite well, Frieda."

Then came my husband. "What are you about, old woman?"

"It is of no consequence, Carl; I am all right again. We have an armistice to-day. Idiss is to be confined to her room, and occupy herself with sewing. Her handkerchiefs have not been hemmed yet."

MORE ABOUT THE "HELPS."

Why Uncle Fritz bestows a bottle of hair dye—Why the latch-key is fetched and Uncle Fritz is not yet elected—About toying with hands and elf-like steps—Why teeth are blue and the Doctor will give away nothing—About luck in money matters and the harmony of souls—About shocking cards and a robber game —Why Herr Kleines flushes.

UNCLE FRITZ had been so kind as to call our house nothing but the Virgin's Cage, since the "helps" had been resident in it, as if I had any need to import vexation from without.

Oh, dear no, I was perfectly able to export some,

and could still have had enough to build up several
mountains of it, it was delivered to me in such abun·
dance ! From Idiss more especially.

And then was it seemly of Uncle Fritz to present a
bottle of hair-wash to my Carl to prevent his growing
grey before his time ? And it had gone bad already.
He could only have given a trifle for the bottle at the
most. What is the meaning of such silly jests ?

And lastly, was it right of him to overwhelm Idiss
with the broadest, most barefaced compliments, when·
ever he came to our house? All the good I squeezed
into her, all the advice worthy of observance, vanished
as if from a solitary sugar-basin, as soon as Uncle Fritz
gave us the honour of his company at a game of Skat.

"Fritz," I asked, "what does it mean ? You make
her quite silly. How can you do such a thing as ask
her whether she knows how beautiful she is ? "—" I cannot help it, Wilhelmine. If she is not made to be
laughed at, who is ?"—"No mother would like her
child to be mocked at, Fritz."—"Then the worthy
mother should train her worthy daughter differently."
—"Fritz, I consider it very arrogant of you, a bachelor, to pass judgment upon others."—"Excuse me, I
am married, only I do not happen to have the certifi-
cates with me."—"Ages must pass before bachelor
instincts will desert you."—"I have never had a leaning towards the Philistines, like your Carl——"—
"What do you dare to say about my husband?"—
"Do listen to the end of my sentence, and you will see
there is no need to fly off in a tantrum. I was going
to say : like your Carl, with all his excellencies, I never
shall be, during the course of my life ; no, not even
if I were to go and be confirmed over again."—"The
highest opportunities would avail you nothing ; that
is why you stay out so late. You are a perfect hea-

then."—"I really do not know when heathens stagger home, but I scarcely think they have already availed themselves of the advantages of the Police regulation hours. Besides, supposing that I do use up an even-ing with the night belonging to it, it concerns nobody but my wife."—"Nice fidelity that is, when the man goes in for dissipation, and the wife bathes herself in her tears at home!"—"What does she do in her tears?" —"Bathes herself in them."—"What a delightful amusement that must be! Could not I see it too?"— "Fritz, if you loved your wife, as it beseems you to do, in the sight of God and man, you would not give her such occasion for grief; as, for instance, the other day when I was paying her a visit, and you sent her word by the boots of the establishment that you would be coming home later. When I asked what you meant by the word 'later' I found that she had already gone to see whether you might not have forgotten the latch-key."—"Have I not got a pearl of a wife?" he ex-claimed delightedly, and his eyes fairly sparkled.— "Much too good for you."—"So I suppose you drop-ped a certain amount of insect powder into her ear?" —"I felt with her silently. The only thing I said was: 'My husband does not care about restaurants.'"

"Does he really never? Your angel Carl!"— "What?"—"He is not so silly. He has given up wor-shipping in the beer-temples, and is able to find amuse-ment in a game of billiards."

"For some time past my Carl has been occupied nearly every evening in his district club, and owing to the elections, he is obliged to be there more frequently than he cares about. What is there to laugh about, Fritz? My husband discharges his political duties as well as you."—"If he goes on as he is doing, I should think he would be made Town Commissioner."—"Well,

where does he play ?"—"I suppose he may venture on
a tiny game after the meeting is over. Walking round
a billiard-table is very healthy exercise ; it balances
heels and head equally ; I mean, of course, after mental over-exertion."—"Fritz, you are talking rubbish !"
—"It is possible," he said, and became quite serious.—
"What is the matter now ?" I asked.

He took out a fresh cigar quietly, nipped off the end
carefully, lighted it slowly, and then said : "I should
have given you credit for a better comprehension of
indigenous languages." — "What are you talking
about ? What do you mean by indigenous languages ?"
—"Such as a person can understand unless he has
tumbled down-stairs the day before. Why did I send
you the hair-wash ?"—"It was good for nothing."—"It
would have been a pity if it had been anything
else."—"Oh, really ! Then it was meant for a salem, or a riddle in flowers ?"—"Selam is the word,
Wilhelmine, and it was to convey a lesson."—"It's
just the same whether it's spelt 'selam' or 'salem,'
one is just as good as the other. And so it was to
convey a lesson to my husband ?" — "No, to you.
I merely wished to make you understand that you
are turning your husband's hair grey before its time
with your training of your 'helps,' and I am honestly sorry for my brother-in-law. Had it been
possible to deal with you otherwise than in a round-
about way, I should have advised you long ago : send
the two nuisances to the rightabout ; they are no rela-
tives of yours."

"If you imagine that this is the Imperial Diet, where
you can be rude with impunity, you have made a pretty considerable mistake, so far as I am concerned. I
request to be treated with politeness, were it merely
for example's sake. What would Frieda and Idiss

think of me, were they to discover that I had been
spoken to in a manner which would not even be permitted in the Vogtland quarter? No, no, my friend ;
you have not been elected yet, so try and behave as if
we were not all barbarians !"

"So you won't listen to me, Wilhelmine. It was
merely a suggestion for your good. Of course, you
can accustom your husband to keeping away from his
home——"

"Has he engaged you as his advocate?"

"Do you know so little of him? No, he never complains of his own accord, but I have just as much
sympathy with him as you have with my wife. Wilhelmine, seriously, make your husband's house pleasant for him again ; it is time to do so."

"Can I influence the young girls, when you, to a
certain extent, pay attentions to Idiss?"

"I only wish to bring to your notice Fräulein Schulz's
extreme liability to regard gentlemen's demonstrative
attention as the genuine article. Do you not choose to
see how she coquets?"—"That child?"—"Watch that
child carefully ; she has lost her belief in the stork long
ago."—"Pure imagination on your part!"—"Should
you ever find an unauthorized lover in her company,
and she stuffs you up that it is a mangle which somebody has lost, I shall not be in the least surprised!"

"Won't you really?"

"If you would not always be looking at the cards
while playing Skat——"—"That is an unfounded cal-
umny."—"I mean at your own, of course ;—but would
occasionally look over them towards the side-table, for
instance, where Herr Kleines plays with her hand."—
"Ah, if that is what you are driving at, that's quite
another tune. I know how to deal with him ; he shall
find out that as he sows so he will reap."

"That was nobly said and still more nobly thought. What is the next company-evening in your young ladies' seminary?"

"Every Friday, as usual. I will make a note of what you have been telling me."

"Good-bye, Minchen, and turn over a new leaf."

Could I have done otherwise than throw the shield of my protection over Idiss? Dared I have delivered her up to Uncle Fritz, for him to find grounds for further reproach? Had I not my own suspicions that my Carl frequently went to the club, because he had no pleasure in his evenings at home?

A change must be brought about; but how? If Frau Schulz had not sent my judgment to sleep by means of my vanity I never should have taken Idiss. And now it was difficult to get rid of her. Matters were different with Frieda. She was developing slowly but surely. She had been uncared for by her father because he was caught in the toils of a person, whose association with his growing daughter he dared not permit. Where are habits that are a matter of course in a well-regulated household to come from under such circumstances? For one thing, when she first appeared at dinner, she would wade into the vegetables up to her elbow, take a helping big enough for three, and then shovel it into her mouth with her knife—a practice that had been forbidden to my children from their earliest youth, and which is so objectionable to them that they cannot even bear to see others do it. Certainly it may be said that every one should eat as suits him best. If he makes no pretensions beyond that— why not? So far as I am concerned, he may lick his fingers away to the bone, but then he must not expect afterwards to be looked upon as a well-brought-up person belonging to cultivated circles.

I knew a young girl who was very pretty, with whom a fabulously rich foreigner, and a count into the bargain, fell in love. But after he had seen her eat for the first time—and she really did mean to do it elegantly, arranging, first a little piece of meat, then some potatoes and a little sauce most delicately on her knife with her fork, and carrying it with a graceful movement to her mouth—her prince retired. She did make a man happy later on, but he was no rich foreigner — he hailed from Moabite — nor was he a count either, but a peat contractor, to whom it was perfectly indifferent whether she ate with her knife or her fork ; and when she suggested to him, " We will eat straight out of the dish, Theodore," he was satisfied with that arrangement too.

Occasionally Frieda manifests a superabundance of zeal, especially since she has been on better terms with Betti. Notwithstanding that, I have been obliged to tell her, " Frieda, hurry should not be noticeable in domestic arrangements ; things go best with a noiseless rapidity, as if they were wafted along on hares' feet, so to speak. And no doubt you move about with a sort of fairy tread, but it is more as if all the fairies put their feet down together. You do pound along frightfully, Frieda."

Then naturally she flies into a rage and sulks, for bitter truths are not pleasant hearing. Whoever has neglected such opportunities for education as God gave him in his youth, is certain to be knocked into shape later on by life. It beats the dust out of people's clothes when they have them on. Neither entreaties nor prayers are of any avail, on it goes with its blows ; and if people weep they are laughed to scorn, for sympathy cannot find standing room in the market-place, though there is plenty for malicious delight in the woes of others.

Idiss, on the other hand, is given to petty pilfering.

Betti had afforded a proof of this in the matter of the coffee-beans, and since Frieda makes the coffee in the morning, and Ida in the afternoon under supervision, it is as good as ever.

We have been obliged to lock away the preserves. We only left out one pot of bilberry jam, and, just as we expected, she had been at it—her lips and the edges of her nails betrayed her. "Ida," I said, "it is not appetising for those who have to eat it to know that you stick your fingers into everything. You surely have not been brought up on the starvation system in your parents' house, that you have to make up for it now ! You will not be curtailed in food or drink, and those.secret bits and sups between times are unwholesome. What but that gives you that constant breaking out on your mouth ?"

Well, she could not easily foist her blue teeth and fingers upon us as an illusion ; that colour, thanks to natural science, is a tolerably fast one. Frieda too remarked, as Ida stood convicted before us, "If I were in your place, I should be ashamed of myself."—"Even if it had been vanilla cream," added Betti.

Now, there is nothing more objectionable to my Carl than blisters on people's lips ; in fact, it makes him quite ill to see anything in the shape of an eruption ; and I had frequently been obliged to request Ida to dine in her room, and suggested the use of Friedrichshall water to her. However, she preferred leaving that beautiful and expensive remedy untouched, and dined with Doris in the kitchen instead of alone ; although I am not at all in favour of bonds of friendship between lady-helps and servants, for under such circumstances the master and mistress are the sufferers. What the one breaks, the other carries

away hidden in her apron to the dust-bin ; and besides, she gets so vulgarized.

Let us hope that I did not hear aright, for sound is de-
ceptive, but I have a very strong idea that Ida and Doris
christened me " the old frump," when there was no
very considerable distance between them and my
back. If I should happen to hear the same slighting
term again, I will give them more than they will like,
for I really have not bargained to be set down as an
" old frump " just yet. But it always smokes in the
kitchen when I want to make something to do there ;
so, owing to my cough, I cannot play the listener
well.

First and foremost, I had to interfere medicinally
in the matter of the eruption, and a son-in-law is useful for such purposes. The Doctor answered my
post-card promptly, and asked with a smile, " What is
the matter, my dear mother-in-law ? Do you find a
difficulty in breathing ? " — " No ; I don't mean to
gratify you so far ; I hope to remain above ground
for many a year to come."—" Of course ; of course.
Where is the seat of trouble, then ? In the stomach ?
A little overburdened, perhaps ? "—" You surely don't
take me for a hungry ' help ' who takes everything
that is indigestible ? No, my dear son-in-law, I am
well, with the exception of a little shortness of breath ;
this time it is Fräulein Schulz who is your patient. I
must tell you that she has blisters on her lips."—" And
you make a fool of me for that, and bring me to the
Landsberger-strasse ! " he said angrily.—" It is only
external," I endeavour to quiet him ; but on he went
in a rage, " It shows great want of consideration towards my other suffering patients. The one thing left
for you to do is to knock me up in the middle of the
night. I really should have credited you with possess-

ing more common-sense. Send the girl to me during consulting hours. Is it really bad ? "

" As soon as one seems to have gone, another comes."

" Let her paint it with Ichthyol."

" Write it down. As you happen to be here, you may as well prescribe for her."

He now proceeded to examine Ida, forbade her taking anything highly seasoned, or difficult of digestion, (as, for instance, coffee-beans, I suggested,) especially old cheese, and kept to his prescription, which proved very beneficial later on. As soon as Ida was dismissed, he asked, "Shall I place this visit to your account, or to the young lady's ? "

" Do you really enter an unimportant thing like this ? I thought you would have done it for love."

" I only give my knowledge to the poor. Before I was capable of giving good advice, I was obliged to spend a large amount on my studies, so we will not talk about 'for love.' So it is to be to Fräulein Schulz's ? "

" Well, scarcely, for it was I who wrote and asked for your visit ! "

" Then it can be put down to my dear mother-in-law."

˙ " But Ida cannot possibly expect me to pay her doctor's and apothecary's bill if she over-eats herself."

" It depends on what Fräulein Schulz's ideas are. Generally speaking, doctors are not bothered about such trivial ailments ; people wait patiently till they disappear."

" But my Carl does not like to see it."

" Then let us put down the visit to my father-in-law."

" Doctor ! When you know how apt he is to grumble at me."

" Do you think then that I am to bear the loss ? "

"Doctor, you are an egoist."

"It is merely external. Fare thee well, little mother."

Why does one take a doctor for one's son-in-law, if
he is productive of so little profit? I thought. But
aloud, I gave him an invitation for Friday. "You will
be sure not to miss our evening for Skat?"

He accepted, and I had the certainty of depriving
him of twice as much as he could put down against
me ; I place myself on the winning seat to the right,
with my back towards the book-case. He had such
tremendous luck in the same seat the other day, that
he got cold feet before the last three rounds. He always wants to pocket everything. But who can blame
him for that?—one never can be fortunate enough
where money is concerned.

Emmi encourages him in his habit, for he puts his
profits into her savings-box, which stands ready for
the purpose on her dressing-table, so that he shall not
forget. When he has lost, he merely taps it with the
palm of his hand, as if something were going in ; but
she adds it up the next day, and says : "Cheating 's
no use, husband." Then he has to put his hand in his
pocket and produce a small surplus, which is invested
later in the savings-bank for the twins.

These are small domestic pleasures. Possibly there
is not much poetry in them, but then they don't cost
much. Were things otherwise with us when my Carl
and I were younger? Hardly ; the only difference
being that in those days the game of Skat was unknown.

At that time I must acknowledge that Skat was to
me as a bottle sealed with seven seals ; there was so
much to be done that the day seemed at least a dozen
hours too short for all that had to be got through.

But now, after sipping and sipping, and sipping over and over again, I have acquired a taste for it, and can only say that it is more attractive than the uninitiated can have the least idea of.

The reason that we played so frequently was to be found in the fact that we were more at home than formerly; for when Felix was not travelling he visited his *fiancée*, and on those evenings we did not go out. If my Carl had an engagement, I remained at home with them ; and if necessity tore me from within my four walls, my Carl chaperoned them. In this solitude the book of knaves was a veritable book of consolation, as the most delightful conversation between an engaged couple is very much like standing beside a person who is looking through a telescope.

Our numbers were easily made up. If we were put to it for a player, we sent across for Uncle Fritz, who came with Erica, or to Herr Pfeiffer or Herr Kleines ; Dr. Paber was sometimes kind enough to come, or Fritz brought one of his friends with him. Sometimes the Police-Lieutenant gave us the honour, and then my Carl produced a bottle of Johannisberg. Generally speaking, there was beer, or some light Mussbach table wine for Dr. Paber ; he likes it, and both as doctor and connoisseur in wines has proved its excellence. For my part, I have learned to value tea ; but it must be first-rate, or else it will have been concocted in vain as far as Wilhelmine is concerned.

Now my "helps" were the cause of a break in the former harmony of souls. Carl paid greater attention to the district club than was quite compatible with his duties as husband. Erica generally declined, and Uncle Fritz followed suit ; and the young people, Herr Kleines and Herr Pfeiffer, were always most useful for filling up, but I had not accustomed them to being invited by themselves. In order that I should not quite lose my little bit of practice, I found myself obliged to arrange an evening At Home for Skat, and I chose Friday on the Doctor's account.

And they came with pleasure. Betti undertook the refreshment department ; and as soon as we had finished with that, the ladies and those who were not wanted for Skat occupied themselves with a round game at the big table.

The same thing happened this evening. The "helps," Emmi, Betti, Erica, Felix, and Herr Kleines had settled down to a low Vingt-et-un. My Carl, I, the Doctor, and Uncle Fritz circulated the knaves.

The scale of victory was most unevenly balanced, the Doctor won one game after another.—"You have got a lucky pig at home, I suppose?" asked Uncle Fritz.—" These are the first cards I have had for six weeks. "You won't grudge me my knave of diamonds? It counts for ten."—"I don't grudge you your good play," said I.—"Very kind of you, dear mamma-in-law."—"Whoever has luck to begin with loses later on," I added.—"Are we going to play or talk?" grumbled my Carl, who had not had a turn at all. "Who leads?"—"You, Carl."—"Spades are trumps."—"Excuse me," said the Doctor, "I am before you. A grand." —"That comes of talking too much !" scolded my husband.—"Really," said the Doctor, "the first time any one has spoken ! Where are the knaves?" and he played out the knave of clubs. As he had the second best as well, he drew my husband's other two and his nice plump spade as well.—"Nothing to be done against it," said Fritz.—" There is some one still living over the hills," I retorted, and made a trick with my ten of clubs. However, the Doctor had enough already, and said triumphantly, " Thirty !"—"If I had not had

the ten, we would have been worse off still," I said, to
put him down.

As I had placed myself in the supposed winning
seat, it was difficult for me to keep an eye on the large
table, where there was a good deal of merriment going
on ; while I was taking up one wretched card after
another ; and if I did happen to do something, somebody overtopped me, or else I made a revoke. I might
just as well have made a voluntary selection of all the
rubbish, so certain was it to be death to me.

"No," said I ; "to sit here like a frog and watch all
the others with their hands full of knaves, is not exactly amusing."—"The gamester is by God despised,
for he to others' gold doth cling," spouted Uncle
Fritz.—"Will you not get Herr Kleines to exchange
with you ? "

"Now that I have a nullo?   Not a bit of it."—"Do
look how he and Idiss are squeezing each other's
hands," Uncle Fritz whispered to me quietly.

A hasty glance revealed the accuracy of his remark ;
the two of them were playing with each other's hands
underneath the table. At the same moment it dawned
upon me why Ida had made herself so extremely grand
this evening.

"Wilhelmine, we are waiting for you."—"Do I play ?"
—"Always the one that bids."—"Who bids ?"—"Why,
you."—"If Uncle Fritz has dealt, the lead is with you."
—"Has he just dealt ?"—"Don't you see that he is
left out in the cold ? "—"Oh, yes ! What has been
bid ?"—"You offered us a tiny nullo, worthy mamma-
in-law."—"So I did. Just give me a minute."—To
make a discovery such as I had just made beside me
at the large table, and to play a nullo with two such
hardened sinners as my husband and the Doctor, is
almost beyond the human organisation. One has only

to know those brothers in iniquity. They lie in wait like tigers, and as soon as ever they find out anything, they fall upon one! But how carefully I played the game; how I avoided their snares! I certainly won, but I shouldn't wish a dog such a trial.

Now that the luck was turning, I was forced to stop; for the only way of making Herr Kleines harmless without drawing attention to him, was to give him my place at Skat, while I took part in the game of Vingt-et-un—which, by the way, I hate, as it is never played without a certain amount of trickery, and generally speaking there is downright cheating over it.

And what happened? He straightway got a solo in clubs with four that ought to have fallen to my lot if everybody had their rights, while I sat down beside Ida, who looked round after her sweetheart so long that I said: "Do not dislocate your neck, Fräulein Schulz; you have only one to twist!"

Erica had lost the most in this robbers' game, because she was too honest to push aces underneath the table, and to unite with her neighbour in secret manipulation of the cards. How can solitary honesty protect itself against the frauds of the many? She has to endure. Or she even smiles at her supposed want of luck, as Erica did, and bears it with gentleness, in the firm conviction that fate is fighting against her.

Herr Kleines won to such an extent that the Doctor began to abuse him. After some rounds I discovered that Betti and Felix had been cheating in company, likewise Emmi and Frieda; that Herr Kleines and Ida had worked in partnership was a matter of course.

"Ah," I said, "now the fraud has come to an end, all winnings are to be returned; my house is not a gambling-hell. You may cheat each other for gingernuts as much as ever you like, but not for money. Out with it."

The revelations that followed on this were very instructive. The certainly very difficult task of redistribution resulted in showing that Fräulein Schulz had pocketed all Herr Kleines' winnings.—" Have you got as far as community of goods already?" I asked her sharply.

" I had left my purse in my overcoat," called out Herr Kleines ; " Fräulein Schulz was kind enough to take care of my winnings for me. Hearts are trumps," and he flung down the card as if he meant to ram it into the table.

After this we talked about one thing and another. Ida was persuaded that she was tired and ought to go to bed, and the gentlemen, too, began to have had enough ; for Herr Kleines, who played a very bold game as usual, fleeced the others to such an extent that never before had so much been lost in our house during the course of one evening.

" That is how people play in Venice and the surrounding woodland.hamlets," laughed Herr Kleines, picking up his ill-gotten gains, which, accurately speaking, really belonged to me. But his mind had not a legal bent.

" Kleines," said the Doctor, "you are too lucky in play ; you are bound to be unlucky in love."—"Who knows?" I remarked pointedly, and he got as red as fire.

When Herr Kleines was saying good-night, I took him aside for a moment. "Young man," I threatened him, "I allow no frivolous sport in my house, either with cards or girls' hearts. Would you like to have the address of Fräulein Schulz's parents, or shall I write to them?"

" Do you wish to make the poor girl miserable for the whole of her life ? " he retorted coolly.

My arms sunk to my side, and he escaped.

" Well ? " asked Uncle Fritz, "what have you done ? "

"Nothing. Fritz, no one is a match for that man. He is capable of marching into church whistling ! "

WINTER EVENINGS.

How innocent pleasure is destroyed—About specialties and execu-
tions—About literature and the tobacco monopoly—The little
story about the two white dresses—Why three stars are put and
Betti reads on—The continuation of the little story—How the
story ends and why Max is pitied.

PETROLEUM is the most accurate measure of time for the winter ; the more of it is used, the longer grow the evenings, and the more difficult it becomes so to shorten them that every one may derive enjoyment from them.

If people are together for a whole livelong day and yesterday as well, and the day before yesterday and to-morrow and the day after to-morrow, what fresh news can they have to give one another, more especially when there are strange ears in the house? If one says this or that, who knows how it will be repeated later on ?

Not necessarily of malicious intent, certainly not ; but the most harmless piece of harmlessness becomes mischievous when taken up by ill-natured tongues, and unfortunately there is no lack of that sort. One is almost inclined to agree with Uncle Fritz, who, together with the more modern professors, is in favour of man's descent from the chimpanzee, for the human creature is just as full of malice as apes are; the only puzzling part of it being who could have fed us while we were springing about in our cages! Therefore there must have been people there.

Our social intercourse had become somewhat limited at this time. "Helps" cannot be left alone, for no wisdom is capable of foreseeing the mischief which they may have taken an opportunity of doing before one returns, and I at least cannot carry on an interesting conversation in society when I am forced to ponder every minute: What drawer are they prying into now? Can they have gone off secretly? I wonder if the lamp has fallen off the table? Shall I find the house one mass of flames, or a fire-engine in the front of it at the very least? How is it possible under such circumstances to devote one's entire attention to the vexed question of whether a singer in the opera has taken a note too high or too low, or whether cherries are cheaper and bigger this year, or were they smaller and sweeter last year?

So I only paid odd visits here and there with my "helps," partly to find out whether people objected to their being introduced, and partly to save them from embarrassment. When one takes out young girls who have not quite a recognised social position, they are of course received and welcomed with friendliness, but still they are given to understand,—another time you had better stay away, for we do not know you, cannot tell who you are, and have no kind of obligation towards you personally. If we receive you in our houses, it is merely to please Frau Buchholz, or whoever the lady may be who is introducing her new "help," fresh from the railway station, amongst the various families.

It is only by slow degrees that the girl succeeds in acquiring recognition and friendship on her own account, that people learn to trouble themselves about her, to like her, and lastly to esteem her. That is to say, if she is worthy of it.

Therefore the best course to pursue is first of all to let her settle down, and then to introduce her at those houses where it is probable that she will not only be welcomed, but where she will be able, with her talents, to play a small part.

We generally spent our evenings at home, but in order to do the theatres a good turn, we often went to them by way of a change, generally in a family party including some friends ; or we went to concerts, or to the Concordia, where people pay their money to see dislocations of limbs, or other things that cannot possibly happen in middle-class life, which they call specialties, and which inspire partly pleasure and partly fear.

On the other hand, the trained seals amused me very much, although I do not understand why they have learned to smoke cigars. I consider it highly judicious, however, that they have been taught how to save drowned people, which they exemplified on a boy, who played at being drowned in a sort of pond, for by this means they might be made useful to the navigators of the North Pole. Uncle Fritz, who was with us, certainly suggested it would be all the same whether an open passage was discovered at the Pole or not, as it would always be frozen over ; but notwithstanding this, there is something scientific about trained seals, and these few groschens have not been thrown away.

The clowns, too, who have discovered how to make people laugh are worth the money. If you think he is going to stand, he tumbles down ; and when he is going to sit, he stands on his head.

Indeed, it is astonishing the way in which people risk their lives to gain a livelihood. "Thank your Creator," I remarked to Betti and the "helps," "that you do not need to balance yourself on chair-backs. If they once got me on the flying trapeze, how low I should lie !"

Not only was their love of sight-seeing satisfied by such means, but the mind, for which small provision is made in specialty theatres, was elevated.

But as the bent of mind forms the character, it was especially its domestic cultivation that was important. Ghost stories are not suitable for this purpose, as Idiss will not sleep alone after hearing them, though they certainly are quite the nicest when told shortly before midnight. Instead of these, we determined on reading something aloud.

Betti suggested the paper, as giving one what was most recent.

"Say rather what is most horrible !" I exclaimed. "All the horrible things that people do, appear instantly in the paper. When a malefactor has been executed, no matter how few spectators were admitted to see it, do not the papers tell us how pale he became, how he was bound, thrown down, how they chopped away at him, how his blood trickled on to the sand, and how heart-rending it was to stand and witness it ? Why does one get it all in print in the morning, before one's breakfast, when it makes sympathetic people feel so ill that they cannot look at roast beef for a week ?

"If one person kills another, he is enshrined in the newspaper ; if any one cheats, absconds, steals, poisons himself and others, the papers take a tender interest in his welfare, even though he be a criminal of past centuries, if crime happens to be flat. As soon as a person wishes to become celebrated for some days, he does something or the other execrable, and the papers indulge him; exactly like the brothers Penn, when they can find no shelter, they break plate-glass windows, and the heated prison opens its doors lovingly to them.

" Many who have done wrong and gone through their penance, wish perhaps that they were rather less well known—who knows what necessity or rashness may have driven them ?—but their wish is of no avail, they are dragged before the general public, the brand of their shame is chafed larger in all directions, when otherwise it would not have been known ; so that it takes more tears to wipe it out, more repentance to rub it away ; but by that time it is too large and it remains.

" The pillory has been done away with, indeed it was not a thing to be tolerated ; but are there not papers which maintain the pillory in undiminished strength ?

" They do so. And we ?

" To speak honestly, we consider it amusing. A paper which excludes such horrors is tedious.

" And what is the real meaning of amusing ? 'Mirth-provoking' is what it means. Are we not a highly cultured folk, when murder, and mortal blows, and filthy vice provoke our mirth ?

" Some people call it 'interesting,' but it means the same thing as 'amusing'; for where pleasure runs short it is apt to be uninteresting, nor does any one attend to it."

The mental supervision of the " helps " made it my duty to preserve them from too bloodthirsty stories ;

for either what you read possesses some influence, or
it is without effect, and may be confined within the
limits of Bradshaw and the current prices of the day.

Betti and I looked out something suitable for our
evening literature beforehand, and when it was necessary to give an admonition to one of the "helps,"
some story was read where the fault of which they had
been guilty, occurred ; that is to say, if there just happened to be one of the kind wanted. When Ida completely scorched my morning cap the other day, while
ironing it, I made her a present of it. Then in the
evening we read about the Hamburg fire, because that
was the most suitable thing we could find, and the
necessity of caution with fire, heated irons, and the
like could be pointed out.

The other day there was a story in Schorer's " Fam-
ilienblatt " which seemed as if it had been written for
Frieda, for she is capable of forgetting her betrothed
over a costume, and there was a deeper meaning in it
which she was at liberty to apply to herself.

When we had finished our meal, and my poor Carl
had been obliged to go to his horrid district club—I
could wish that they ordered better cigars among
other items of their electioneering expenses, for he
often comes home reeking so dreadfully of smoke,
that one imagines they must have consumed the whole
tobacco supply—we sat down to our work at the big
round table (another old heirloom), and I gave Ida
the magazine containing the story of the "White
Dresses." After Ida had blown her nose, during which
performance she half buried herself under the table, to
hide her soiled handkerchief, for she has only hemmed
three and a half, she began :

"It was her tenth birthday."

"Whose birthday ? " interrupted Frieda.

" Patience ; we are sure to find out about it. Go
on, Ida, but with a little more expression."

" It was her tenth birthday," read Ida, " and a Sunday as well, so it was a double day of rejoicing. Her
mother had seemed full of secrets the last few days, and
stayed up late at night long after her father had retired to rest. The little one had a good idea that
something was on foot, for the lamp-light just fell on
her bed through the open bed-room door, and aroused
her more than once from her sleep and dreams. Then
she would speculate as to what the meaning of that
clear light could be, but she had too little courage to
ask about it, and so she went to sleep again, to dream
further dreams about her dolls, her toys, her school
work, and her knitting, which was hardly a source of
joy to her.

" However, on the morning of her birthday it was
given to her to know why her mother had sat up so
frequently. The secret was handed over to her in the
shape of a white dress, trimmed with lace—cotton lace,
it must be admitted, as large expenses could not be
incurred—and with a sash of red silk ribbon. The
ribbon was not new either—the mother had worn it
before ; but what is chemical cleaning for ?

" It was a real beauty, this white dress; no princess
could have had a finer one, or at least none more fashion-
ble, in the mother's opinion, who had borrowed the pattern from one of her acquaintances, a person working in
a first-class dressmaking establishment in the Friedrich-
strasse, who therefore knew very well what was stylish
and what not. ' And how grand the child will look
when we go out together this afternoon ! ' exclaimed
the mother, who did not find the praise contributed by
her own small family circle sufficient for the work of
her hands. ' Our child need not be ashamed to be

seen, more especially in the new dress. We will buy a new hat to suit it on our way; she could not wear the old one, anyhow. I have seen one in a shop window that really is not a bit dear.'

"'I think she has enough with the dress,' the father quietly answered. 'You know, wife, that we must cut our coats according to the cloth; my salary is only a small one. And then, I should not like the girl to get vain. That would be the very worst present for her birthday, and might be bad for us all in the long run.'

"'But, husband, is the child to look like a scarecrow? What are you thinking of?—a new dress and an old hat would not go at all well together. Are the people we meet to ask, What kind of a scarecrow is that, with a new, white dress and shabby, worn-out hat? No; it would be better for Matilda not to put on the dress at all, than have the finger of scorn pointed at her; I would rather have sat up at night and worked myself to death for nothing; rather not go out at all to-day, though I have been looking forward to it so much; rather——' But here the degrees of comparison necessary to the woman for a description of her woes, came to an end, and therefore the argument of arguments—a flood of tears—put in its appearance. The child cried too, without knowing why, and the hat was agreed to. But the birthday feeling was gone.

"Dinner was quietly eaten, without the merry chatter that was usual on such occasions, and after the meal was done mother and child went to dress, as they wished to have something of an afternoon. During this period the father read the paper, which he and his neighbours shared, but he could not fix his attention on what he was reading; more than once he glanced up from his paper and looked straight in front of him into a far, far distance, as if he were trying to gaze into the future.

"At this moment the bed-room door opened and his child came out, dressed in her white frock with the red sash, and beaming with delight. Her eyes sparkled bright and clear as only children's eyes can sparkle; her cheeks glowed in happy excitement, and the fair curls framed the merry life in a golden glimmer, like spring sunshine waking the blossoming buds with its kisses. Her father got up, wishing to fold his child in his arms, and press her with delight to his heart, but she pushed him away and said : ' Papa, you will crumple my new frock.'

"'Don't you love me any more then?' exclaimed the father.

"'Certainly!' answered the child ; 'to-morrow and every other day, only not to-day! I must take great care of my new frock !'

"The father did not say a word, but went into the bed-room to reproach his wife seriously about the wrong path in which she was leading the child, about the foolishness of letting dress seem of more importance to her than the natural stirring of the emotions. His wife answered quietly that the child must begin to think a little about her appearance, she was quite old enough to do so—he, being a man, could understand nothing about it. While this conversation was going on, the child—happening to be alone—had pushed a chair into the middle of the room, placed herself upon it, and was looking in the glass with the greatest delight at her new white frock with its red sash, made out of the chemically-cleaned ribbon.

"When the family returned home in the evening, the discord had all-but disappeared. Many an eye had rested with pleasure on the charming girl and smiled at her. A susceptible disposition cannot be indifferent to the charm which a fresh expanding human rose spreads around it ; it is that charm that leads the imagination to people heaven with angels in the form of lovely children, such as poets describe to us in song, and painters represent on their canvas, and it was that self-same charm that drew the glances of the passers-by in the Park now and then towards the child in the white dress.

" This flattered the mother's vanity ; she drew her husband's attention to the sensation that the girl was creating, and jogged his elbow each time that somebody noticed the little one, and these small signs gradually dissipated her anger over all that had gone before. She occasionally called to the child with motherly care : 'Matilda, hold yourself straight ; the people are looking at you !' And Matilda did as her mother commanded.

" It seemed as if for this evening sleep had deserted the little bed, to which it found its way so easily at other times. The little one lay awake for a long time, and dreamt with open eyes of the glistening silk dresses which she had seen ; of hats with flowers and feathers on them ; of gold ornaments and glittering stones. Ah, could she but have such things ! Things as beautiful or even more beautiful than those ladies had, who drove past her, and whom she had seen in the brilliantly illuminated Park, laughing and jesting as they walked to and fro. How would the people look at her then ? she wondered. She never cast a thought towards her dolls and toys—they were deposed from this day forward."

  * * * * *

" Is the story finished already?" asked Frieda.

"There is about as much more," answered Ida·

" but there are five asterisks here, to show that we may take breath."

" They signify a pause, or that a certain amount of time elapses between the parts," thus I proceeded to instruct youth which has not much experience in literary details. " When an author wishes to arouse thoughtfulness in his readers, he attracts his glance to such stars, for is not the star-bestrewn sky chiefly created to make us thoughtful? And now let us interchange ideas. For instance, how do you like the little girl, Ida?"

" What little girl?"

" Why, the one you have just been reading about!"

Ida was confused.—" Aha, the good effects are showing themselves; the story is as efficacious as the contents of a chemist's shop!" I said to myself, and therefore I considered it advisable to encourage her in giving her opinion. " Speak out your mind; there is no tax on thoughts."—" I—I," she stammered, " I— when I am reading aloud, I never really know what I am reading about!"

Betti smiled, and went on with her work without looking up.

" What do you think about it, Frieda?" I endeavoured to draw her into the conversation.

" I cannot understand anybody making such a fuss over a washing-dress!" answered Frieda. " And then to go to Kroll's in such a get-up; I think it's simply vulgar!"

" There is not one word about Kroll in the story!"

" Where else could they have gone to?"

" We will continue. Betti, you take the magazine. Fräulein Schulz will listen. I really should prefer reading myself, but then, you know, my breath. Now, mind, with expression and impressively, Betti."

Betti read on :

"A number of years have gone by. The baby shoes
had wandered off to the old-clothesman long since,
the white dress at last was turned into dusters, which,
if they are lucky, will celebrate their resurrection in a
paper-mill. But the child had blossomed into a lovely
young woman ; the bud had fulfilled its early promise.

"The father knew what a dangerous gift of fate
beauty is when it is not closely hedged in by rank and
riches, and so he watched over his daughter's movements with Argus eyes, to the great grief of her mother, who would have liked to dazzle people with her
child.

"Offers were made to the daughter to act as lady-
cashier in *certain fashionable establishments*, and remu-
neration for her services was offered, which was well
calculated to keep care for their daily bread far from
the family—that care for a sufficient competency which
increased with the years, in proportion as their de-
mands upon life became larger with the child's increasing growth. It was impossible to hold aloof from
everything, to bury oneself completely in one's household ; it was due both to the girl and themselves to
take part in such-and-such pleasures, nor would it be
seemly that there should be a semblance of poverty.
What would people think of that? Nor was every
kind of intercourse advisable, unless one intended
giving up the hope of the girl's making a good match.

"So cares accumulated, and the more they made
themselves at home, the less was seen of Contentment,
which ended by only paying a very occasional visit,
though formerly it had been one of the family.

"Admirers were not wanting for the daughter, but
poverty was in close proximity to beauty, and all looked askance at such a bride, with the exception of one

who was not frightened by it, as he himself enjoyed
its most intimate acquaintance. He was not able to
offer the girl a brilliant destiny, but he was rich, immeasurably rich in love for her. He was too little of
a philosopher to be able to embody even suggestively
an idea of happiness, but he felt in the depths of his
inner consciousness that something grand, splendid,
unutterably beautiful must exist in the world, about
which he never could become quite clear, although he
had a distinct presentiment of it, and indeed almost
believed it within his grasp, whenever his thoughts
were busy with the lovely girl, whenever he lingered
beside her.

"He had not told her yet, how dearly he loved her,
how he would brave the greatest difficulties for her
sake, would strain his powers to the very uttermost
for her, for the labour of his hands was all that he yet
possessed. That was what he had to offer her beside
his love ; he lacked only words to give expression to
his honest thoughts.

"Matilda would have been wanting in the instincts
of a woman had the love which was glowing for her
in the young man's heart escaped her notice ; she felt
the warming breath of its glow, she saw it shining
forth from his eyes, and felt its reflexion burning on
her own cheeks ; it seemed to her as if a marvellous
life streamed out from him, which made her heart beat
more quickly, and yet she behaved as if he were indifferent to her, like all the others. He was not what
people call a good match. Ah, had she been willing
to share want and misery with him, she would have
told him that she cared more for him than for any one
else on earth ; but it so happened that she had had
her waking dreams of silks and satins, of precious
stones and glittering jewelry, and having lived herself

into this dream as completely as if it had been the reality, she was unable to give it up. So she discouraged the young man's courtship, and paid no heed to reality, but let her imagination paint the future with the most brilliant colouring.

"One colour alone was wanting on her palette—that of love. Her wishes were to have their fulfilment, her mother cared for that. She knew that her daughter was beautiful, very beautiful ; she had known instances which demonstrated clearly that youth and beauty had arrived at fortune more than once. And if this had happened to others, it might well come to pass that a rich man would be caught by her daughter ; then matters would mend for all of them.

"First and foremost, the theatres must be visited, in order that her daughter might be seen ; her fortune was not to be found in the simple circles of her own rank ; so much experience had taught her. Time was passing, for she had completed her twentieth year. Economy was practised in the household, many little pleasures of life were given up, the necessities of the table could be still further reduced ; the father was obliged to submit : he always had two votes against him.

"The only time that the two women dared not venture on one word in reply was when he threatened them : 'Should my daughter return to her home one day a dishonoured woman, we part company.'

"That was one reason that gained for Matilda the repute of being as cold as she was beautiful. People told each other that marriage was the only means of modifying her ideas, and could tell laughable stories of what had happened even to so-called irresistibles who had endeavoured to win the favour of this prudish young lady, and been repulsed with scorn. The second reason, however, was the young man of whom Matilda knew that he really and truly loved her. Had one of the many who surrounded her, resembled him even to some extent, she would have given credence to his promises.

"When a man came at last, who asked her to be his wife, she shuddered at him mentally; but she had not the courage to say 'No,' for he wooed her with glittering gold, with jewelry and pearls, with everything that her ardent wishes had been longing for so long in vain.

"He was a man upon whose features a dissolute life had left its traces, whose lips could only smile in scorn, whose glances made her cheek burn when they rested covetously upon her. She did not know that good society shunned him as it would a leper, that he would not have dared to ask for the hand of a daughter of a house that cared for its reputation; she knew nothing of his past, nor of his present life. She did not know that he had wagered high that success would crown his efforts to possess her, and she gave her promise to belong body and soul to the man of whom she felt a secret dread.

"So the goal was reached, so the dream that she had dreamt in her childhood received its fulfilment.

"Once again there was a white dress adorning her, for her wedding day; but this time it was a dress of heavy white silk. Diamonds glittered at her throat, myrtle and orange-blossom perfumed the wavy golden hair. How lovely she was, and how little the man at her side resembled her; the man whose touch she could not avoid, for she was his—had been bought by him with gaudy tinsel!

"And again she stood before a glass, as on her tenth birthday, again in a white dress. She thought of that

day, and wished that it had never dawned for her.
How she then had envied those fashionably-dressed
ladies, who strolled about the Park illuminated as
with the brightness of day ! Now she was more beautifully dressed than any one of them, but she had become the wife of a man without love, without even a
touch of love. She had waved happiness from her
when it was being borne towards her; she would have
been happy with the man who could find no words to
tell her how dear she was to him, and so hot, heavy
tears fell upon the white dress, now that it was too
late—for ever."

"Well, Frieda," I asked curiously, "what is your
opinion about it?"
"If one does not know the people, what can one possibly care about the whole story?" she said, with utter
lack of sympathy.
I looked at Betti, Betti looked at me. It seemed as
if we were both ready to say the same words :
"Poor Max!"

AMONGST OURSELVES.

Why ashes are scattered and fruit is refused—Why Wilhelmine
would like to bewitch, and why longing is voiceless—Why Wilhelmine is a pattern, and Herr Kleines like a flash of lightning.

IF a person has married her daughter, she has got
rid of her. This eternal truth permits itself neither
to be shaken nor moved, for it agrees with what has
happened to me, although my eldest daughter is still
on the way to the hymeneal altar.
Some weeks ago I said to my Carl, "How about the

coming Christmas ?"—"What do you mean, Wilhelmine ?"—"I am racking my brains as to where it ought to be kept," I made answer, and looked at my Carl while doing so, as if I did not comprehend him. So he dutifully brought his powers of reflection into action, but a considerable space of time was required before the needful Edison light began to burn, and he arrived at the result, "It will be difficult to manage, Wilhelmine."

It was of course clear that Emmi and the Doctor intended having a tree at home for the twins, and would have no thought for the Landsberger-strasse. Then there was nothing positive inscribed in the records of the future, as to whether we could reckon certainly on seeing Uncle Fritz at our house, for he is not to be calculated upon, when it is a question of submitting to the reasonable arrangements of other folk.

Ida spent Christmas week in Zehlendorf, and took Frieda with her. Although Frieda and Ida were not especially devoted to each other, still Frieda accepted the invitation thankfully, probably in order not to be forced to say that she certainly had a father's house, but no father with whom she could celebrate the festivities ; that she had no trace of kindly feeling towards his present wife, who never should have been allowed to cross the threshold over which her mother had once been carried forth. It must be hard to have to fly from a father's heart at Christmastide, because he has disposed of it unworthily.

On the other hand, Betti and Felix were to be depended upon ; but surely it would be impossible to celebrate a family festival in the absence of half of the family.

While my Carl was still busy thinking matters over, I asked him sharply : "Is that all you were taught in the night-school?" whereupon he brought forward quite a novel idea, expressing himself to the effect that we might all go to the Doctor's, and lock up our own house.

"Carl," I said, "there shall be a Christmas-tree at home here so long as I live, even though I may have to sit alone in front of it and water the gingerbread with my tears, because of the world's ingratitude."— "Wilhelmine, you exaggerate."—"How? That is news to me."—"You are irritated without reason."—"Without reason?" I inquired sharply. "Do you wish our daughters to become complete strangers to us? If I am not to be allowed to have my children with me on Christmas-eve, if I am to be tolerated like a stranger on such a day at my son-in-law's, you had better kill me off at once and cremate me, greatly as I usually object to the process, and scatter my miserable ashes to the four corners of the world. What good can I be to anybody?"—"Wilhelmine, to say too much is to say nothing at all."—"Really!"—"Now please, do not make me angry."—"As soon as Betti is once married, we can take up our abode in the streets on Christmas-eve."

I had long since given up having the control of my children. Had I not given my daughters to the men they loved, and renounced therewith the holiest rights? Had I not reconciled myself to the fact that the greater portion of their love was given to a man unconnected with myself, and that only the smaller share remained for me—a sort of habitual love? Had I made this sacrifice, or had I not? I had done so.

But now came the test—Christmas-eve. Ought they not all to have said, "Mamma, we can only spend it with you ; our home is with you ; our love for you is the same as of old"? And Uncle Fritz, too, ought he

not also to have said, " Wilhelmine, I never could at
any time—with the exception of the campaign—have
any other thought but of passing this holy evening
with you " ? And yet what hesitating, vacillating answers he gave when I begged him to come to us with
Erica—" I don't know whether it can be arranged,"
he said. " Erica has promised to run down to Lingen
for Christmas."—" And of course you go with her ? "
I exclaimed.—" Probably," he answered, " you know
that divided pain is doubled joy ! "

" That is what comes of taking a foreigner to wife,"
I thought to myself. As he is so set against her relations, he certainly cannot calculate upon the popular
diversions being pleasing to both parties. However,
there is many a one who partakes during the honey-
moon of dishes that have been most abominably burnt,
and swears that they give him a foretaste of Paradise,
until at last, having had enough of such bills of fare,
he satisfies his hunger first with something eatable at
a restaurant, which naturally creates dissension. Perhaps that is the reason why Uncle Fritz lets himself
be gently inveigled into going to Lingen this year ;
but next year, on the contrary, he will distinctly decline the apple, by which I mean to signify the grandmother, whom I consider to be a veritable poisonous
morsel—a simple mass of unwholesomeness.

Nor could Uncle Fritz himself deny this, for whenever, during the early days of his married life, he used
to get home a little late from his musical union, " The
Whooping Cough," Erica always provided bilberry
soup, or apple-sauce and biscuit, and such-like messes
for dinner the next day, for all of which Uncle Fritz
cherishes a deeply-rooted contempt.

Finally and at last his patience gave way, and. he
asked how it was that he could always calculate on

her worrying him with fruit soups after he had been visiting his friends? Did she mean it as a kind of joke? On hearing this, she was extremely upset, and had then said that she did not understand him at all. Her grandmother had bid her lay specially to heart, that thin sweet soups for dinner on the following day were the best remedy for men who were irregular in coming home; there was nothing wholesomer in the world.

"She is a dear old lady, your grandmother," Uncle Fritz had answered to this explanation: and when Erica discovered that the invalid diet was nothing but disguised malice, she asked his forgiveness over and over again—a boon he willingly granted her. For as soon as ever she lifts her big blue eyes imploringly to his, there is nothing he can refuse her. My penetration is absolutely at fault as to what the reason for this may be; were it not uncultured, I should believe that she had bewitched him. But wherewith and how can that be done?

And so if he really did intend going to Lingen, it could only be because Erica had summoned the magic charm of her blue eyes to her aid, or else because he had a crow to pluck with the grandmother. This latter might certainly be worth the fare.

As my Carl did not develop an inventive faculty, I said, "If my own belongings do not choose to come, I shall invite strangers. Herr Max is unfortunately away travelling, but Herr Kleines is sure to like to come."—"Will you not invite Herr Pfeiffer too?"—"I'll do that also. If the others choose to keep themselves to themselves, I will show them that we can remain by ourselves." Herewith matters were settled for the time being.

My invitations were accepted, thereby enabling me to carry my point.

And so the twenty-fourth of December approached. We had doubtful weather on that day, which accorded well with my frame of mind. I did not feel at all in a festal spirit, for I could not disguise the fact from my-self that the wisest course might have been to transfer the common festivities to the Doctor's house, but then what would it have looked like to back out of one's invitations ?

When twilight came I could stay at home no longer ; I felt I must be on the spot while Emmi was giving her presents.

Franz and Fritz, the twins, were too sweet—fit for preserves, as Amanda is always saying—and even if they have not attained to a high degree of intelligence so far, still they did notice that this evening was some-thing out of the common, especially Fritz, who alto-gether takes more after the Buchholzes and has superi-or mental powers. He looked at the fir-tree with a thoughtfulness and feeling that could hardly have been expected at his age, while Franz displayed a stronger inclination for the toys, and more especially for the eatables. Everything that they got was in duplicate, and that looked extremely pretty ; the little shoes, the wee stockings, the tiny Sunday hats and dresses, it was all quite charming, and so practical— even the playthings were mostly unbreakable. Grand-mamma Buchholz contributed two money-boxes, ele-gantly varnished and bearing their respective names. My Carl had taken care that they should rattle when shaken, and this gave the Doctor special gratification. He said that civilised humanity could not begin to save too early.

However, we had to leave, in order to fulfil the du-ties that we had taken upon ourselves. On our way home my Carl said : " How nice it was there ! Don't you repent of your obstinacy? Can you women never get hold of the fact that you are not infallible?"

"One can understand it well enough," I answered, repelling this defamation of our entire sex; "but——"

"But?"

"One does not always want to understand it. But please do not talk about subjects that do not concern you."

Betti and Felix were waiting for us when we got back home. We gossiped for a little, and after Herr Kleines and Herr Pfeiffer had made their appearance, the tree was lighted up. Every one ceased speaking when it was alight, and a solemn silence filled the room. For there were no merry children about us, and the grown-up people who stood round the tree may well have wished themselves back again in the days whose pleasures were pure as heaven's light. And longing is voiceless.

The mutual presents that were being given first re stored conversation. The two gentlemen expressed their thanks for being allowed to keep their Christmas-eve in a family circle, in the doing of which Herr Pfeiffer reached the lowest depths of his voice, and Herr Kleines was not wanting in politeness. How-ever, his hungry appearance warned me that it was time to adjourn to dinner. Just as I was on the point of issuing an invitation to this effect, unexpected visit-ors came in, and who should they be but Uncle Fritz and Erica.

"Good gracious!" I exclaimed, "are you not at Lingen?"

"As you see, we are not," replied Uncle Fritz. "But if our coming is inopportune, just say so, and we will go back again, re-light our tree, and remain at home."
—"I like that! Why, this is grand! You could not

have designed a more delightful surprise for us. Just think, what would a Christmas without you have been like for me?"

I took him aside : "Did your wife reconcile herself easily to not going to her own people?"—"Capitally," he answered.—"Did she see the wisdom of it at once?" —"At once."—"But how was it possible?"—"I got Dr. Wrenzchen to prohibit the journey as being bad for her health."

I looked at him questioningly; he nodded with a smile. "Fritz," I exclaimed, "you have only been married for such a short time, and yet you behave quite astonishingly like a husband! Where did you learn to do it?"

"It is a special gift," he answered. "Besides, I have taken you and your Carl as a pattern."

I was on the point of paying him back for this sally, but the door opened, and the Doctor and Emmi, accompanied by Dr. Paber, came in at the same moment. This so overpowered me that I was unable to say a single word. Now all of them were there together. Affection had led them hither. I had only persuaded myself that its extinction was imminent, that the new home caused the old one to be forgotten, as well as ourselves who had remained behind in it.

When I had managed to collect my thoughts, I said : "Children, it is really delightful to have you all assembled here. But whether I shall be able to make the carp go round, is quite another question. If the fishmongers are closed, we must fill up the interstices with sandwiches."

Herr Kleines hopped up to me, in a series of comical skips, and said : "There is nothing easier than that. How much?"—I appraised their capabilities : "The Doctor can play a good knife and fork, Uncle

Fritz does not require much pressing, Dr. Paber must not be put on short commons—from six to eight pounds." I had scarcely said how much more we should want before Herr Kleines exclaimed : "I will get it ! " and hurried out of the room. There was no means of holding him back. He had shot down-stairs like a flash of greased lightning, so that I barely had time to call after him, " Be sure that they have hard roes ! "

Repentant sinners are zealous in rendering services, in order to be taken into favour again. But for all that, he is only to be invited to large parties—his manners are too familiar for smaller ones.

Herr Kleines arrived after an interval with the carp. He had driven into town in a first-class fly, and sure enough had hit upon a fishmonger who was still open. Of course they had persuaded him into taking soft roes. But that is what always happens when gentle-men make purchases, only they decline to see it.

However, it was no matter, for there was suffi-cient hard roe in the first portion which had been pre-pared for the gentlemen to have enough ; we ladies declined it, except for just a little taste.

I have seldom seen people enjoy their supper more than our guests did this evening, for in the meantime it had got very late ; fortunately, we all had abun-dance. And why should they not have liked it ? All of us merry folk were intimate ; we were all either re-lations or friends ; and the tapers of the Christmas-tree shed a gentle glow, like messengers of peace from the days when none of us knew what parting meant.

A BALL-ROOM CHAPERONE.

Why Berlin requires robustness, and what is a sufficiency for a
   junior class—Why the table rang again, and the father remained
   in leading-strings—Why oratorios are run off the reel, and
   money does not give happiness—Why Carl coughs, and ball-
   room partners are looked up—Why war is engendered and Idiss
   has to go to bed again—The higher arts of cookery and cheerfulness—About truth being inculcated, and lumps of sugar—
   Why Wilhelmine is not a murderess and Idiss looks like
   whipped cream—About national songs and turtle-doves—Why
   Betti is jealous and Idiss's market value increases.

WHENEVER I visit Erica, she receives me with sucn
a courteous grace, that I feel quite cosy and comfortable directly ; and now that her establishment has
been completed, and the last things got according to
her liking, her home is just like herself.

How pretty she has made it look, with her flower-
stands and a large fan-palm, which together form an
arbour in the room ! There are comfortable little
arm-chairs in it, and a tiny rustic table with slanting
legs, which makes one fancy that it is a corner for the
dolls, but we grown-up folk establish ourselves beneath the broad leaves, and feel ourselves freer from
constraint.

She attends to the plants herself, and they give back
their verdure in gratitude.

And how charming she looks in her garden, as she
calls the corner ! She always wears light colours, although she is fair, but her delicate complexion seems
to throw the fragile materials into the shade, which,
as Uncle Fritz says, are just barely good enough for
her. Were he a Crœsus, or any other banker on a
large scale, I think he would complain at not being
able to get something dearer than the manufactories

ever produce. But she thinks everything too good for herself.

She does not care for jewelry. A ribbon, a bow, a flower is sufficient adornment for her; she understands arranging these simple adjuncts in exquisite taste, though it may be quite different from the fashion. However, when she goes out, being just as much in the fashion as the rest of humanity, in order not to attract notice by her divergence from prevailing customs, she only makes a fleeting impression, and her manner becomes timid and constrained. This is why Uncle Fritz calls her his " Edelweiss," which displays itself most charmingly in undisturbed solitude.

I admit that Berlin requires more robustness, more strength and power, but Uncle Fritz has enough of those qualities for both.

Erica thinks a good deal of me. I can see that quite well; even in the small matter of pouring out coffee for me, she does it with so much care that there should neither be too little, nor too much to slop over into the saucer, but just what makes it look most inviting. And this is one of Nature's ancient truths: " As it's offered, so it tastes."

When taking her altogether, her conversation and her opinions, one gradually becomes conscious that she has barely a conception of what we understand by hatred; she retires like a snail whose feelers have been trodden upon; one feels that she could suffer dumbly, but as to showing any one a trace of unkindness, she simply could not do it.

And who is there that would hurt her?

And if any one tried it—'ware Uncle Fritz! The other day, when we were sitting in the palm-garden, that is to say Erica and I, gossiping, Uncle Fritz came in rather unexpectedly, for it was just during business hours, and he had a big envelope in his hand, which he held aloft in triumph.

"If you feel inclined for it," he exclaimed, "we will go to a ball given by the United Singing Clubs. Here is the invitation. It will be a capital affair. Good-day, dear Wilhelm! How are matters progressing in the penal settlement? Is my brother-in-law still alive?"

He sat down beside us, and placed the invitation card, which was printed in gold, on the rustic table. "Well, what makes you so dull and stupid?"

"Well-bred folk never answer impertinent questions," I retorted severely.

"And you are not pleased about it, Erica?" he turned to his wife.

Now for the first time I followed his glances, which rested in consternation on Erica. She was silent, but her features expressed timidity and fear. I had never seen her look so strange.

"Are you not well?" he asked anxiously, and with one push of his chair he was close beside her; he drew her head to his breast and kissed her forehead. "Erica!"

She smiled again. It was a sad, melancholy smile with which she recovered from her torpor, but it grew more cheerful, and gradually the last cloud disappeared from her face.

"Forgive me," she whispered; "it was only a memory that took hold of me!"

"A ball-room memory?"

She nodded assent.

"Gentlemen are sometimes boundlessly enterprising at balls." I gave Uncle Fritz a key for his better comprehension.

"I have never been at a ball yet," said Erica.

"Then how can you remember——"

" I thought that I had forgotten it," Erica continued ;
" but just now, when Fritz came in and asked whether
I felt inclined to go to a ball, it seemed to me as if it
had only just happened."

"As if what had happened ? "

She glanced towards Fritz for permission.

" What was it ? " he asked, gently and quietly now.
" I have no secrets from my sister ; she has been my
mother confessor since my youth."

" Well, yes," I answered ; " he was up to some mischief every moment.   The blows that he escaped would
have been enough for a respectable junior class.   However, that is the way with Berlin boys ; fortunately the
wildest amongst them are afterwards——"

" The best," interrupted Uncle Fritz.

" We won't make quite such a definite assertion."

Erica smiled.   " He is the best," she said.

" Only one should not let him know it, or he will
think too much of himself.   You were going to tell us
about your ball.   Had not the dressmaker sent your
dress home ? "

" Oh, yes, she had ; even the new shoes with the little
rosettes had been ready a fortnight before the evening !
It was a children's ball to which I was to be allowed
to go.   My father had made me the promise.   He had
asked, just like Fritz, whether I was inclined for it,
and I was scarcely able to answer for joy.   I had never
had an amusement like that—never before.   My grandmother always insisted that pleasures destroyed the
soul, and that I was too naughty——"

" You naughty ? " Fritz burst forth.

" Certainly," answered Erica naïvely.   " Should I
have deserved beatings if I had not been ? "

" You ? "   Uncle Fritz flew into a passion.   " They
have given you—— May they be——" He made the

little table ring again with a blow from his clenched fist. "Go on," he said angrily—"go on. So you were to go to the ball?"

"I was to be allowed. I could hardly sleep for a whole week beforehand. You may imagine how vain I was. I put on the new shoes secretly, and tied the blue bows. How afraid I was of crumpling them! But I could not help myself. And as for the ball itself, I pictured that as being like an evening sky with sunbeams and rosy clouds. My heart began to beat at the mere thought of it."

"My sweet wife," Uncle Fritz said, and kissed her.

"When the day of the ball arrived, as it became dark, I was told—'Go and dress, Erica; it is time.' The servant helped me. 'You will not sit out a single dance,' the girl said; 'you are sure to be the prettiest there.' How is it, I wonder, that I have remembered it all—to the very words that were spoken? I opened the door of my room and went to the stairs. But how strange it was; there was no light burning in the parlour down-stairs. 'May I come down?' I exclaimed. They were to admire me in my ball costume—father, grandmother, the little brothers and sisters. Nobody answered. Once more I called out, 'May I come?' Then——" Erica stopped, and the grief again made her eyelids heavy, and threw dark shadows over her face.

"And then——"

"First I believed that it was a delusion, and stared into the dark room with open eyes and ears; but once again I distinctly heard my father's voice saying: 'Go and undress, Erica; you are not going.' And while I still kept fancying that it could not be true, my grandmother exclaimed: 'People must learn to give up betimes. Be careful with the shoes; they have only been lent.' Oh, how distinctly—how distinctly!" ·

Uncle Fritz had compressed his lips—he was boiling over. Indeed, I felt myself as if my nails were growing into my fingers. Erica saw how furious her story had made him, and she added soothingly : "It was to be a trial ; I was not always submissive. They intended my good ; you must not be angry with them, Fritz."

I had involuntarily drawn further back, as I could not but expect that the little table would now get the remainder of its punishment. However, there was no such display of force as Fritz is capable of when he is excited ; he only looked at Erica with a glance of unspeakable love. "Yours is a heaven-given heart, my wife," was all he said. Then he clasped her to him, and enfolded the fair head with his protecting hands.

It was incomprehensible to me that the father should lend himself to such a cruel system of education ; but no doubt the old woman intimidated him from his early days, just as she had done with Erica. She had helped to scrape together their little bit of money, and in her obstinate severity she never would allow her son to be independent ; he therefore remained in leading-strings during the whole of his life. Fritz had told me that while he was still courting.

Now, too, I understand the charm which binds him so fast to Erica—her soul is as beautiful as her face. As neither of the others said anything, I felt that it was my duty to fill up the pause. "A charming specimen of antiquity !" I remarked.

"Who ? "

"Why, the grandmother."

Uncle Fritz got up. He seemed as if he could not get over what he had just heard, and was endeavouring to choke down his excitement by marching up and down the room with clenched hands, a process which is more reasonable than wreaking one's anger on pieces of furniture, because it is cheaper. My Carl is never vehement towards defenceless objects.

Gradually Fritz got quieter. " Shall we accept the invitation?" he asked.—"I should like to see a ball for once," answered Erica.—" So you shall. And you shall have rosettes on your shoes and a blue bow as well. And you, Wilhelmine, you will come too."

" What are you thinking about?"

" Air your 'helps' for once, or else they may get full of moths. Young girls must have some fun. And you yourself, the abbess of the whole, will be benefited by some recreation, or do you imagine that the old nuns never danced? They jumped about like good ones, I can tell you."

"Fritz, please oblige me by sparing me your hyperboles ; they have not the slightest artistic value in my eyes. My Carl must give his consent first of all !"

"That's all right. So that point is settled."

" How so?"

"If you consent, your Carl will do the same. Or do you think he won't? Wrenzchen will join us, I'll undertake that. There will be singing, and he is fond enough of listening to it. Just fancy, Erica, three singing societies have entered for the festivities ! 'Gravity and Mirth' head the list, and our 'Whooping Cough' is amongst them. Whole oratorios will be run off the reel, and all sorts of other rubbish. Do be pleased about it, Erica ! There are some splendid voices among them, especially baritones. Wife, do be glad ! "

Erica smiled. "It would be too charming, if you would take pity on me, Frau Buchholz," she said.

" Am I not there?" exclaimed Uncle Fritz.

"You would surely not neglect your friends on my account?"

"You are right again. How clever the child is!" smirked Uncle Fritz; "and only in Berlin for the second time!"

"It does not depend upon locality, but on the amount of intelligence with which one starts," I corrected his silly speechifying. He was offending Erica. How can she help not having been born on the Pariser-platz? But my esteemed brother and consideration! None need exist for his requirements. It is as indifferent to him as mittens in August. Were it not that one fortunately knows him from another point of view, he would keep one in a chronic state of wonderment.

While he was walking up and down, he had got hold of a fresh idea. "Erica," he said, "if you have a *tube*-post-card lying about anywhere, we will summon the Doctor hither at once."—"You had better leave that alone," I warned them, "or else he will enter the visit to you."—"That won't hurt, if he is accurate."—"Fritz, money alone cannot give happiness."—"Agreed. But one must have some of it."

Erica had been looking for a *tube*-post-card on her writing-table, but none was to be found there, as generally happens when one is in a hurry, and she went out to have one fetched.

When she had vanished, I said: "Fritz, what a grandmother! She certainly must be a witch of earlier days who has escaped the flames. Is there no royal court of justice which could interfere?"

"Leave the old Jezebel to her own devices. When I come to think it over, she is the real reason of Erica's becoming my wife."

"A horror like that?"

"When I saw how the old woman ruined the life of her family, I determined positively to save Erica at least from her clutches."—"And so you took your Rickchen to yourself."

"Don't use that name, please ; Erica does not like it."—"I presume a diminutive is not grand enough for you ? "—"Her grandmother called her by that name." —"Of course, then——"—"When the old hag wanted to hurt her, she used to call in the gentlest possible voice, 'Rickchen ! Rickchen !' till the little one was close enough for her to get hold of her gold curls and give them a sound pull."—"I should have bitten into her bony knuckles ! "—"Yes, you would. You unfortunately were never forbidden such enjoyment. At first I used to call Erica 'Rickchen' in jest, but she begged me not to do it, and told me why."—"Fritz, I am afraid that the old wretch has pinched her and pushed her against the corners of the table. Just let her once come to Berlin again, and I will give her such a talking-to as will make her ears tingle even when she is lying in her coffin ! Of course, Erica must go to the festival. I hope that I can answer for my husband."

Uncle Fritz told his wife that I was going to chaperone her.—"I shall be delighted," said I. "And if Mamma Buchholz should see fit to pass over a few dances, my clever, intelligent sister-in-law will not complain. There are reasons for so doing."

"Wilhelmine, you are a pearl ! " exclaimed Uncle Fritz, and gave me such an approving slap of his hand that my shoulder-blade quivered again.—"Augh, you are a brute ! "—"Curious," he laughed ; "when I hit, it always hurts the other person more than myself ! "— "You had better hammer away at your tables," I scolded. "By the way, how many tickets are you going to get ? "—"I shall take a dozen straight off, to make a round number."—"At half price ? "—"We shall see ; though many committees decline to be moved by the groans of numerous heads of families."—"It would be very nice if one could save a trifle ; times are so miserably bad."—"So they are. It was only yesterday that another horse fell down in the Friedrich-strasse."

When Uncle Fritz begins his nonsense, it is advisable to take one's leave. I therefore did so, and went.

The fight with my husband for his consent was hardly worth speaking about. "What an expense our grand journey to Switzerland would have been, or to the Salzkammergut, which lies a day's journey further off," I explained to him ; "and now that I am voluntarily—Carl, what are you coughing for? I accent 'vo-lun-ta-ri-ly'—relinquishing it, the expenses for the ball need hardly be taken into consideration at all ! Besides, we are taking a dozen tickets, and will be sure to make a small profit by so doing."—"We must take them together," assented my Carl, like a good man of business ; and when I told him that our whole entire family as it stood was to meet there, he became still more accommodating, and ordered his dress-coat to be cleaned with benzine, and ironed.

Can there be another husband who is more considerate, merely comparing him with my brother?

Betti was enchanted when she heard that we were going to a ball, and that every objection had already been nipped in the bud. "I shall only dance with Felix !" she exclaimed.—"That would look very peculiar," I answered.—"What need I care about that?"—"If you don't, I do. I am the chaperone."

Now the question was to devise ways and means for Ida and Frieda. The dresses were there, and as Max had just returned from his last travels, Frieda was provided with a dancer. But where were we to get a partner for that luckless Ida? We agreed that the three gentlemen must settle it, for we could not expect Dr. Paber to burden himself with her, and Kleines, together with Herr Pfeiffer, were excluded. A ball is really not given for the purpose of throwing unguarded young girls before lions. That was at most only the fashion with the ancients.

Some light was shed upon the question when Felix promised one evening to provide Ida with a respectable gentleman.

I bought my "helps" in the following manner: " Young ladies, if your behaviour during the next fortnight is exemplary, you will be allowed to go to a ball at Arnim's hotel as a reward. But if, on the contrary, you give me occasion for displeasure, nothing will come of it. I shall look through your wardrobe and chest of drawers myself, Ida, and hope to find everything in the very best order. Untidy folk stop at home." This warning seemed to make no impression for the moment ; they flew off like sparrows.

Max was back again. He found Frieda changed for the better, and was glad of it. Yet—had he had her about him for weeks, like myself? No. It is lucky that affianced brides do not always know what their affianced husbands are about; that they believe firmly he is thinking uninterruptedly of them, or staring unceasingly at their photograph in a cigar-case. And it is just as fortunate that the reverse holds good also, otherwise the business of marriage would be prosecuted with less energy. Had Max known that in the bottom of her heart Frieda merely considered him as a friend to take care of her, he would not have been deceived by the few graces she has acquired, or the small amount of ill-breeding she has laid aside.

Now, as formerly, she was neither hot nor cold, and

their first meeting after a fairly long separation passed off as if he might have extended his journey for a considerably longer time. He, however, was caught anew by her prettiness, and more devoted to her than before.

The preparations were actively taken in hand. We had decided in favour of simple white, but each dress was to be trimmed differently, and the most tasteful patterns were sought for in the book of fashions. The "helps" behaved fairly according to my desire; a cessation of hostilities prevailed to a certain extent, and each one thought her dress the most charming, and far more beautiful than the other's. And yet dissension crept into the harmony of the ball tailoring!

Whoever failed to see in Max a well-built man ought to pay an early visit to the eye hospital; and Ida, too, seemed to be of this mind. Wherever Herr Max was, there she was fluttering about likewise; and she was so cat-like and velvety in her manner towards him, that I was just about inculcating rules for her behaviour. However, Frieda took charge of the matter on this occasion.

A praiseworthy fate so arranged that my husband was absent when the skirmish took place.

I had missed the beginning, in which one word led on to another; it was only the loud exchange of speech in the next room that caused me to interfere.

"Frieda! Ida! What a dreadful din!" I exclaimed "What in the name of fortune is the matter now?"

"She says——" screamed Ida.—"She says——" exclaimed Frieda against her.—"She said——"—"No, she said——"—"Not a word of truth in it!"—"Fräulein Schulz began it!"—"That is a lie!"

"Ida," I commanded, "hold your tongue. If there were no more than a rabbit against you, suspicion would fall upon you. Frieda, how was it?"

" She has done nothing but jeer at me the whole afternoon——"—" Imagination ! " said Ida, interrupting her.

" Fräulein Schulz, either you will take the trouble of retiring to your room, or you will hold your tongue. What caused the quarrel, Frieda ? "

" I don't choose that an impudent hussy like that should be running about after my intended husband." —" Indeed ? " asked Ida impertinently. " You may just as well know that I cannot get away from him. Besides, what is there about you to attract him in the long run ? "

" An absence of spots, at least ! " Frieda snubbed her. " He amuses himself at your expense. That is all."

Ida gave vent to a derisive " Bah ! Have you any further grievances ? He has promised me three dances, and he is going to wait for me in the ' choosing partners.' "—" It's a lie ! " exclaimed Frieda.—" Indeed ? " —" Yes."

" Ida, is that true ? " I asked very seriously.

" We have settled it," she answered ; " but he will scarcely confess to it when Fräulein Frieda makes such a barbarous row."—" Who makes a row ? "— " She ! Who else does ? Why, you have just heard her ! "

" Fräulein Schulz, if you begin to plot intrigues, I, for my part, cannot take you with us. In a word, your behaviour is not the proper kind for a ball-room. You will remain at home, and go to bed early."

Now she began to weep and implore. She asked me to forgive her, and promised improvement on all points.

I thought it was very nice of Frieda not to bear malice after Ida had given her solemn word of honour not to dance once with Max. Ida made a positive promise about this, and so the "helps'" differences were adjusted. The parties were separated by my taking Frieda with me.

"My love," I said, "do avoid these outbreaks. If anybody is injured by them, it will be myself."

"I controlled myself as long as I was able. But she must leave my intended alone."

"Aha!" I thought; "Herr Max is not quite so unimportant to her as I had supposed. That may be considered as a good sign—a very good one indeed. Only my having to pay so cruelly for it is not good."

"Frieda," I then said aloud, "please give me the valerian drops—they strengthen one a little, though the effect may not be lasting; the bronchial tubes worry me after any annoyance. However, when we once have the ball behind us, I shall request Frau Schulz to receive her Ida back again. I do not see why I am to stand on guard, when the wide world is open to her."

This determination Ida strengthened still more, by her bad behaviour on the day of the ball itself. Kindness was of just as much avail with her as teaching puppies to read.

Betti was still a little behindhand with her dress, for she had determined on making an alteration at the last moment, for which I did not blame her, as she was not going to be put in the shade by the "helps." While Betti was busy with the dressmaker, we confided the care of the dinner, to which Herr Max had been invited, to Frieda and Ida. Frieda was to take the opportunity of giving her intended a sample of her cookery at the same time; for this fact remains true, that she had made praiseworthy progress under Betti's superintendence. For the rest, I could take an occasional look into the kitchen, and it is not very difficult to roast beef. Game and such things do certainly demand greater experience in the very buying of them, and the art of feeling poultry is a gift in itself. Doris served up the gravy soup and Ida the macaroni stars ; vegetables, potatoes, and *compot* were arranged in the same way, the latter consisting of dried fruit which had been stewed. "Be sure you don't forget the cover," I impressed on Ida, "so that the plums may swell out properly. My husband likes them best like that."

Why had I not had more foresight, and had the dinner fetched from a restaurant, in portions in white porcelain vessels placed one on the top of another, and fastened together by leather straps ? Because one never does learn wisdom, nor imagines that young girls who are going to a ball in the evening become half-witted in the morning. And yet it really must be the case.

When I betake myself to the kitchen the "helps" certainly are actively employed. But how ?

Everything which had been placed on the fire was boiling, I will not say at a gallop—no, rather in mad career. Wheels alone were wanting to the machine, otherwise it would have been a fair locomotive.

"Ladies," I exclaimed, "I presume that you are practising the art of incendiarism ?"—"You said yourself that the roast beef must have a hot fire to begin with," Frieda defended herself.

"Of course I did. But you have made the stove red-hot, as if the Three Children were going to give a concert in it ! Doris, why did you not interfere ? What a waste of coals ! "

"Fräulein Frieda said, such were Madame's orders," answered Doris. "I don't go anywhere near

the fire-place if the young ladies have the chief command."—"But, Doris!"—"No, I'm not going to do it.
If anything goes wrong, the cook has done it; but if
it succeeds nicely the young ladies are praised up to
the skies. I have not liked being here for a good
many fortnights now, and thank goodness I'm not
married to the place either!"

Another word from me and Doris would have given
me warning. That was a thing to be avoided on such
a day as this. Otherwise, off she should have gone.

Punishing Doris by taking no notice of her, I instructed Frieda to damp down the fire, and have the
baking oven so far cooled that the meat might be put
into it with a quiet conscience, and told her to bring
me the pan. "Oh, Frieda, what an unreasonable
quantity of butter you have taken!" I was forced to
exclaim, on seeing the big lump she had destined for
the roast. "It certainly is true that good butter does
not spoil anything, but it oils the way to ends not
meeting, and easily acquires a metallic flavour."—"I
have never noticed that," said Frieda.—"Madame is
thinking of the groschens," Doris put in her word.—
"Doris, you have not been asked."—"Stuff! Butter
was said, and I was meant! I know all about it!"

"She shall learn how to fly, shortly," I determined
in my own mind, and left the field.

Now what may be the cause of this distinct mutiny
on Doris's part? If she wants to go, why does she
not approach me in a becoming way? Who has made
her rebellious?. She shall be interrogated to-morrow.
There's a ball to-day.

As Betti could not leave her dressmaking to itself—
indeed, there was even a difficulty about her being
finished in time—the pleasure devolved on me of looking after the preparations for dinner, and as I thought

that it was about time to provide against mischief, I made my way towards the kitchen, where hilarity and merriment seemed to prevail as I approached. So I quietly opened the door in order to see what the fun was.

It was Ida.

Would any one have thought it possible? The godless creature had put on my singed morning cap, had fastened my second-best knitted woollen vest round her, and was acting for the edification of the two others!

"People may keep house on a good deal; a little may also be made sufficient, ladies," she said; "lay that to heart." Then she walked up and down mincingly, as if it had been me, only of course there was not a trace of likeness, and she cleared her throat as if suffering from asthma, and she grinned and danced and waggled about with outspread arms as if she was going to flutter, behaving, generally speaking, as if she were quite crazy. "Doris," she went on in her mimicry, "Doris"—in a high, piping voice, whereas I never speak loud or shriekingly—"believes probably that butter does not cost anything; the baked pike is swimming in grease! That is the way to make a hole in the milliards. My husband does not care about grease; it does not suit my Carl. He likes to eat them best the way I bake them. Is that not so, my Carl?"

Doris and Frieda laughed until the tears poured down their cheeks; and the more they rolled about, the more absurdly Ida went on.

Then Doris suddenly became aware of my presence, while I, as unsuspected as an archangel, looked on from the slips.

"Oh, Lor'! the old 'un!" she shrieked, flew like the wind into the store-room, and slammed the door behind her.

Frieda had become very confused, and crept shame-
facedly to the kitchen table, where she occupied herself aimlessly. Ida quickly tore off both cap and
knitted vest, and endeavoured to hide them behind
her back.

"How is the dinner getting on?" I asked with icy
calmness.

I had not deserved that. To wound me in such a
way! They are welcome to caricature me, for all I
care. But my Carl!—that is the last straw.

"Just as you told us," Frieda answered timidly.

"That is well."

And to instigate Doris against me! As if I ever
spoke evil of her behind her back! Oh, no; I always
impress the truth straightforwardly on my servants!
Of course, now it was easy to see why Doris had been
finding fault just before. Ida had been slanderously
carrying tales; which accounted for the firm friendship between the two.

"Take care that the dinner is served punctually
Frieda."

"Certainly."

I took my departure without having so much as
glanced towards Ida. She was to be made to feel what
it was to be mere vapour for respectable people.

Betti came to consult me, because the dress wrinkled
about the sleeves. When she heard what had happened, she insisted that Frau Schulz should be written
to, and that Ida be allowed to join her parents.—
"Quite out of the question," I said.

There was a knock.—"Come in."—Ida appeared.

"What do you wish for?"

"Ah, Frau Buchholz, I really did not mean to do
anything wrong!"—"When?"—"Just now, I mean."—
"Just now?"—"When I—when——"

"It is well that you are here, Fräulein Schulz. I was just going to ask you whether you had any message for your mother. I may possibly write in the course of to-day—or with greater quiet to-morrow."—"No,—none that I know of."

"You may go, Fräulein Schulz; or did you wish to communicate to me that you would prefer not going to the ball?"—"You surely cannot wish that?"—"It would be better; for every one can see at once that you have been tasting things," said Betti.—"I touch nothing," answered Ida.—"Who will believe it?"—"I declare that I have not," Ida asseverated.—"Your lips betray you."

Ida drew her handkerchief quickly from her pocket to hide the brown ichthyol that she had smeared on her lips, but in doing so she tore forth divers trifles as well; baking plums, pieces of lump sugar, and dried pears flew about the room.

"What have you to say now?" Betti exclaimed.

"Somebody must have put them in my pocket on the sly."

"It could not possibly have been otherwise!" I said. "How would it be if you took your departure now? Doris can lay for you, if you would like dinner in your room."—She withdrew backwards.

The dinner was horrible; I could just manage to cut a few eatable morsels from the middle of the roast for my husband and Herr Max, and the stewed fruit had been turned into a ruined mass resembling soaked brown coal.—"I suppose they come from some antediluvian soup-kitchen?" asked my Carl, leaving them untouched.

"Dinner is never very grand on the day of a ball; there are so many more important things to be seen to," I said, to explain away the scandalous cookery.

" Where is Fräulein Schulz ? "

" Probably engaged with her toilette for this evening."

" I think that she is writing," said Frieda.

" The best thing she could do," I thought. "If she tells her mother that she has become a nuisance, I shall be released from a task that only becomes more unpleasant the longer it is put off.",

. When we went off later to make ourselves ready for the dance, Betti said : "I really cannot understand you, mamma ; how could you keep so quiet over Fräulein Schulz's impertinence ? I should have treated her very differently."

" Betti, in the first place, I did not want to lower myself in her eyes ; and secondly, I have taken an unshakable resolve to have her bundled off to Zehlendorf the day after to-morrow. I have experienced the worst with her. It cannot be surpassed ; and this conviction lent me control and strength. You may thank Providence that you do not see a murderess, or something of that description, sitting before you in your mother. Ida had brought it to that pass. But whoever has once experienced the fostering care of the law, will keep watch over his actions rather than plunge into endless expense."

In order that my husband should have no occasion for remarks, I hurried everything forward ; and when it was time for us to start, two flies-full were quite ready.

The ball had already begun, though there were late-comers still to be expected. The effect really is too overpowering when people rustle through the widely-opened folding-doors into the brilliant room, and when those who are already there direct their glances towards the entering guests and whisper to each other,

"Who are they?"—"Oh, they are So-and-so."—"Indeed; that is who it is!" Then the toilettes are admired, and people's unaffected manner, so far as it can be attained, holding their hands as if the kid gloves had been born with them; and one feels as if in a swing, or as if cold water were trickling down to one's feet.

Betti and Frieda calculated on their *fiancées* as partners to begin with, and likewise on Dr. Paber, who had joined my son-in-law's party, and had arrived shortly before us. Dr. Paber belongs to those who honour the good old proverb, "Live and let live," and who see that unattached gentlemen must do penance at balls for partaking of the family fare.

We grouped ourselves into a sort of connected range of wall columns, in which Frau Assessor Lehmann joined, and she too invited several acquaintances to help in the elongation of the string of onions.

My three girls went in white, only that the cut of each dress was different, and that each had on a different sash. Frieda looked extremely well. Perhaps she provoked more attention than is seemly in an affianced bride. There was something out-of-the-way charming about Betti. She had a puffed trimming, exquisitely adorned with small green sprigs, which presented quite a bride-like appearance. Ida, in her muslin dress and broad, flaming red sash, was very like a dish of whipped cream with currant jelly; it was impossible to torture the gentlemen by expecting them to dance with her, more especially as some remarkably pretty girls adorned the room.

However, Herr Felix had taken upon himself to procure her a partner. I do not remember what his name was, but he was a kind of giant cut short, back slightly rounded, bright-eyed, bold in his attitudes, although his legs turned inwards, and remarkably taken up with himself. The great oaf was more than good enough for Ida.

The rooms filled gradually, and dancing was going on with great spirit by the time Uncle Fritz was visible with Erica.

They attracted attention. And how? By Erica's unaffected simplicity. The dress was made quite plainly, but it was of the finest cream-coloured cashmere, such as was more the fashion formerly, and her only adornments were, a light pale blue velvet ribbon round her neck, and the same in her fair hair. This toilette might have been called childlike, but it bestowed such a virgin charm on the young wife, that the sight of her positively called forth veneration. And it is impossible to describe how her big blue eyes looked admiringly at the glittering, billowing throng, or how timidly she kept to the side of her handsome husband, whose face beamed in his overflowing felicity. Betti hurried up to her and said, "You are the most beautiful of all!"

Erica cast down her eyes and reddened.

The distinguishing feature of this ball was the splendid performances of the singers in the intervals between the dances; and they did not sing lamentations either, but merry marches and waltzes, which regaled the ears of us elderly ladies more especially.

Besides this, they acted a scene in which music was introduced—from the "Volkslied"—which afforded a charming variety between the dances and the eating and drinking refreshments.

The room was cleared at a given signal, and dwarfs and gnomes came tripping in to the strains of a merry march, some drawing and some pushing a frame resting on wheels, which, being shrouded in glittering gauze, presented the appearance of a snow mountain. When this had been placed in the middle of the room, the forest spirits lay and squatted round the mountain, seeming as if they had settled down for their winter sleep, the music meanwhile growing softer and more conducive to slumber.

Suddenly a French horn resounded, and peasant-lads marched through the door with their treasures, in the most diverse costumes, four pairs always being dressed alike, as Tyrolese, Suabians, Swiss, Frisians, Appenzellers, or any other costume that peasants wear.

These all danced several minuet-like figures, and seemed to pay no attention to the mountain or the gnomes surrounding it.

Then a chord was played upon a harp, followed immediately by a second. The orchestra was silent, the dancers stopped and listened, and the sprites began to move. The harp sounded again, but this time it was softly accompanied by the strains of a pleasing melody, the white covering slid slowly down from the structure, and a charming young girl became visible, dressed in a grey-blue skirt and brown bodice, cornflowers at her breast and in her hair, a stringed instrument in her hands. She was the Genius of National Song.

At her feet sat the knight and the goldsmith's little daughter, the hunter with his cross-bow, a small brother and sister, the hermit, the valiant man-at-arms, and the maiden at her distaff. A couple of turtle-doves billed and cooed together on a green branch, and a roe peeped forth from among the boughs. Everything that National Song tells of was joined together in a *tableau vivant*, which turned slowly round so that every one could see it. And while this was being done, the gentlemen sang a collection of the finest National melodies, which gradually passed into a dance tune. Once more the costumed throng moved to and fro in the mazy dance, and then they left the room as they had entered it.

There was only one opinion about this delightful representation, which had been invented by Fritz's friend—Dr. Theodore Mann. Had he only seen how Erica could find no words to express what she wanted to say, he would have been richly rewarded. But he had to wield the conductor's *bâton*.

After this the ball was continued with renewed energy. I was in no mood for dancing after the experiences of the day ; but Uncle Fritz insisted, although I had dressed in black. He is a magnificent dancer, careful and sure, but light and elastic in his movements withal. I begged him, if it were possible, to introduce Ida to some partners, as she had been sitting out for several dances, to which he answered, "At once."

When the next Schottische was beginning, four men came up together, who appealed to Fritz for an introduction, and requested the honour of being allowed to engage the young lady for a dance. From this moment she became one of the most sought-after partners. That there was some mischief connected with this, was certain ; and that Uncle Fritz had set it afloat, was still more certain.

Frieda, who was not equally fortunate, grew visibly sulky, and behaved just as shrewishly towards Max as she used formerly to do ; he certainly had committed the mistake of neglecting her completely for a whole dance, and Ida was sufficiently deceitful, notwithstanding her promise, to precipitate herself on Max in "the ladies' choice," and waltz off with him.

Frieda called him over the coals on the subject. He

answered more forcibly. She grew more and more violent, and—I do not know whether I saw rightly, but she had raised her hand, and he grew deadly pale. Turning short round, he left her standing there. Something had happened.

Frieda now wanted to go home. " When we all go," I told her. There were the most abominable commotions in prospect again for to-morrow between Frieda and Ida, Frieda and Max, Max and me ; myself, Frieda, and Max, Ida and myself, and between me and Doris. And lastly, between me and my Carl, who must stand by me, for I did not feel equal to encounter coming events alone.

However, even that was not all. On the contrary, Emmi came as well. " Where is Franz ? "—" Emmi, why are you so excited ? "—" I ask, where is Franz ? " —" I have not got him in my pocket ! "—" He has gone off surreptitiously." — " To see a patient, no doubt."—" Mamma, for some time lately he has vanished about eleven every·evening."—" My child, he is a doctor."—" That is what he says too, but Frau Lehmann knows better than that."—" What does she know ? "—" That he is deceiving me."—" Nonsense ! "— " Frau Lehmann knows the world; she does not trust her husband either."—" Well, Herr Lehmann is not your husband ; what have you to do with Herr Lehmann ? "—" Mamma, there is proof sufficient in the fact that Franz can desert me here at the ball. I am going now with Frau Lehmann; if you see Franz, tell him that he knows well why I have done it. I will come to you to-morrow. Perhaps I shall bring the children at once."—" Emmi ! "—" Have you not had your suspicions of him too from the first ? "—" But what an idea ——"—" You cannot deny it, mamma. Oh, you saw through him ! "

Frau Lehmann gave her a sign, and both went towards the door.

This was to be a nice ball for me! Everybody was enjoying him or herself to the utmost. Lights and music, merriment and life, wherever one looked; I alone sat there with nothing but worries and cares.

Then a gentle hand was laid on mine. "Why are you so thoughtful?" asked Erica.—"I am tired."— "Then we will go."—"Are you not enjoying yourself?"—"I should never have thought that a ball could be so charming."—"It is your first, but when you are a chaperone you will think differently. Have you danced much?"—"Only a few times with Fritz."

"That is right; he holds his partner firmly, and dances with circumspection when necessary. He thought of my amusement, too. There he comes."

Uncle Fritz agreed to our leaving. He fetched my Carl from one of the side rooms, where he had been having a game of whist with some elderly gentlemen. Frieda, whose eyes were filled with tears of rage and mortification, was longing to go; Ida alone wished to stay. "I am making such a sensation," she said; "I am engaged for five more dances!"

Nor was this untrue, for her programme was covered with names.

"Fritz," I asked softly, "how have you set to work to turn this horror—that is what I call her—almost into the queen of the ball-room?"

"A little Stock Exchange manœuvre, Wilhelm. I spread the report that she was an orphan, with eighty thousand thalers at her disposition; and as many people prefer enjoying their parents-in-law cold, her price went up in the market at once. I wager that many gentlemen will pay their visits to-morrow."

"This is the last straw! Children, let us go. I

really do feel ill. Being a chaperone is not only trying during the evening—ah, no!—she has to go
through the hardest part before—and frequently too
afterwards. Fritz, wrap Erica up well, so that she
does not catch cold."

BUILDING PROJECTS.

About conspiracies and the rule of three—Why Betti has no judgment and the Doctor will not be sent away empty—Thoughts
about stained glass and distant nurseries—About envenomed
ink and powers of destruction—About Feodorovna and the un-
burnt letter—Why the kitchen smoked.

THE morning had scarcely dawned before a hollow,
subterranean noise frightened away the sleep, which I
had had difficulty enough in wooing when I lay down,
for it does not permit itself to be either commanded
or coaxed like a cat. Neither flattery nor scolding is
of any avail. It winks itself off if it does not intend
coming.

"Carl!" I exclaimed; "Carl! do you hear the
knocking?"

"Sleep on quietly, Wilhelmine; I am sure that you
are still tired after the ball."

"I wish that I were, and could sleep through a spell
of four-and-twenty hours."—"Are you so worn out?"
—"Oh, no; but what one sleeps through, one does
not experience! Carl, where is that hammering?"
I raised myself in order to listen the better.—"Do stay
quietly in bed."—"Carl, the walls are positively trembling. What is the meaning of it?"

My husband, who had got up, cheered me by saying:

"Do not excite yourself unnecessarily, Wilhelmine; we are beginning our building."

"Beginning what?"

"Our building. The masons are breaking down the walls between this and the building lot beside us."—"You only tell me about it now?"—"In order not to spoil your night's rest. You are too fond of tormenting yourself with superfluous cares."—"Had you only told me one word about it, I am sure that I should not have waked up; I could have had my sleep out most beautifully. When one knows what causes noise, it is not in the least disturbing. But it is just the way with all men; when the wife is buried beneath falling stones, it is quite time enough to tell her that the house is being pulled down. I cannot stay in bed another minute."—"I would strongly dissuade you from getting up; you will come to grief much more comfortably on a mattress than off it."—"Carl, you are heartless; what did you drink yesterday?"—"Your good health."—"Is that an answer?"—"This is how it was. I drank with Felix to the success of the building, and to our all being allowed to see the fulfilment of the hopes which we connect with it, old as well as young, and to your getting well over all the attendant bother. Betti was of opinion that you would sleep so soundly this morning, that we might easily begin then."—"Just think of it, Betti was in the secret too! Well, well; I am just good enough to be made the dupe of a conspiracy!"—"Minchen, will you do me the favour of not getting out of bed wrong foot foremost?—you have a leaning that way to-day. I shall expect you to recover your good temper later, for architect Krause is coming to breakfast at eleven; we have important matters to discuss which are waiting for your verdict. Be good, old woman; snuggle down under the counterpane and drowse away for a bit. You know Krause is a nice sort of fellow."

Before I could groan out to him, " Is not the measure for this ill-starred day filled to overflowing yet?" he was gone. " Let them build," I thought, sinking back on my bed in the weakness of despair. " Everything is out of gear ; why should not the poor, innocent house come in for its share of suffering? Meanwhile, they have humiliated me."

Why was I so silly as to worry myself about other people? How delightful it would have been quite alone with my Carl, just two or three friendly rooms, one with the morning sun on it, a modest servant, far away from Berlin, somewhere on the border of a forest ; the larks sing—some hens as well—four—six, I suppose it ought to be—Carl is too fond of new-laid eggs—and a cock—each lays one on alternate days— the best daily—that makes eighteen eggs a week—no —once six is six, and one-and-a-half times five—no— every other day goes three times into six—three times five are fifteen—makes twenty-one altogether. All wrong ; for the hens don't keep Sunday—so it is two into seven—won't go. What am I to do with the two half-days ; they lay whole eggs, surely? The sum grew more involved with each fresh addition ; I could not get it right, and the first half of the rule of three had disappeared by the time I had just written the last number on the wall in my thoughts.

The door opened and Betti came in. " Well, mamma, had your sleep out?"—" I have not closed my eyes, child."—" You were in a lovely sleep when I looked in just now."—" You mistake ; since papa went away, I have been lying awake here."—" But it is after ten already !"—" Ten?"—" Will you get up and dress?"—" I am so tired out."—" Your coffee has been kept warm ; I will fetch it for you. Breakfast is ready too ; the gentlemen may be coming."—"If you say so, I suppose I must have had a little nap, but only a very little one."—"Shall we say for about three hours?"—"Betti, is time charged with electricity too? It never used to fly like that."

A morsel of refreshment is always strengthening, and as Betti made herself helpful to me in my dressing, my recovery progressed fairly—I even had strength to ask after the "helps."

"Have Ida and Frieda been fighting with each other already?"

"They avoid each other, with angry looks."

So their account had not been settled yet.

"Has Doris given notice?"

"Mamma, Doris was instigated to rebellion by Ida ; she has begged me to say a good word for her to you."

"Has Emmi come yet?"

"Emmi? First thing in the morning?"

"She intends leaving her husband."

"Mamma, you are dreaming still!"

"She is coming to us with the children. Frau Leh-mann has advised her doing so."—"Mamma, I do not like Frau Lehmann at all, especially since they have come into money and only keep up intercourse with people who live in great style. I never had the least doubt that she was a very ambitious woman ; she always wanted to push herself forward, but did not quite know how it was to be done. And now that she has got to the front, no doubt she supposes that the way to fashion is family scandal. She has by no means caught the knack of the real aristocrats yet."— "But supposing the Doctor really should have given Emmi grounds for jealousy?"—"Franz thinks a great deal too much of her and the twins. I will speak to Emmi."—"You can have no opinions on such matters yet."—"Mamma, Felix and I are keeping a great secret to ourselves. He revealed it to me, in order that the past should never throw a shadow across our happiness—in order that he should never merit the reproach of having deceived me."

"That he loved another?"—"How do you know?'
—"Supposition, child; supposition."—"But it was before he had seen and known me, mamma. And yet you cannot conceive what torments I endured, how I suffered through his sincerity. I felt as if I had been immeasurably rich, and was now reduced to beggary at a stroke. I could have envied the stone his foot trod upon, such was my adoration for my idol. Do you understand the heartache that his confidence caused me?"

What was I to say? The thought which had often troubled me in secret, that she would learn it just at the moment when it could work the greatest mischief, was past; she knew it now, and it was well. For unpleasantnesses always come to light just when they are least wanted. There was no object in telling her that her supposed great secret had caused us trouble enough already. But I wondered how she took it.

"Does it make you love him less?" I asked, after a pause.

"I love him more deeply and truly," she said. "The sorrow has subsided, and everything is clear and above-board between us. And Emmi must not commit a folly; I will try to dissuade her from it. A sister is nearer to her than Frau Lehmann."—"Is the Doctor to get off entirely? It seems to me that he is the guilty party."—"Your authority had better be exerted over him."—"Authority? Of course. But supposing he

shows me the door?"—"Franz would never forget
himself so far as that."—"He would not push me out ;
it would be done in all friendliness, naturally, but I
should find myself outside all the same."

Frieda announced that the gentlemen had come in
for breakfast. She looked pale and confused. "Frieda," I exclaimed, as Betti went off, "Frieda, what is
the matter with you?"—"Nothing."—"I thought that
you were feeling sorry for your behaviour of yesterday
If Max is angry with you, who can blame him for it?"
—"He will come round again ; if not to-day, it will be
to-morrow ; but Fräulein Schulz has had three big bouquets sent her, and she keeps on pluming herself about
it.   Then she keeps on telling Doris that she danced
and another person sat out.   That is a hit at me."

"It is a matter of total indifference to me."

She went off looking very much ashamed, but as I
had quite made up my mind to send Ida to the rightabout, I had not the remotest intention of taking either
side against the other.   Otherwise there might have
chanced to be a mild thunder-storm.

My husband, the architect Krause, and Felix had
not begun their breakfast before I appeared.   We sat
down, and the conversation soon turned on the building.   They showed me their plans piecemeal and by
degrees, accompanied by a piquant morsel here and a
glass of wine there.   The building of the manufactory
received my approval ; but when the cat was let out
of the bag, I soon saw in what direction it was jump-
ing, and I learned to my horror that our dwelling was
to be divided into two halves ; the one for us. the
other for Felix and Betti.

"No," I exclaimed, "I will not give my consent to
that !   Had we not better go into the workhouse at
once?"

And yet how prettily the architect understood strip-ping the peel from the nut! Our house has its advantages, that is true, nor can we two alone turn it to account; for even now, when certain rooms are used for storing goods, it is too big; but who can bear say-ing good-bye to an old friend that is to be altered be-yond recognition? I could not, and I could not make up my mind to it.

"Wilhelmine," said my Carl, "we must limit our-selves to fewer rooms for a time, while the building is going on, and there will not be room for Fräulein Schulz. Do you not think that this is a favourable oppor-tunity for returning her to her mother's arms without further reasons?"

"Yes, my Carl; if the house must be altered, the 'helps' must go. But, tell me, Herr Architect, can you arrange to add a bay-window, as is so much the fash-ion now?"

"Of course."

"And what do you think about stained glass?

"I consider it excellent for chapels and cathedrals, but I think white window-glass is more appropriate for practical purposes. One wants some light in a room."—"Mamma," said Betti, "don't have it. When Frau Lehmann lies on the lounge in her boudoir with the stained-glass windows, she looks ugly and pale green, like a sick haddock."—"You were going to Em-mi's, child."—"Directly, mamma; but I should like to know first what is going to happen about the house."

"You have no time to lose."—"Then make up your mind, mamma, so that I may be off."—"But what will Emmi think about the building? She might perhaps fancy that you are being preferred to her!"—"She thinks it would be advisable," answered Betti; "but the Doctor tried to dissuade Felix." She crimsoned to the roots of her hair and hesitated.—"Why did he dissuade him?" I inquired; "what grounds had he for dissuading him? Out with it."—"I will whisper it to you."

Betti whispered it quietly to me.

"Carl," I exclaimed, "I am determined now! We will build."

Hereupon we toasted the building in bumpers, and shook hands over the affair.

But oh, this doctor! What had he said to Felix in order to frustrate our building projects? "Be sure you don't settle down on the same floor, or the women will sit upon you." That was what he had said! Scandalous! The inspection of the plans and a thorough overhauling of the house, which led us from one room to another, and gave us occasions for measurements, examinations, decisions in favour now of this, and now of that, cooled down my wrath against my esteemed son-in-law; but his unfeeling remark was put in pickle for him until further notice. He shall hear more about it some day.

When the architect had gone, I said to my Carl: "It is a real blessing that there are men to be found like Krause. You will see the dwellings are going to be charming, and above all, practical. With what careful view to its purpose he has taken the nursery into consideration! We cannot hear the slightest noise at our end, not even when the eldest gets a few knocks, however loudly he may yell."

"Minchen," laughed my Carl, "there is not even one yet, and you are looking forward already to his being soundly thrashed! Go on at half the pace!"— "I only say, supposing such a thing should occur! I do not permit violent measures;—not under any circumstances. I can be with Betti in a second to pre-

vent the occurrence of anything wrong. Grandmamma is the only person who knows how children ought
to be dealt with. The Doctor has not the dimmest
notion on the subject, nor Felix the least idea. How
pleasant it will be, not to have to cross the street !"—
"Hem," said my Carl.

Doris came and brought a letter ; the address betrayed Frau Schulz's handwriting.

"Aha," I said, "she is sure to beg that we will keep
her offspring !"—"Have you written already ?"—"I
hope Ida herself has communicated to her that her
position has become untenable. What other reason
could she have for writing ?"

Meanwhile I had opened the letter and was reading it.

"Carl," I exclaimed, "the blow prostrates me ! This
passes all bounds. Oh, how shameful ! No, how
abominable !"

"Wilhelmine !" my Carl came closer to me, as I was
sitting there like a living corpse.—"Such a creature !
Is it credible ? Her daughter would be physically and
morally destroyed in our house were she to remain a
day longer in it ! Just listen !"—and I now went on
reading to him : 'My daughter has been silent and
suffered long enough'—'suffered' trebly underlined.
Now, Carl, I put it to you, who has suffered, Idiss or
I ? 'In the simplicity of her heart she did not venture
to complain ; perhaps, too, it was fear that closed her
lips. I will not take this occasion to call you to account for the fact that she was slighted, that she was
threatened with imprisonment, with violence, for frivolous trifles,'—Carl, she was only sent to bed occasionally—'that she suffered hunger,'—Carl, suffer hunger
with us !—'that maddening necessity drove her into taking scraps secretly, and that she was scolded for the fact

when crumbs were found on inspecting her pockets.'—
Carl, are cooking apples, scraps ? Are lumps of sugar,
crumbs ?—' As I said above, I will not call you to account for this, because I wished that Edith should be
treated strictly ; although I certainly did not intend
brutality to be understood when I spoke of strictness ;
but that my daughter should be kept at degrading
work, that she should have been forced to sew buttons
on Herr Buchholz's underclothes, that obliges me to
assert my rights.' "—" Is that true ? " asked my husband.
—" What ? "—" What she says about the buttons."—
" Carl ! When I mend all your linen myself, and put
in the patches so carefully that they are not to be
seen ! They are manifest lies. Why did we get a girl
like that into the house ? "—" I told you at once that
she did not please me, but you reproached me with
my want of knowledge of human nature. Do you not
remember ? "—" Please don't get angry with me, my
good Carl. I have made a mistake. Don't be cross.
But the letter has not come to an end yet. That
woman must have dipped her pen in envenomed ink.
Just fancy, she wants to get something else out of us !
She writes : 'You will return the money paid for my
daughter's board, as you cannot possibly assert that
starving her is the same as boarding her ! '—Ida has
starved herself fat and plump. Had we only known
that this was awaiting us, I should have had her
weighed to start with.—' I also demand an indemnity
of one thousand marks for my ill-used child ; which
you will, I hope, pay down amicably. I wish to express my regret that a matter from which I had promised myself the best results, should have ended so de-
plorably, and I beg to remain, with the expression of
my high esteem, your most obedient, D. Schulz.--
P.S. I shall fetch my Edith away to-day, and expect

that the other matter will be in readiness for me.'—
Carl, must we hand over the money?"

"Has your contract been made in writing?"—"Only
by word of mouth, and nothing was positively settled."—"Then she must go to law."—"Carl!" I
screamed in my fright, "not before the court?"—
"Where else?"—"I shall not survive it. But, then,
on her side she must pay for what Ida has broken.
The cream-jug was worth at least ninepence, besides
her other endeavours in that direction. She possesses
astonishing aptitude for breakages. Just let the
mother come!"

"I will take her in hand," said my Carl. "I shall
have you ill, and I don't want that. Leave the matter
alone until I come back; I will get advice from a solicitor." He took the letter and went off.

Could such meanness have been thought possible?
But I was served quite rightly. Why did I listen to
her smooth words, when Frau Schulz praised me as a
pattern of domesticity, and exalted me to the skies?
It was your vanity, Wilhelmine, which played you that
trick; you made up your mind to show the woman
how unexceptionally you could educate Ida, how she
would sing your praises; otherwise the first week
would have taught you that your strength was not
sufficient for such obstinacy. Now you are left sitting
like a blockhead, Wilhelmine, and such a blockhead!

Betti found me fairly in a state of despair and de-
pression when she came; but she brought good news.
It certainly was no trivial matter for Emmi that her
husband had almost totally neglected his home for
some weeks. She had believed him at first when he
told her that he was treating a rich and travelled Russian, who insisted on having all the Doctor's spare
time in return for a brilliant honorarium; but when

Frau Lehmann had seen the Doctor one fine day during the dinner-hour in a carriage with a veiled lady, she began to get suspicious. Although he now owned that the Russian's wife was his patient, Emmi's suspicions increased; for why had he not told her the truth at once? In order that she should not harbour silly thoughts? That had been done with Frau Lehmann's help. Yesterday, when the Doctor vanished from the ball, she had come to a determination to put an end to this state of things; but the Russian lady had died during this very night. "How terrible, mamma, to be called from a ball-room to a death-bed! Verily, a doctor's life is not an easy one."—"And Emmi has given in now?"—"The Doctor took her with him to-day to the Russian's house; she saw the dead woman, and took flowers for her, although she resisted doing so at first. Then the Russian thanked her for the roses, and asked her to forgive him for having laid claim to her husband's time so frequently and for so long. His care had been successful in holding back the fleeting life for some weeks, and he was thankful to her for every day, every hour gained. Then he made her a present of a gold chain which Feodorovna used to wear. I hope that whenever she looks at the chain she will remember that it is better to have confidence in one's husband than in a so-called friend."—"Yes, Betti, if they were all as wise as you."—"I have gone through my share of trouble, mamma."—"I have not yet." And now I told her the latest news about Ida and Frau Schulz. She was ready to fall down flat.

Frau Schulz appeared shortly before dinner. She was shown into the drawing-room; and as my husband had not returned from the solicitor's, I was obliged to do the honours. But they could hardly be

called that. "Where is my daughter?" she asked,
after she had taken a seat.—"In her room, probably."
—"She is packing up, I suppose?"—"Possibly."—
"You have told her that I was coming to fetch my poor
child?"—"No. She thought it wise not to show herself to me, and I that it was still wiser to leave her completely alone."—"Then she hardly knows that I am
here?"—"Not from me."—"I have been greatly deceived in you, Frau Buchholz."—"Don't mention it;
I can return the compliment."—"Can I do otherwise
than believe my Idiss? Can you contradict the complaints she has made to me?" Upon which she drew
a letter from her pocket and held it towards me. It
was from Ida, and contained all the accusations the
mother had brought against me in her document. "I
wonder whether Ida would have the effrontery to persist in her lies in my presence?" I thought. "There
is only one person," I said to Frau Schulz, "who can
contradict these assertions, and that is Ida herself.
We will have her called. Or, better still, we will go
up-stairs, and you can remain behind the half-opened
door, so that you may hear every word while I am
talking to Ida."

She demurred, but I held fast to my suggestion.
When I walked into Ida's room she was lying on the
bed, resting after the fatigues of the ball. I had not
been so fortunate. "Ida," I said, "I believe that you
wish to leave us?" She was silent. "Have you ever
been wronged?" No answer again. "Have you ever
suffered hunger?" Not a word.

How triumphant Frau Schulz must have felt behind
the door!

"What have you to complain of, Ida?"—"I don't
complain."—"Then why did you write this letter?"
She opened her eyes wide and stared at the paper.

"I—I did not mean anything by it."—"Did you not think that you would hurt me by writing it?"—"I did not intend that. Mamma should have burnt it at once."—"But she has given it to me. Ida, how could you allow yourself to behave like that?"—"Frieda told me you had said that you would turn me out of the house, and so——"—"And so?"—"I determined to write first."—"And to throw all the blame on me?"—"I did not mean it to be as bad as that."—"You were only thoughtless—is that it?"—"Yes," she said, barely audibly.—"I will put the best construction I can on that. And now, Ida, be honest. You have much to make amends for, Ida. We will not part in anger. I am sorry for you, my poor child, but we cannot remain together. Your mother is here, and will take you away with her." Frau Schulz came in. Ida turned away. We left the two alone together.

It was a long time before Frau Schulz came downstairs again. She was very quiet. My husband, who had really prepared himself for a violent altercation, and had hedged himself round with all manner of legal devices in our favour, expected nothing less than this complete change of position, which held out hopes for a peaceful solution of this more than burning question.

"She neither could nor would absolve her daughter from blame," she expressed herself, although there might have been mistakes on both sides. Idiss had acted unadvisedly; all the more so, because, to judge from the attentions of her partners, her daughter must have been a great favourite. Three magnificent bouquets ought not to be under-estimated. Then she asked what sort of a person Herr Kleines was. I referred her to the Police-lieutenant, who would be able to give accurate information.

She may try her luck, but every registry office would revolt against bringing those two together. If, on the other hand, she imagined that I kept a marriage bureau, she was in the same predicament as the man who took Blücher for a defunct tenor, because he was placed close to the opera-house.

Doris was sent off for a commissionaire, and mother and daughter left the house. Frau Schulz did not insist further on her thousand marks, and as she had not paid me for the girl's board at all yet, this point likewise was not mooted. She was a veritable slow-worm in the matter of moneys to be paid by her.

That evening, for the first time for ever so long, my husband forgot his district club, and Doris sang away in the kitchen. I went to her and asked her why she was so merry.—"It's too fine, this building," she answered. "We shall see some life about the courtyard now, and then that Schulz girl is not standing behind one everywhere any longer. O Lord! Idiss was her name, and that was about all she had to boast of. A horse might have been her godfather."

"Doris," I turned that subject aside, "as there are workmen in the house, one of them might take a look at the range when he has time. It has often smoked very badly."—"There was quite another reason for the smoke," laughed Doris. "When Madame showed herself, Idiss, who's now gone for good, used to take a big piece of firewood, and fill the kitchen with its smoke. That played the mischief with the asthma, and Madame had to go. Well, I do say that she was a real deep one. However, it can't hurt the range to be freshened up a bit. A half-day's work over it will do it good."

"It was simply sinful the way she knocked the things about," I was forced to allow with much head-shaking.

"And shall we be taking another fresh Idiss?" asked Doris.

"No; if uselessness be all that one can claim from a person who contributes towards the expenses, I have been forced to enjoy more of that article than I could have had any idea of up to the present time. People must not want too much of a good thing, Doris."

"That is just what I say."

BACK FROM SCHOOL.

Acquaintances more closely looked into—About elegant conversation, with intersprinkling of foreign words—Why Mila cannot get acclimatised and Wilhelmine will not dance—About a minor state of siege and optical delusions—Why cannibals are supported and people bite themselves—How educated folk behave and how the post discovers people.

I ADMIT that the Police-lieutenant's wife had frequently intimated to me in private that a revolution would take place as soon as her daughter had returned from her Swiss boarding-school; but as to what she really intended, that was only put into words a couple of days before the expected arrival, for she probably thought, that if anybody wants to offend anybody else, it is more agreeable to do so gently and gradually than suddenly and at once.

"You see, dear Frau Buchholz," she said, "I fear that I shall be obliged to look more closely into the list of our acquaintances as they stand at present, on my Mila's account; for of what avail are the most refined manners, if the child is to relapse into ordinary habits? If one considers the immense outlay merely in extra charges for private lessons and the external requirements of society, one is anxious that such enormous expenses should not have been incurred for nothing."

" You might as well throw the money into the Spree at once," I answered ; "then you would at least hear the splash it made ! "

"Oh, no," she answered rather snappishly ; "you make a radical mistake about my Mila ! Nothing has been thrown away on her. She is bringing a marvellous dress-improver with her ; but who can tell whether it will keep in its place ?"—"I should sew on a broad piece of tape to strengthen it. Fancy the horror of a possible slip ! "—" How—on Mila's part ?"—"No ; of the avalanche that might come thundering down behind her."—"Oh, ah ! Really, it is hardly *comme il faut* to allude to such secrets."—"But they are worn."— "Deportment requires that they should be. But I rather intended to convey that the extreme perfection which Mila has acquired may perhaps be lost if her companions have no understanding for it. What use will the most perfect Parisian accent be to her, if it falls on stony ground ? "

"Let it fall," I said, to reassure her; "you and I have got through the world without it. And indeed, now especially, when half the bills of fare are written in German, it is as good as useless. You need not have spent anything upon that."

"It would be difficult for our opinions ever to coincide on that point," said the wife of the Police-lieutenant, and drew herself up majestically. " Every one has his own ideas about distinction. It will be my business to see that she is kept up to the mark, and does not contract the manners of a rustic."

"Contract the manners of a rustic is perhaps a little severe ! " I ventured to interpose.—"Certainly not.

The other day I was at a party, and when the young people were dancing later, two men had to hold the sideboard steady, otherwise the bust of the Apollo Belvedere would have tumbled on our heads."—"The architect was probably to blame for that. Nowadays they build everything so thin and tottery."—"A person possessed of grace can dance upon a rope without anything falling down; but then the art can only be acquired from the French. They are always *chic*."

"I can well believe that French manners and customs suit French women excellently well," I answered; "but it is an open question as to whether their style of manners would do for others. Uncle Fritz thinks, too, that it would not be desirable to plume ourselves on our ape-like aptitude for copying the French."—"*Naturellement*," she exclaimed, "he knows everything better than others! But he will be astounded. Of course I expect him to circumscribe his expressions somewhat, as indeed I hope that our acquaintances generally will help me in showing the respect due to my daughter."

Her personal offensiveness was comprehensible to me without the aid of a telephone, but I considered it right to swallow down the anger that came bubbling up, and left her for the present to wait for an answer.

In the days when it was a question of saving her Mila from the snares of Herr Kleines, I was good enough for her; and when anything goes wrong with her now, she comes to borrow experience from me— a thing which one is willing enough to give, because one has it—and now it turns out all of a sudden to have been plunder. For what was the long and short of her many words? "Buchholzes, you are not sufficiently cultivated for us, for our daughter has been educated in a boarding-school!"

In former days there certainly would have been a summons ; but as one grows older, one ponders over the unseasonable, and considers consequences. It is easier to get angry than to be reconciled ; and where a rent has been made in friendship, the patches are always visible.

Immediately after this she became very pressing, and insisted that we should take part in the festivities she was going to have on Mila's return, and especially emphasized : "Your brother must not fail us. I should be glad for him to convince himself how unjustifiable his verdict is. It is only a French education that teaches one the true *savoir-vivre*."—" I suppose she knows all about it," I thought, and assented.

I kept from my husband the conversation I had had with Frau Police-lieutenant, partly to obviate the misunderstanding that it certainly would have raised, partly because I felt convinced that this kind of high-and-mightiness would be sure to abate. But I did give a message to Uncle Fritz to the effect that he must watch himself more carefully, if he wished to find further favour in her eyes. However, he laughed and said : "Wilhelmine, let us hope that at least she won't drop her food about ! "

It did strike me as being remarkable that Mila should return in the middle of term-time, and let slip a half quarter's education paid in advance. But it was of course possible that she had completely finished learning ; and I did not care to inquire, for when a person does not intend to tell the truth, he says something else, which leaves the questioner as wise as he was before. Later, however, a Bengal light was thrown on this darkness.

It was very fortunate that I had no need to get anything new, although extra exertions would probably

be expected.   They are hardly so very high, that my
brown moiré would not be quite dress enough.

The great day arrived.   Mila had arrived the evening before, and her solemn introduction could now
take place.

We were invited for eight o'clock.   My Carl ventured on a fly, for it had been raining so heavily for
some time, that the stones had begun to get soft.
Since science has taken up with the weather, it is
rarely dry when one wants it ; but that is the case
with everything that learned men turn their hands to
—they are too unpractical.   Uncle Fritz said at once
that he would not take his wife in such bad weather,
so he appeared later on all by himself.

When we entered the room I saw at a glance that
our hostess was a gulf beyond me in the matter of
toilette.   She glittered towards us in a moss-green
plush, gold beetle shoes, and a coiffure that had been
constructed by a professional hair-dresser.   A panorama could not give a more literal description of her.

At such moments the astonished gaze must be a
silent one, therefore I did not say a word, though she
seemed to have a burning desire that I should burst
forth into extraordinary sentiments regarding her
adornment.   However, I behaved the whole evening
as if the dress were an old acquaintance of mine, which
was visibly displeasing to her ; but where aristocratic
manners are expected, people do not talk about the
outward appearance.

As I was about to greet Mila in my old accustomed
fashion, she made me a curtsey, with one step backwards and deep inclination of the upper portion of
the body forwards, so that I involuntarily exclaimed :
"Good gracious, Mila !"   Upon this she recovered
herself, and gave me her hand.   "I am sure you are

pleased to be back home again?"—"Ah," she answered,
"it will be difficult for me to become acclimatised!
Chère maman must modify much, *si cela doit me convenir.*
One-o'clock *déjeûner* and six-o'clock *dîner* has become
d'usage—how does one express it?—second nature to
me. *Cher papa* will learn to accommodate himself,
though he does say that it won't do."—"Formerly you
liked our ordinary customs well enough."—"*O mon
Dieu,*" she exclaimed, "I had not seen the world then!
But will you permit me to.present to you one of my
school-friends, who remains here for some weeks to
afford me opportunities for conversation?"

She hopped away, and brought back a young girl
with her, who was dressed like Mila in rose-coloured
poplin, wore just the same high-heeled rose-coloured
shoes, and looked very nice up to her eyes, which had
a slight squint. I did not discover really what her
name was, as Mila now set to work with true Parisian
elegance, and the other girl assisted her with great
loquacity.

While I was considerably embarrassed by the incom-
prehensibility of their chatter, the Police-lieutenant's
wife was positively transfixed with ecstasy, although
I have my doubts as to whether she could follow it
thoroughly, for she listened with suspicious attention
to every word, and her grin of approval suffered from
noticeable uncertainty.

As a means of escape from this discomfort, there
were several guests on hand, whose acquaintance one
had to make; so with the words, "You know it beautifully, Mila," I separated from the two rose-coloured
friends and their parley-vooing, in order first of all to
be introduced to people in the lump.

Many of the faces were quite strange to me, but as
it was not the correct thing to ask who they might be,

I sat down and drank a cup of tea which was handed to me by a white-gloved hired waiter.

"One cannot go very much beyond a hired waiter,' I thought, and made myself acquainted gradually with my neighbours.

The lady sitting beside me on the sofa, certainly gave one the impression of having been re-dyed. But she was not at all bashful ; on the contrary, she asked me at once to join a Dogs' Home society to which she belonged.

"Estimable Frau Lehmann," I parried her request, "human beings come first with me, and then animals."—"We accept the smallest offerings," she appealed to me further ; "at all events, I may send you half-a-dozen tickets for our next evening entertainment with a little dance ?—the net profits are destined for the Home.'

"No," I said, "I do not dance for dogs. But to prevent you thinking that I am stingy, I will send you a donation, and persuade my husband to do the same." Upon this she gave me her visiting card, from which I learned that her name was not Lehmann at all, as I believed that I had heard, but that she wrote herself Lemoin. "I presume that your name is spelt according to the newest orthography ? " I asked her jestingly.—"We come from the colonies," she said.

Her husband was a teacher of the French language, she explained further, and had to brush up Mila's knowledge ; for, between ourselves, she was inexcusably wanting in grammar, and surely that was the principal thing. Did I perhaps know of a couple more scholars, they would be very welcome to her just now, as times were bad. Owing to the association she could not devote herself to her household as she would like, but if she gave herself no trouble, nothing would be done for the poor animals ; latterly she had spent a dreadful amount of money on flies, in order to get hold of actors for the representations given on the evening of the entertainment, and her husband had been obliged to dine at the hotel. Some lessons would be a great help to them.—I quite took her word for that.

Now came Uncle Fritz. Mila endeavoured to produce a great impression with her dancing-master curtsey, but the charm did not work with him—he had seen too many ballets for that. He made some courteous remark about her appearance, in which he was correct, and behaved generally speaking as if she had returned from a short journey to Rixdorf.

After greeting each other, the gentlemen became absorbed in a political conversation ; and when they once begin on that, they might as well be in an undiscovered quarter of the globe : they are absolutely unapproachable and not to be converted. Why is it not prohibited, as we are placed in a minor state of siege ?

In order to enliven the ladies' conversation, Frau Police-lieutenant showed us a magnificent bouquet which had been sent to Mila that morning. She had pondered long over the question from whom it might have come, and had at last hit upon Amanda Kulecke, whom she still expected. We praised Amanda with one accord for this attention ; indeed she really is a splendid girl, though she may be a little too tall and remarkably downright.

Mila hastened frequently to the entrance to see whether she were not yet coming, until her mother told her that she really might remain quietly seated. Her tripping step and graceful floating in and out of the room certainly was objectionable, especially as she held herself as if she wanted to say : "Do look how monstrously genteel I am in my movements !"

She was much too affected for my taste, took up everything with two fingers in her exaggerated refinement, holding the others up and far apart, as if they were on the point of flying off. She had either been too long in the educational establishment already, or else they had let her leave it too early.

Amanda now appeared. Mila rushed towards her and embraced her so warmly, that the heartfelt joy of meeting each other again produced quite an agreeable effect. "I have got something that I really must tell you," said Mila, endeavouring to draw her away; but Amanda answered: "There will be time enough for that, child; I must first make my excuses to your mother for having come so late."

"You have a long way to come," Frau Police-lieutenant remarked graciously. "But you have come, and that is the principal thing. Mila has been quite longing to see you, to thank you for those lovely flowers."

"Flowers?" Amanda questioned in astonishment. "What flowers do you mean?"

"I was speaking of this magnificent bouquet," the hostess said, and pointed to the costly bunch of flowers.

"Nonsense!" laughed Amanda; "my means don't allow me to indulge in luxuries like that."

While she was speaking, Mila kept on making signs to her, and exclaimed: "You are pretending! Just acknowledge that they come from you!"

"Rubbish!" Amanda repeated; "not a bit of it!" —"Come, come!" Mila insisted.

The general attention had been directed towards this discussion, and the Police-lieutenant, who had approached the ladies, said very emphatically, "We believe that the flowers came from you, Fräulein Kulecke."

"It was an optical delusion," answered Amanda.

"Have you no idea as to who sent them?" the father asked Mila sternly, and looked at her with severe scrutiny. She got more rose-coloured than her dress, and began to talk French. "You can speak German to me."—Mila shrugged her shoulders and was silent.

Personally my suspicion fell at once on somebody who manages to nestle into families by means of bouquets and such-like courtesies, but I kept this ray of light to myself. The Police-lieutenant was so upset, that it seemed advisable to make no further stir about it. Perhaps he, too, was of my opinion; but notwithstanding divers allusions, I behaved like the Sphinx, who strews sand on the most important questions, without moving a feature.

As Amanda had arrived, we could sit down to table. The places had been arranged in such a manner that all those who were well up in French sat together, while the other end did not need to put any restraint on itself, and was allowed to talk commonplace German.

Uncle Fritz soon set the conversation going, and told us that a man could become a large landed proprietor in Africa for fifty marks; he had the greatest inclination to take part in it, and what did the others think about it?

The Dogs' Home lady thought that there were problems to be solved which lay nearer to us. Until the Dogs' Home had been called into existence, she could feel no interest whatever in endeavours towards colonisation.

Uncle Fritz explained that for his part he expected great things from the colonies; it was only the other day that he had sent to the South Seas a big box full of cheap bronze men-at-arms, each one having a ban-

ner on which was written : " No ceremony," * as they
could not be got rid of here owing to the quantities
in which they were produced !—"I call that giving
superfluous support to cannibalism !" Amanda Kulecke exclaimed angrily.—"Not so," Uncle Fritz answered : "the figures give greater pleasure to the
savages than to us, as they have already artistically
improved the process of distillation. And it was high
time that the Camerooners should be made happy by
means of our Middle Ages."

This discussion was accompanied by perch with
melted butter and boiled potatoes, the latter of which
had been kept standing rather too long. While the
plates were being changed, Herr Lemoin rose and
proposed a toast in French. This was probably the
culminating point of the grandeur, to attain which he
had been invited, notwithstanding his want of clean-
liness. Mila looked her approbation at each sentence,
and her mother behaved as if she also were capable
of passing judgment on it, with the single difference
that when Mila nodded to the right, she nodded to the
left. I admit that French is very useful when people communicate secrets on post-cards, which the
domestics are not intended to decipher, or for school-
work, but it is somewhat defective when used as
a vehicle for table-talk. I understood nothing of it,
but as it is his business, I took no further offence.
The man must live, you know. Then we had a saddle of
roebuck and turkey, both fairly well flavoured, but, as
we soon discovered on tasting them, they had been
sent in from an eating-house, and the sauces were
handed wrongly as usual. The Police-lieutenant,

---

* *Genöthigt wird nicht.* An announcement often seen displayed,
as indicated, on Berlin tables, to imply that visitors are left to take
what they like.—TRANS.

who noticed this, therefore said to Mila, who sat obliquely opposite him, "Hand me the sauce for the turkey"; whereupon she, to show her willing affection, jumped up quickly and reached the sauce-boat across, with the words, "*Voilà papa.*" But in her haste, or perhaps the graceful pose of her fingers got in the way, bang went the *voilà* on to the table in the middle of the green-gages, which were to have been handed later.

"All the more room when things are well packed," exclaimed Uncle Fritz, meaning to put an end to the incident with an innocent jest; but he had made a mistake—it was not in its place here, for Mila pushed away her chair from the table, flung it over in her rage and hurried into the adjoining room, accompanied by a universal stare.

Her friend remained anxiously seated, and squinted dreadfully in front of her. She only speaks such broken German that nobody can be a whit the wiser for the fragments, nor had she understood what really happened, so that she was obliged to make shift with looking miserable. Of course it was not pleasant for any one of us; for, although our hostess showed no outward signs of disturbance, I noticed incontestably how vexed she was internally, and how she exerted herself to appear indifferent. What else would account for her getting red and white alternately, and chewing away at her under-lip? When a human being bites himself, he is simply raving.

Mila remained away. Amanda endeavoured to soothe her, but without success. "I do not know what I have done to her!" Amanda complained on her return. "Mila inveighed against me as a faithless betrayer, and hit at me with the heel of her shoe. I should not have expected such treatment from her."—

This communication was by no means adapted to increase the general enjoyment.

Meanwhile the hired waiter had covered over the accident with a fresh napkin, and placed an apple-tart upon it, which seemed to look very nice, I admit, but which nevertheless had not risen properly. Well, I partook of it in order to offend nobody, but I really could not praise it.

When supper was finished the gentlemen adjourned to the smoking-room, and we ladies remained by ourselves.

Frau Police-lieutenant had disappeared, probably to deliver a sermon to Mila, and verily she did not require a pulpit for the purpose. My own opinion is that Mila had not been properly grounded before she was sent away. Her character had been neglected, and so the education would not stick properly.

Amanda sat down beside me, and was quite unable to set her mind at rest about Mila's behaviour. "Do you consider that well-bred?" asked Amanda.—"Oh, no; the truly cultured person makes no noise! He neither flings chairs about nor administers blows."—"But how could she so forget herself?"—"It was on account of the flowers," I whispered to her.—"How so?"—"Mila wished you to say that the bouquet had been sent by you. Did you not notice how she was winking at you?"—"How can I know what her intentions were?"—"You have not learnt such tricks, and it is no harm that you have not. Perhaps it may be better for the mother to discover now at once what o'clock it is, than when it may be too late. So much, however, I do say, she will tempt me in vain for the future; I do not mean to go on the war-trail again. Self-sacrifice is thrown away with such people."—

" What do you mean ? "—" Nothing, Amanda ; I was
only thinking of something ! "

The gentlemen had finished their smoke, coffee had
been partaken of, and there was nothing to interfere
with the return home. Frau Police-lieutenant showed
considerably more sense than she had done before, for
she said to me in confidence : " There will be much to
improve. Mila has brought back a good many things
with her that do not please me."—" She will get on
the right track again,". I said by way of consolation.—
" And you will be sure not to forget us ? "

As it had turned out a starlight night, Amanda joined
our party as far as the nearest cab-stand, from whence
she drove to the Bülow-strasse. To have a double
night journey and be kicked into the bargain, is what
I call unpleasant.

My Carl now told me that the Police-lieutenant
quite intended to solve the riddle as to who had sent
the bouquet, even if he had to make a reconnoitring
tour through every flower-shop.—" Has he possibly a
suspicion of anybody ? "—" He conjectures that it may
be Herr Kleines, for Mila had to leave the boarding-
school in the middle of the term, owing to the continuance of her correspondence with him. Besides
this, he made a business tour in Switzerland, on which
occasion he visited her. Her father brought Mila into
his immediate neighbourhood, in order to have her
under his supervision ; and notwithstanding this, he
is unable to watch over her."

" So that is the reason ? What is the use of sending
people away ? The post is too quick at discovering
them. It really ought to be absolutely forbidden."—
" That certainly would be an effectual measure."—
" However, Herr Kleines really is inexcusable ! " I exclaimed.—" I like him," contradicted Uncle Fritz.

"Had it not been for his offering of flowers, we should probably have had to wait some little time for the blow that told to Mila's disadvantage. It has now been proved that she is just a little overspread with veneer. As soon as she loses her temper, the polish disappears."—"There is still something of the Landsberger-strasse remaining in her," I answered; "she will pull herself together again. Good-night, Fritz; here we are at home. Give my love to Erica, and tell her, that if the weather continues fine, I shall expect her to-morrow afternoon, or else I will pay you a short visit—that will do just as well. Fritz, be glad that your wife had not to be sent to a boarding-school!"

THE KRAUSES.

About the *archæopterix* and the devil—About Greek, Latin, and diamonds—Herr Krause as despot—Frau Buchholz as the lion's friend.

THE building ran its course for the present, and only encroached on my domain so far as the cellar and boiler were concerned; but so much is certain, that nothing more desperate can be conceived than masons in or about a house. Only those who have suffered from the infliction themselves are entitled to speak; those who do so without experience, and do not agree with me, deserve to have them quartered upon them. This plague was spared to Egypt.

I expressed myself the other day to this effect at the Krauses, for one could but assume that it would flatter a master if one remembered school-teachings, proving thereby that a good deal of knowledge is retained.

But he knew better how things had gone, and flung Pharaoh and all his mishaps to the winds.

" Research has arrived at results that are in crying contradiction to tradition," he said.—" He who cries is, generally speaking, in the wrong," I answered.— "Science never errs, because it proves. In former days people learnt from books ; now, on the contrary, they are taught by nature, straight from the crust of the earth which preserves the testimonies of the past." —" From the earth? Then I suppose that an inordinate amount of intelligence has been thrown up in the process of drainage?"

" Dear lady, you misapprehend science," retorted Herr Krause ; " the aim it has in view is to prove that every species of being has been evolved gradually. It could not tell us for a long time from what birds had descended, but it has now been demonstrated by the discovery of the *archæopterix* that they proceed from reptiles."—" What do you mean by reptiles ? "—" Lizards, frogs——"—" Herr Krause, with all due deference to your superior knowledge, I should like to see the frog which could prove itself to be the father of, let us say, a wagtail. Possibly lizards may be in a position to do so ; but I fear that it would give them too much trouble."—" The changes were accomplished very gradually during periods extending over millions of years, until at last man formed the last link of the chain. The *archæopterix* is one member of our common line of ancestors, and it affirms anew the fact that everything living has originated naturally, and not been made by a creator. We are happily rid of old wives' superstitions."

" Herr Krause," I replied to his over-confidence, "you pleased me better before you adopted these antics. Confess yourself that you are no longer as con-

tented as formerly. You used to be much merrier."—
"Is that to be wondered at, when one cannot get on
beyond a trifle of fixed salary? Have we no cause to
be vexed, when we see the standard of luxury rising
all around us, when others enjoy life in all directions,
and we have to be contented, though we possess
a thousandfold more knowledge? And when life
has come to an end, what have we got out of it?
The knowledge that it was not worth having been
begun."

"Then it must be all one whether people find out
from what the birds are evolved or not?"—"You re-
fer to the *archæopterix*? You may estimate the high
value that has been placed upon it by the fact that it
has been sold to England for five-and-twenty thousand marks."—"Old things fetch unreasonably high
prices!" I retorted. "But it may be possible that a
vegetable diet has affected your spleen, Herr Krause,
since you have abjured meat."—"Vegetarianism is absolutely conformable to nature," he defended himself.
"Fruits formed the nutriment of our ancestors."—
"Indeed! And where may that have been? It was
just on account of eating fruit that Adam and Eve
were sent across the border."—"If you persist in a
point of view that has been so completely exploded, I
am afraid that I must give up further discussion," he
retorted rudely. "Does not progress exist for you?
For all I know, you may still believe in the devil."—
"Don't you?"—"How can you believe in a bogey
like that in our enlightened age—a phantom with
claws and tails and horns? Just fancy," he exclaimed
aloud to the rest of the company, "the devil still ex-
ists in all seriousness for Frau Buchholz!"

"Why not?" I answered. "Perhaps he would not
be nearly so bad, if only he were properly tamed." I

was not going to be put down before Frau Krause, who was already looking high and mighty.

"He has carried off a good many already," Frau Bergfeldt upheld me.

I must explain that we were all at the Krauses', whose son Edward had just been confirmed, and they wished to celebrate this chapter in his life. Frau Krause told me that her husband considered it narrow-minded, but as Edward was soon going off to sea, which was so malignantly dangerous, she looked upon it as her duty to neglect nothing. People could be sure of nothing. She is in dreadful anxiety, but the boy sticks to it that he will be a sailor. A ship has been decided on, too, upon which he is to make his first voyage.

When she came to us to invite us, she cried pitifully. "He will be so far away from me," she moaned, "and his trunk is packed already! Ah, how many wishes I have folded in with his clothes that he may return to us in safety! how many sighs! Who will take care of him and preserve him from bad companions and from drinking brandy? Sailors play the most dreadful pranks with their health."—"Frau Krause," I said, "if he loves his parents heartily, he will always be thinking about them, nor will he do anything that could cause them sorrow. I do not know whether they have impressed that upon him. The hour is sure to come, when children will be grown up and sit in judgment on their parents, as to whether they have done rightly by them. Then comes the question as to whether they can feel the heartiest gratitude, or have forcibly to suppress bitter reproaches. Not that I mean anything by what I say!"

"That is not the question with my Edward. Boys will be boys; they are not always sitting round the stoves like girls, and are therefore more difficult for those tð understand who have none themselves. He happens to have no inclination for the dead languages, and that is the case with many."—" Why are the languages not buried, if they are dead ?"—" How could a scheme of study be drawn up under such circumstances ? "—" Something living might possibly be found for the purpose."—" But how is one to understand the German speech of scholars, without knowing Greek and Latin? However, Edward always objected to scholars, and fled to Hamburg in order not to become one. And since that time all his desire has been towards the sea. I cannot thwart him; but, however, he will not be utterly forsaken, for my deceased mother accompanies him as guardian angel." —" Who ?"—" Have you never heard of the spiritualists ? "—" Surely not the table-turners ?"—" There is something in it, Frau Buchholz ; the spirits really do manifest themselves. What will people not do in their distress ? I was advised and I went.

" The spirits were not in force on the first evening, but the second time they wound up a musical box in the dark, and rapped everywhere and did all sorts of things. The third evening a spirit manifested itself, and that was my deceased mother."—" In the regular way, with a cold hand ? "—" No; first by rapping out the words, and then by writing. The medium was unconscious, and the spirit was in the fingers with which she held the pencil. It was my mother. She wrote my name accurately, and her own as well, and many things of former times."—" But perhaps it was all an imposture ! "—" Impossible ! A professor was present, and even high families take part in the *séances.* They are conducted on strictly scientific principles. Will you not go once and be convinced ? "—" I am much too enlightened for that, Frau Krause; but if it tranquillizes you for Edward to be looked after by a spiritual nurse-maid, I am very glad of it."—And—would you believe it?—that offended her!

"Edward has attained the regulation height, and seems strong enough for his profession. He can scarcely wait for the time when he is to be off. Foreign coasts attract him so much," said Frau Krause; "and indeed there is much more profit in watching elephants and llamas in their natural state than in captivity. Is that not so, my Edward? And if he is fortunate, why should he not find a huge lump of gold, or a number of diamonds? Only, you must be very careful that they are not stolen from you, Edward; it would be wisest for you to sew them into your lining —nobody will think of their being there!"

My husband remarked, that being a cabin-boy, it was unlikely that opportunities would be afforded him of watching for llamas and searching for gold— it would be a question then of being at his post. Captains were not given to indulgence.

"Blows are more plentiful than ha'pence," Frau Bergfeldt contributed her quota of nautical experience. "If any does not obey, he gets plenty for his back. A distant cousin of mine once had to go through it; but never again! You ought to hear the tales he tells. With a rope's-end, he says."

I suppose the conversation had become too professional for Frau Krause, so she asked Frau Bergfeldt whether the gentleman who had behaved in such a civil manner on the occasion of her coffee-party, was still lodging with her.—"He has left me," she answered. "The amount he thought of himself was unbearable. Then the constant waiting on him, and I without a servant! But now I have let my rooms furnished to a man who does not mind if my husband gets fidgety occasionally. He will get on well some day."—"How?"

"He is writing a tragedy."—"You don't say so!" —"Only wait and see; he will earn his thousands by it."—"But first of all people must like it."—"There is no doubt on that point. Everything that has been composed heretofore, is wrong; the theatre generally is falling into decay. It must be radically altered. He will revolutionise the rotten state of affairs."— "That almost sounds as if I were listening to Wichmann-Leuenfels himself!"—"Do you know him?" Frau Bergfeldt asked in astonishment. "It is the very man."—"I congratulate you."—"And so you may. He is strongly endowed with genius."—"How about the rent?"—"He is just engaged on the last act, where the torn shroud is to be displayed on the battle-field. Nobody has been so bold hitherto."—I asked whether he was punctual in his payments.—"If the piece is successful, he will pay up arrears on the nail." — "I should have no confidence in tragedy writers."—"Just have patience. You might feel very happy if everything were as sure as the piece. He reads some of it aloud to us every evening. It is splendid, I can tell you."—Frau Krause had served up supper, but things remained as uncomfortable as they had been from the beginning. The cold things were eatable. There were roast beef, cut-up fowl, sausages, and an enormous quantity of cakes in Edward's honour. Then she tapped a red wine, certified wholesome, but good for nothing but toasting with. Whether the wine tasted so sour owing to the sweets or whether it contained the acid in itself, I was incapable of discerning; but it was economical, as everybody guarded his glass against being refilled.

Meanwhile Edward kept on filling his mouth with cakes, and his mother provided him continually with fresh big pieces, until Herr Krause said at last: "Adelaide, will it agree with the boy?"—"He is confirmed!" she screamed at him. "Do you wish to embitter his last hours under the parental roof? Had you shown yourself more loving towards him, he would not be leaving us. But you are a despot! Oh! I shall not survive it!" and her tears began to flow afresh.

Herr Krause made a savage face, and the youth went on eating. This formed our entertainment.

Although the afternoon had really only just begun, we took care to say good-evening as soon as possible, and Frau Bergfeldt too insisted that she must leave, as it was getting too late.

This is the only occasion on which we agreed in all respects.

When people have guests at their house, matters should not be so arranged that they languish for the further side of the door, and emerge into the pure evening air with a feeling of relief.

In order to do away with the bad impression caused by the Krauseian festivity, and to get rid of the taste of the wine, my Carl hailed a fly, and we drove to the Löwenbräu. We insisted on Frau Bergfeldt coming with us. What good does she get out of existence? The old man is breaking up visibly, and requires constant care, even though Augusta does relieve her. And of course she has her own domestic concerns to attend to. I can only hope that Herr Leuenfels's piece will bring in something; otherwise, where is she to get it from?

The Löwenbräu tavern was packed close with guests, there being hardly space to wind our way through

the crowd ; but when the Berliner sees a thirsty man
in difficulties, he economizes space, and so we too
found accommodation.

Frau Bergfeldt had not yet seen this beer saloon,
where one takes one's glass of beer in all sorts of
corners ; whereas in the Spatenbräu, artificial railway
arches have been fitted up for the purpose ; and so she
was enchanted with the pretty wooden walls, and the
paintings, brilliant in their classic black, as well as
with the stylishness imported by the beer wagons.

And how delicious the beverage tasted ! My Carl
embarked on a quart measure straight away. The
fact that they brew beer in Munich which finds its
own way down people's throats, is said to be due
to the circumstance that they are more sparing of the
water there.

And now at last we could have a rational conversation, which we had been obliged to forego for so long.
Frau Bergfeldt displayed an intelligent understanding
on the subject of our building when I told her what
trouble we had had about the cellar, because Doris
would not venture into it alone when she wanted to
fetch anything, owing to the way the masons went on
with her, for which reason I was always obliged to go
too as protector ; and also what the kitchen looked
like while the boiler was being put to rights, which
they messed about at for nearly two days. On that
occasion I had reproached one of them—it was the
elder of the two—with the fact that I had never before
met with such dilatoriness, to which he merely answered, "Quite so "; and when I remarked that they
might have finished the job in half a day, he said,
"Quite so." But what was the cause of it ? They
were having their little jokes with Doris. However, I
then said, that shall not be so any longer, and promptly

took up a permanent position there, the consequence of which was that work progressed rapidly. And what did he say when I said, "Well, do you see now?"— "Quite so," he said.

We conversed on domestic subjects while my husband was ruminating over the smoke of his cigar, the only occasional interruption being caused by the bellowing lion, which is pinched every time a fresh barrel is tapped. When it growls the public rapidly empty their glasses, and their knocks summon the waiters. A truly cosmopolitan bar!

My Carl was desirous of hearing the lion howl once more; but Frau Bergfeldt reminded us that her old man was decrepit, and that Augusta would certainly be getting impatient.

We took her back to her house, and said that Augusta might as well drive part of the way with us. Augusta was soon ready. She did not say much, and seemed as if she were unwilling to be questioned. I fear the Bergfeldts' affairs are hopeless.

We clattered through the long streets. It was past midnight already. We saw lighted windows here and there; some of them high up, some low down, and some again between the two, irregularly distributed, just as they happened to come.

What caused the lights to be burning? Was it merriment, or did anxiety dictate it? Joy and sorrow are often only divided by a partition in Berlin, and are ignorant of each other's existence.

Joy soon flies away; care has crutches, and is often importunate; no disinterred remains or table-rapping avail against that. If it be looked at straight in the face, as Augusta does, it will soonest take its departure.

THE SILVER WEDDING.

About a brilliant wedding and the bridesmaids—Why Mila is disappointed and Amanda wants to throw things—About reason
being under restraint and about the old elder-bush—About pine
groves and finishing touches—About weddings and exhorta-
tions—Why a piece of muslin is charming, and Herr Brandes
speechifies—About the hand-organ and the wedding tour.

BETTÍ was displaying obstinacy again. Nine thousand reasons were adduced to her for having her wedding celebrated with at least as much pomp as the
marriage of her younger sister, which is still occasionally referred to as having been magnificent; but her
answer remains ivariably the same : " No display."

Was the silver wedding to run its full-blown course
and Betti to be portioned off with a splendour that
might be knotted into a handkerchief? No; but a
middle way might be struck out. We were still surrounded þy the old rooms, just as they had always
been, though sentence had been pronounced upon
them; the doors were still in their accustomed position; every piece of furniture was still in its place;
the house was still our old beloved home; and so I
proposed there to celebrate the day, which was to be
one of honour and joy for both of us.

This pleased Betti and my husband as well, though
he would have preferred promulgating a huge bull,
including some hundred guests, gathering all his business friends round him, and inviting the families of
our acquaintance in tribes; but virtue triumphed, and
he accommodated himself to my views with commend-
able rapidity, in the sentence, "As you like, Wilhelmine."

"Now, do you see, old man," I jested, " you really

comprehend quite quickly, if you are given a week to do it in."—" Discretion comes with years," he retorted. —" You surely don't mean to insinuate that I was wanting in it formerly ? "—" Could you consider me capable of such high treason ? "—" Carl, I am not quite sure, but I often have a vague idea that you are quizzing me." He kissed me, and said just the one word, " Old woman ! "—Well, that made it all right.

In contradistinction to the Doctor, Betti and Felix determined on making a wedding tour, for which purpose they had selected Dresden and Saxon Switzerland. They will be obliged to stay at a hotel anyhow on their return, until their rooms are ready for them. My husband and I, as well as Frieda, intend settling down in the upper story, which, especially on our side of the house, will remain almost untouched. This will probably occasion some discomfort, but really not nearly as much as having the "helps"; and as my Carl had been obliged to suffer from them, it would be presumptuous on my part to decline enjoying the building worries with him.

It was further determined to bring only the family together for the celebration, but on closer consultation we remembered the bridesmaids, who could not be drawn from among the nearest relations, and therefore Mila and Amanda were taken into consideration. The Police-lieutenants could not be left out. Felix too had some friends.

"And what do you think about my book-keeper and the two clerks? Though they do not usually associate with us, still they ought to be among the number on a day like this."

"Carl, Herr Brandes is retiring, and the two young men make no pretensions. They will esteem it a great honour if you invite them."

As there was one seat left, we put our heads together as to who should be asked to fill it. "What
would you think of our inviting Dr. Stinde?" said my
husband.

"Carl, what are you thinking about? Did you not
read in *Voss* that his humour was running dry? What
should we do with a stupid customer like that at our
wedding? Is he to spoil our little mite of pleasure
with his criticisms and fault-findings, because he does
not understand our ways?"

"Formerly you had a very different opinion of him."
—"I take my opinions from the paper; that can surely
not be untruthful."—"Heaven forbid!"—"Carl, why
do you say that 'Heaven forbid' so dubiously?"

"Do you remember an occasion on which the *Post*
showed its love for its neighbour by hanging an imbe-
cile congress-table speech on to somebody, which had
neither been made by the somebody, who was not
there at all, nor by anybody else?"—"Quite right.
It had to put up with a good deal, and has not washed
the stains away yet. Carl, the *Post* ought to have Idiss
on its staff; the girl would feel at home there. But
do you know what? I'll have Frau Helbich. She
stood by me in trouble and sorrow, and she ought
to rejoice with me on my wedding - day. She certainly is nothing but the mistress of a tavern, but
she helps others when they are suspected and accused
instead of spreading false reports about them. Besides, she might have been made on purpose to be
Herr Brandes' table-companion."

Mila and Amanda accepted their invitations to be
bridesmaids. Mila came and made inquiries as to
whether the wedding would be on a very large scale,
and seemed disappointed at the small number of
strangers, probably because she had calculated on

there being a large circle, with opportunities for making herself conspicuous. But if she wants to dazzle people, we are surely not called upon to bear the expense!

Amanda, on the other hand, agreed with Betti. She remarked, with her fathomless sincerity, "Who can blame her for it? The man she was first engaged to lies in the churchyard, a miserable suicide. Had she totally forgotten him, she would not have been worthy to be called his affianced wife, good for nothing though he was."—"Amanda, you do not know the circumstances. Emil was a good fellow at bottom, only he was too weak. Ask Augusta Weigelt about it."

"Possibly. He was not to my taste; but Betti cared about him, and I should not be inclined for noisy festivities were I in her place. I imagine that the happiness of loving and being loved is so great, that everything fades before it, dancing and shouting first and foremost."

"I hope that you will come to know it, Amanda. I should be delighted to get an announcement of your engagement."

"I am all for freedom and independence," she said shortly.—"I thought so too at one time; but then came my Carl, and led me into another path of life." —"Where is the harm in my remaining an old maid? I am not anxious to marry a man who would make me unhappy. If I did, he would certainly wish that he were seated on the top of the column of Victory, and had no need to come down."—"Why so, Amanda?"— "Because I should have everything for him—nails, teeth, the whole set of crockery, and whatever else there is that might conveniently be thrown at his head; but no love."—"Take care; that is blasphemy, child. If a person has plighted her troth at the altar, she dare not create a scandal."—"It will be a considerable time before my father's daughter says Yes."—"Still, I don't like the idea of throwing things, nor do I believe that you would do it."—"A sick bullfinch can wind me round its finger, Frau Buchholz ; but if I notice that my bit of money is the attraction, I do get furiously offended. Am I to be a mere appendage to my dowry, a piece of unusable flesh thrown into the balance, because such is the way of business ? I would rather end my days as a beggar ! "

"But supposing the right man were to come, Amanda ? "

She gave a start, as if the question had touched a sore spot, and said sadly : " The right man sometimes passes by and does not see the burning eyes that are gazing after him. It is a mercy that one can cry them back into their place."

"You may be of good cheer," I answered ; "there are several right ones." — "That depends," she retorted, shaking her head.

It was suddenly borne in upon me that Uncle Fritz had taken considerable interest in Amanda at one time, and that it was probably he who she had hoped would woo her, until he made his choice in Lingen, with the love her dreams foreshadowed, without greed for money, led simply by inclination.

In those days I did not care about the match, advised him off it, and was well satisfied when he gave up going to the Kuleckes'. But now Amanda's heart was still bleeding, and that laid a weight upon me. So I said soothingly, " Amanda, the illusions of life are so great that it is often years before we can perceive our mistake. The man who is destined for you has certainly not passed by yet ; for do you not see, my child, had it been so, he would surely have halted ? But you must not throw things."

She laughed out loud. "Only the sofa-cushions just now and then!"—And before I could turn round she exclaimed, "How pretty you are to-day, Grandmamma Buchholz!" and flung her arms round me and kissed me on the mouth and cheek.

If only she had been half a head shorter! But Schweninger has no remedy for height—his cure is for fat, and that is often liable to return.

Brotherly love took the preparations for the festival off my hands. "You are the festal sacrifice, and have got to keep quiet," Uncle Fritz commanded, and we yielded, in order to leave him full freedom for all he wanted to do in conjunction with the men of the ell-wand. When reason has been laid under restraint, one obeys willingly.

Spring had come upon us unnoticed, just as a cloudy sky often clears up; the air was warm and soft, and although we often talked about and counted the intervening days, still the wedding-day overtook us much too soon. It stood suddenly before us in the midst of our turmoil and tailoring. "Children," I groaned, "we are not nearly ready yet, and to-morrow will be the day!"

And how quickly the day before flew past! We stayed at the Doctor's until dinner-time, and when we returned home, Uncle Fritz was still there to prevent our inspecting the rooms that he had had in hand.

Then came the night, and then what a morning!

Strains of flowing, swelling song awoke us. Fritz's musical friends serenaded us from the courtyard. We cannot wreathe a day so that it should have festive garlands, but if it greets us at dawn with elevating strains, then it too has put on festival apparel. "Carl," I said, when they had embarked on the third piece, " I have often objected to the ' Whooping Cough,' but did I know that it could be like this ? "

Uncle Fritz knocked. " Are you not up yet, slug-gards ? "—" Directly, directly ! "

I suppose he could not exercise patience, consider-ing what he had to do. When I reached the stairs I had to come to a standstill, I was so overcome ; and my Carl was quite touched when he looked at the garlands that were wreathed round the banisters, and at the flowering shrubs that turned the entrance to our sitting-room into an arbour, while it was itself converted into a fir grove, in the midst of which Betti and Emmi stood and then hurried towards their par-ents. Nobody else was there. Thanks, my Fritz, for this hour !

After a while Frieda brought breakfast, and Uncle Fritz followed her. " My dear brother-in-law," he said, " for five-and-twenty years you have managed to get along with my sister. You deserve to have a statue erected to you ; I know her from her youth up ! "

" You ! You ! " I exclaimed. " You will never im- prove ! " And then I held him in my arms.

Frieda congratulated us and turned to go. " No, no, Frieda," I interposed ; "you must stop here." She looked quite delighted, for I had not been able to use the familiar " Du " since she had found pleasure in Ida's scoffing jests in the kitchen ; to-day, however, it came back to me quite of itself.

Even the breakfast-table was surrounded with ever-greens, and a vase with a small branch of elder-tree was placed in the middle of it ; however, the branch had more buds than blossoms, two or three on the whole. " The bush in the garden means to do its part," said Betti ; " the first tiny buds have opened

this morning."—They had not much perfume, but the
old bush meant well; and if we have had our pleasure
out of it year by year, to-day it delighted us more
than ever.

And now appeared Doris, with her white apron on,
and carrying a pound-cake. She wished to congratulate us, she said, and hoped the cake would prove a
success. We cut·and tasted it. It was excellent. "It
is exactly the way my mother always made it," she explained, "only more eggs, more butter, and a larger
quantity of raisins."—"A capital recipe," I praised
her; "we will make the next just like it."

"I am glad of that," said Doris, and marched proud-
ly off.

"Will you have a look at the drawing-room and see
whether you like it?" Uncle Fritz now asked. "We
shall take the doors off later on, and will then possess
a space for the festival of sufficient crowdedness. ·The
tables which are laid have been placed in the back
room, and will be brought in for the chief feed. Vict-
uals will follow from a court restaurateur." —"And a
hired waiter, Fritz?"—"Two of them."—"Why, that
will be gorgeous!"

He opened the doors. Inside them also the walls
were covered with fir-green, which would do no harm
whatever, as the paper had been hanging for the long-
est possible time. My picture was placed there, and
looked as if I were promenading about in a pine grove
whose branches were interwoven with silver thread to
typify the green and silver wedding. It was unique
in its way.

And then just to look at the temple of offerings, as
Fritz called the table on which the presents had been
arranged, with the most exquisite baskets of flowers
and nosegays! If they can do it anywhere, they un-

derstand how to arrange flowers in Berlin; but I never yet had seen anything to compare with these, so fragrant they were, and all of them with silk ribbons and visiting cards fastened to them. And among them the presents, ranging from a nominal to high value; nor were they contributed solely by relations, but also by business friends of my husband's, to whom, as it turned out, Fritz had given sundry hints. "We cannot accept these!" I exclaimed.—"Take them without further ado," Fritz answered; "they will squeeze the cost out of the next order they give."

The other table belonged to Betti. What a sight that was to look upon, with its numerous letters and telegrams, many more of which arrived in the course of the day! Visitors came also, and so the morning simply melted away under one's hands.

It was not until Betti, Felix, my husband, and the Doctor drove to the registrar's office that an interruption took place, which I intended devoting to myself. But I did not get much good out of it, as Augusta Weigelt had waited for this moment.

"Augusta!" I exclaimed, in astonishment at her entrance.

"Just a very few minutes," she said quickly; "I do not wish Betti to see me, but I must wish you every good thing that the human heart is capable of feeling."—"You put me to shame, Augusta."—"No, no. It is your friendship which has so often revived my drooping spirits when I was on the verge of despair; you are my support. I know that you will help me if the worst comes to the worst, and my determination never to let it come to the point of having to hide myself from your clear-sighted penetration, is the spur that urges me on to attempt gaining the upper hand by my own efforts, and it has been successful.

Your severity has taught me to test everything whether it be foolish, your goodness strengthens my confidence in life. Where should we have gone without you—I, my children, my husband? Backwards, ever backwards."

"Augusta," I answered her, "you over-estimate me in this particular, and that ought not to be done. Many things come to pass that we have no idea of. Tell me, how are things going on at home, Augusta?"

"They are all well and happy at home, except the youngest one. I fear that she will not remain with me long. And I am so fond of her! Mamma sends her congratulations; it is difficult for her to get away —father cannot be left without somebody to look after him. She begs that you will accept this little gift."—Augusta unrolled a small parcel, and handed me a charmingly worked reticule. "I have done the embroidery; the thimble in it is from mamma. You are to use it for whichever you like, your sewing, or crochet; there had to be something of silver in it, that is the proper thing."

I thanked her heartily and said: "Augusta, never forget that we two are old friends and will remain so."

She said good-bye, and I sent many greetings with her.

So nothing came of my intention to rest. Uncle Fritz returned and took possession of the rooms to give them the last finishing touches, nor had we much time for delay.

First of all, I helped Betti with her dressing, and then set to work on myself, to array myself in my new grey silk dress. It was made of German silk, extremely beautiful and very tastefully worked. Frieda, who was helpful in handing me things, expressed herself to the effect that it was very aristocratic. Then Emmi put the silver wreath on me.

"The number of the guests was almost complete," she said. "Uncle Fritz had turned the entrance-hall into a reception-room, which was very fairly filled already. As soon as the clergyman arrived, papa would fetch me. Fritz and Franz had come too ; they were going to be good and not disturb any one."—"That may be taken for granted with Fritz, but who will go security for Franz ? You had better go to them and keep them quiet. For a solemnity may easily be screamed to death."

Now at last I had a moment to myself, but the long-intended collective backward glance was not a success. My heart was too full.

I sat there neither awake nor yet asleep—nonentity seemed to be laid upon me until my Carl came.

I had not heard his entrance, and only noticed him as he stood before me with outstretched hands to raise me up. We looked at each other, face to face. He read my eyes, I his. Then my glance fell on the silver spray of myrtle on his breast, he looked down on the silver wreath in my hair, and said lovingly, " Come, silver bride."

I laid my arm in his. Speech was impossible to me.

As we were going down I regained my composure after the first steps ; I could even bear to listen to the notes of a harmonium, which was hidden behind some plants. Doris, who was listening about near the entrance, in search of information, said : "They are all of them inside already."

This was the fact. The invited guests were sitting in a half circle composed of several rows, Betti and Felix being in the middle, on one side of them Emmi and the twins, on the other Erica and then Frau Police-lieutenant. I took cursory note of this while we were slowly advancing towards the clergyman, who was waiting for us on a slightly raised platform. The music was silent, and he began his address.

"He had been called hither for a double purpose," said the clergyman, "to bless an old alliance of hearts and to consecrate a new one. A green wedding was the name given to the solemn service in which a young pair implored that the blessing of the Most High might rest upon their wedded bonds, but it was called silver when the commemoration of their early vows was to be celebrated after a lapse of five-and-twenty years The green wreath was a symbol of the love that springs as mysteriously into being as do the leaves and blossoms of which it is composed, which begins by peeping forth timidly, but then presses forward towards the light and finds its blessing in revealing itself. Sprays and flowers wither and crumble into dust, but love grows and becomes steadfast; tried in the warfare of life, it becomes constant and strong like refined silver.

"And so the green wreath was changed into the silver wreath. Every year and every hour of the year have done their work on it, and now the past presents it in its glittering beauty. Let happy thoughts be dedicated to the past and to those life-joys it has strewn along the path. Nevertheless days had been, of which we say they please us not, but they exercise the heart in patience. Patience helps us not to despair, but to put our trust in all humility in God's goodness, which we experience often and richly in our own persons, if only we choose to recognise it. And experience brings hope, confidence in the unchangeable love of Him from whom proceedeth all good things. Him let us thank; may His blessings rest upon this happy pair!"

While he was speaking thus, I felt that something

had taken hold of the folds of my dress, first on one side, and then in the same manner on the other. It was the grandchildren, who clung to grandmamma, and looked up with childlike eyes at the strange man in his long black robe. God bless them too, these darlings of us all! God bless them!

And again, as we had done five-and-twenty years ago, we gave each other a hand, my Carl and I. How tightly he clasped it ; oh, how tightly!

I really only recovered my composure when I was sitting beside my Carl on the chair that Betti had just been occupying, for she and Felix had now advanced to the clergyman. Being still too greatly touched by what had taken place, I was unable to follow the pastor. I certainly did hear words, but they fell abroad like loose crumbs, and I only had an indistinct vision of the two youthful figures. However, my pulse gradually slackened and my sight grew clearer. Betti looked almost too severe for a bride, but on the other hand there was a look on Felix's face like the rosy dawn of a day that promises to be rich in happiness. I only noticed his white necktie, which gave me the impression of having been frequently washed already.

I looked at the witnesses of the marriage : they were faultlessly attired. I looked about me ; the gentlemen connected with the business had put on brand-new satin ties, and the younger of them, Herr Hoff, even went the length of having on an under-waistcoat bound with red. It seemed strange to me about Felix, for he is generally as careful of his appearance as a lieutenant got up for a party, the only difference being that he does not curry-comb his head when entering a room full of people. And then the fashion of the thing! There are none of the sort to be had.

But had I not seen it once already? Where could

it have been? That is it. In Tegel, during the days
of the midges, Felix lost his necktie in the water on
one occasion, and Betti made him one out of the mos-
quito curtain. That was when they had seen each
other for the first time. And now he was wearing it
on his wedding-day, in remembrance of those bygone
days! How he must have loved and valued it in order
to treasure it up so faithfully! I never should have
thought that a little bit of muslin could have looked
so charming!

Now I could have derived the greatest enjoyment
from the marriage address, but it was just over. I
could only tell Betti by my embrace that I was spending the delightfullest day. "And you, my child?" I
asked.—"If only my thankfulness could be in proportion to my happiness!" she said.

We now saw more than ever how cleverly Uncle
Fritz, as leader of the whole, had arranged everything.
While the numerous congratulations were being continued in the entrance-hall, which by the aid of hang-
ings looked at the very least like a councillor of commerce's, the hired waiters were transporting the tables
so rapidly to their proper places, that the meal could
be begun in the shortest space of time. We bridal
couples were placed opposite each other at the principal table. The Police-lieutenant took in Erica; Uncle
Fritz, Frau Police-lieutenant; Frau Krause was given
to the Doctor, which caused him to express dissatisfaction later on, for she wailed to him unceasingly about
her Edward, who had already sailed. If the wind
blows through the streets, she trembles for fear the
ship should be capsized, and the weather reports in
the papers keep her in a chronic state of anxiety. But
the spirits had promised to tell her of every danger.
After this the Doctor gave up listening to her silly

talk, and entertained himself with the claret instead. For him spirits are nothing but erratic bed-sheets.

Every single course of the dinner came from Otto Bellmann.

"You can take some more with perfect safety, if you like it," I said to my Carl ; "and just fish the crayfish out of the turbot sauce ; there are not enough of them anyhow to satisfy the Doctor's appetite ! "

The Police-lieutenant gave the first toast in honour of the silver couple. It was a little long, but choice as regards language. He wished us a further five-and-twenty years, until the golden wedding, and that we might all be at our posts then. Then we had another course, and Uncle Fritz drank to the health of the young couple. But as usual, there were marginal notes. What was the meaning of his dragging me into his speech and congratulating Felix on getting me for a mother-in-law, as there were worse? Then the bridesmaids' health was drunk, the Doctor doing duty this time ; then that of the best man ; then that of the ladies ; then that of the grandchildren ; then that of the married people, coupled with the Police-lieutenant ; then that of Uncle Fritz. Good Heavens, how they did clink glasses ! We stood almost as long, glass in hand, as we sat for purposes of eating, and the ladies had constantly to take care that they did not get spots of red wine on their dresses. But it was jolly—awfully jolly—very jolly indeed.

Last of all, we had got to the ices, and the champagne had been handed round, Uncle Fritz having chosen a Lorraine brand for the purpose, highly to be commended, and plentifully supplied, when Herr Brandes knocked for silence. He requested us to pardon him for taking such a liberty, but he wished to be allowed to say a word. Everybody's health had already been drunk ; there was one wish he would still like to express. When he had arrived in Berlin, many years ago, the town was not the same as to-day, when it is praised by every one who gets to know it. It had been extended and beautified, the old had been obliged to give way to the better new, for there was too little space for both. This was the state of affairs at present in the Landsberger-strasse, in the Buchholz house. The business had become extended, and builders were at work pulling down, in order that it might be able to develop. He hoped that their old luck would remain true to the house, that it might prosper, in a smaller way, just as the city of Berlin grew and blossomed on more extended lines; he begged us all to join him in the toast: "Long live the firm of Buchholz and Son! Long may it live!" "*Hoch soll sie leben, drei Mal hoch,*" we all sang, and my Carl went round and thanked Herr Brandes.

When dinner was finished, we had our coffee in the entrance-hall, the tables were cleared away, and a small dance was to be set on foot. However, this failed, owing to the pianist having left us in the lurch. "Surely we can contribute as much as we shall want ourselves," Uncle Fritz suggested, but nobody pressed forward towards the piano. Every one began to make excuses. He was sure he could not do it well enough.

Upon which the Police-lieutenant exclaimed : "Mila, you have enjoyed such wonderful instruction in Switzerland!"—Fritz conducted Mila politely to the piano, and requested her to play a polonaise. Mila bethought herself for a moment, and then began. Well, we marched according to the waves of sound she produced, for time there was none, and so Uncle Fritz begged for a waltz. Felix and Betti revolved a certain number of times, but that would not do either.

"Is that a waltz?" I asked.—"One of Chopin s,"
answered Mila.—"I suppose it is more of a waltz to
listen to than to dance to?"—She retorted, "She did
not play rubbish," and got up pertly from her seat.
After this Betti and Emmi produced an old book of
duets. These were serviceable, but then they wished
to amuse themselves too. Let it suffice to say that we
were in a complete dilemma. Then Herr Hoff came
to the rescue, and asked whether he might fetch his
accordion? "Of course," said Fritz.

He returned after a while with his accordion. But
what was it? A huge hand-organ! "No," I said, "I
cannot allow that."—"Just play away," commanded
Uncle Fritz.

Herr Hoff could play the newest dances very invit-
ingly, and with plenty of go, which pleased the young
people mightily, though Frau Police-lieutenant made
long faces at it. However, her disapproval abated
upon Uncle Fritz engaging her, and as he put his best
foot foremost in dancing with her, she thought later
that it really was most obliging of Herr Hoff to sacrifice himself by being orchestra.

So there stood the expensive piano, and the lessons
had cost many a groschen! To what purpose? After
all is said and done, a concertina is much cheaper, and
answers the same purpose. They ought to be more
studied.

What with dancing, singing, and refreshments, it
grew increasingly lively, and was something like an
unconstrained festival in forest glades. This was due
to the firs. The departure of the young couple remained unnoticed. We should have liked to keep
them longer, but they had to get away by train.

Then the Police-lieutenant's family took leave, and
the Krauses, and so on, one after another. As soon as

the last had taken their departure the merriment ceased. Only the candles were still alight, the empty chairs were all standing about in disorder, and glasses and plates where they just happened to have found a place. The festival had come to an end.

"Are you tired, Wilhelmine ?" asked my Carl, as I was resting a little wearily.

"Sit down beside me, Carl, and let me lay my head on your breast, quietly, peacefully. It has been a grand day ; how beautiful the memory of it will be ! "

WESTERLAND.*

Why Doris leaves and Herr Kleines emigrates—Why Herr Weigelt is dependent and an educated man is turned into a parcel— About the ideal in art and general change of tissue—About strengthening weeks.

THE chimney had already been taken down, and workmen were engaged setting up machinery in the factory, during which process Felix's presence was absolutely indispensable. The young people had taken up their abode in a hotel as a sort of elongated wedding tour, for it looked horrible at home, and as my Carl had got hold of some new ideas, the pulling down of the walls was more extensive than I had been originally led to expect ; we were therefore crowded together in a constantly diminishing space, and Frieda was about me all day long. So we became better acquainted with each other ; and as troubles end by bending the strongest will, I gained her confidence

* A small strip of land in Holstein, bounded by the German Ocean. There is an island of the same name close by.—TRANS.

too. She had gone too far the evening of the ball, and great as was the power of her beauty usually over Max, the sceptre broke when she believed, in her anger, that she could allow herself everything, even to bodily threats. He came neither the following day nor the next, and so matters went on. The total destruction of the dinner on the day of the ball may have had something to do with his holding back.

Max had given Frieda up ; he sent us no news about himself ; we only knew that he was in Africa. Frieda became more depressed daily after the celebration of our silver wedding. She had hoped that Max would at least write his congratulations to us or to Felix, and that there would be some mention made of her ; but as there was not a single sign of love or life forthcoming, she feared the worst. " He has probably only disappeared for a time, and will turn up again somewhere," I strove to soothe her ; but she said : " Even supposing he is alive, he is angry with me. I have forfeited his love by my own fault. At the wedding I saw the meaning of being and making happy. I desired only to receive, and would give nothing ; I considered myself perfect, and was full of faults. Oh, if he only were to come back, I would serve him as well as I am able, would be what I am through him alone, would live only for him ! And now he is dead."— "Nothing certain is known on the subject, Frieda."— "He is lost to me."—I pitied her deeply, and determined to keep her always with me. If anybody had to be her stay, I was the person. My interference may have had just as much to do with the turn things had taken as she herself had by her former behaviour.

If Max could only have seen her ! Trouble had gradually lent a melancholy expression to her features, which deprived her smile, when it did come, of the boastful look which used to chill people who approached her. Her voice sounded softer when she begged for anything ; there was something in its ring that expressed thanks in advance for the favour to be granted. There are many who have a heart concealed somewhere, but it will not speak when it ought, and this had been the case with Frieda heretofore. It could give utterance to its feelings now, but Max did not hear it. I found Frieda grow pleasanter from day to day. She gave herself a great deal of trouble even when I was out of temper, for which provocations were flying about wildly.

First and foremost came Doris. She seemed particularly anxious to have notice given her, with orders to leave at once. There was no further question of cleaning up, as the rooms would be filled with dirt again directly; and whenever I went into the kitchen, I found an oft-forbidden mason sitting there. So dirty as they looked, too ! "Doris," I said, " I allow no nonsense."—" Quite so."—" Do you not wish to remain longer with me ? "—" Quite so."—" But have you anything to complain of in any way ?"—" Quite so." —" Are you thinking of marrying ?"—" Quite so."— " But surely not with a mason's apprentice ? "—" That is exactly it."

So that was the upshot of the matter. Had Idiss been more careful of the boiler, I need not have sent away a trained servant. It would be beyond my powers to instruct some pampered person in her work in the present state of confusion; and a decent woman would certainly not enter such ruins.

And then, secondly, that Herr Kleines !

Well, he came to see me one fine day. " Mercy on us," I exclaimed, "how ill you look ! Have you been chased through a needle's eye anywhere ? " He really

might have been threaded into a medium-sized darn-
ing-needle, his skeleton hung so loosely together.—
"Protect me from that Schulz woman!" he cried.—
"From whom?"—"From the mother and daughter.
The old hag persecutes me; Idiss says that I have
promised to marry her."—"Is it true?"—"No."—
"Well, who is telling stories?"—"Idiss."—"Then you
are well out of it!"—"Do you call it being well out
of it, when that Schulz woman applies to me twice
every week?"—"She only worried me by letter."—"I
won't have her letters taken in. But if you could only
hear the fuss she makes! And changing my quarters
is not of the slightest use; she manages to find out
where I am directly, from the Police-lieutenant. Do
please take me in, Frau Buchholz; she is afraid of
you."—"I am very sorry, but we are building."—"I
have changed my lodgings five times already, and five
times I have been obliged to fly. It is enough to drive
a man out of his skin and make him sit down by it."

"You should have done that long ago."—He looked
at me interrogatively.—"I mean to say you should
have given up your mode of life; it has never been
what it ought. Really, if a plaster-of-Paris cast were
taken of you, you would be a medical spectacle for
doctors, but not for families."—"Because families are
stupid and prudish," he answered. "I shall emigrate."
—"That would be a wise proceeding on your part;
for, honestly speaking, I imagine that we are much
too old-fashioned for you here."—"Skat is played so
badly, too," he said, and went away. — I wonder
whether he referred to me when he talked of bad play?
If this were the case, the ocean is not broad enough
to separate us.

As Frieda offered her services for every kind of
work, Doris left us on the first, and we two kept house,

with a charwoman to do the rough work ; but it was
not agreeable, especially as the weather became warm
and the summer turned Berlin into a furnace.   However, salvation was near, and it came from Emmi.

The Doctor owed her some compensation on account of the Russian lady, and this could only be
done by bringing out the mammon—which Emmi surely too had earned by having been deprived of him for a
week !—for a journey.   And how amiable it was of
them, to invite me to seek recuperation at Sylt under
their protection !—a place which was to work wonders
for my nerves and asthma.

They all advised my accepting it, and so I consented.   But only under the condition that my husband
would go to the hotel, that Frieda would take care of
the Doctor's rooms during our absence, and that we
should take Augusta Weigelt's youngest child with
us, for the doctor had said that sea air would help to
pull the little creature round,—it was on the road to
recovery.   This also was agreed to.

Herr Weigelt asked what he could do for me, when
he heard about it.   I told him, "Hold Augusta in
honour."   He answered, "Frau Buchholz, a woman
like my wife really is a woman !" and he could get no
further.   A pulpy mass of dependence, that man.
Could he not have said simply, "Certainly"?   However, it must be acknowledged that he is not extrava-
gant, and that he works honestly.   But supposing he
were without such guidance !

So it came to pass that we all met at the Lehrt station late one evening, with trunks, hand-bags, and um-
brellas.   The Doctor was fully primed for the occasion, as Herr Jeckel, the bookseller, had sketched a
plan of the journey for him.   He knows so well every
place where a change has to be made, where the train

stops for a time, and where one has to travel by slow train, that they ought to have made him councillor of locomotives, or something of that description, long ago, for he arranges routes so admirably that a person wishing to go to Kötschenbroda, may steam off to Eidtkuhnen for his amusement, owing to the combination of changes—an amusement that probably yields a percentage to the State.

Either the emolument from the Russian was not sufficiently good to allow of sleeping-berths, or else my son-in-law felt more inclined for the old fashion of spending wretched nights in a train. The carriage being one which had a passage in the middle, prevented every attempt at stretching ourselves out, and if the children did not exactly crawl about, they squalled unceasingly till Morpheus opened his arms to receive them. "A very beneficial journey to a watering-place!" I suggested.—"It cannot be arranged otherwise, dear mamma-in-law," said he in mock pity; "we do not happen to belong to the aristocracy of finance!" —"Miser!" I thought inaudibly. "If the roubles really are going to be spent, why must one's unfortunate corpus, which is travelling in search of repairs, be subjected to the rack first? People certainly do say that nothing can hurt you if a doctor be present, but there are degrees of tenderness, according to how one sits, and subject to one's own judgment."

The times in the tables were all correct, the only thing being that the trains never kept them, so the difficulty of reaching Sylt with twins had to be solved by means of State aid. Even the man most completely endowed with reason, turns into a parcel here. But he does reach his destination.

When one has managed to arrive at this extreme point of the German Empire at Westerland, where huge hotels and architectural villas for visitors have sprung up beside peasants' houses, one asks, " And where is the far-famed German Ocean ? "—" Beyond the dunes," they say, for they only speak the Frisiac language to each other, and one goes through the town, towards the sandhills, up the steps, and then !

Yes, then.

Then it seems as if volley after volley were being fired to greet the king's birthday ; one clap of thunder after another is caused by the waves, as they fling themselves on the dazzlingly white beach, in such mighty force that all one's worries are forgotten.

We made our way down to the many hundreds who were walking along the sands, or sitting in their beach basket-chairs, or lying flat down sunning themselves. Many were digging holes in the sand, in which they take up their abode after ornamenting the walls with flags ; others built castles, like the children. The grown-up folk had holidays and music as well, and convalescent homes with fluttering pennants, black—white—red, and flocks of silver-grey sea-gulls, which are so tame that they will catch pieces of bread thrown up to them in their bills. The sea rolls on uninterruptedly, and flings its spray high into the air, which being saturated with salt is health-giving to those who inhale it. " Being here will do me good," I said.— " All of us," suggested the Doctor.—" Yes, certainly ; there is so much health in it, that none need go empty away."

We were more satisfied day by day with our lodgings and the care taken of us. They cook excellently, and, which is a matter of great convenience, there is no redundant luxury of toilette, although the society is good, being drawn from the cultivated classes. Everybody is there just as he is, and that is beneficial to health, which suffers under restraint, and economical at the same time.

My weak condition was, it must be admitted, a mere matter of detail. The Doctor, and, influenced by him, Emmi also, had left their nurse behind from motives of economy, and the care of the grandchildren was laid on grandmamma's shoulders. This was the reason of their amiable offer to take me with them !

He revelled in the open sea, while I only required to breathe, and Emmi took warm baths to start with. The result of this was that I had to sit about on the beach alone doing nurse. Mercifully, I got some assistance during the very first days of our stay, in the persons of Herr Spannbein and Ottilie, whose acquaintance we had made while in Italy ; they were here, too, accompanied by Quenglhuber and the young Spannbeins. I really cannot describe the pleasure of meeting each other again.

Herr Spannbein paints sea landscapes now, and Quenglhuber seems pretty nearly to have given up his historical crotchet ; for the natural finds a readier market, and he cannot force the public back into the past by means of his criticisms. He complained bitterly of being forced to make way for younger critics, of whom he insists that they write the most utter rubbish, while they in their turn make the same remarks about him.

" The ideal must be utterly destroyed," he coughed, for he has grown old.—" Tell me what is the ideal really ?" I asked.—" Do you not know ?"—" No."—"Well, the ideal is—good heavens ! you must surely know what the ideal is ?"—" No, I don't."—" Nothing can be simpler. Well, the ideal, or rather idealism—but fancy your not knowing it ! Absurd !"—" Go on, please," I said. After collecting his thoughts for a

little, he began : "Idealism, in contradistinction to
realism, is the idea looked at objectively as an example
of the sublime in human affairs ; or *vice versâ*, it is rel-
atively the æsthetic perception of matter. But it is
all nonsense ; you know perfectly well what ideal
means ! "—"Could you not tell me the same thing in
German ?"—"But I was speaking German."—"Really !
Ah, well ; there must be a deal of hard work to do
before Art can hang on our walls ! But you are a
grandfather and I a grandmother ; why need we trouble
ourselves about it ? "

The young Spannbeins were veritable sand-boys.
They were unwearied in constructing dams as a protection against the waves, and said, "This time they
are strong and firm." Then came the tide and
licked their work away, like Fate, which flows in upon
us and destroys what seemed to be indestructible.
I wonder whether the factory will ever come to anything ?

My Carl wrote regularly, and told me, amongst
other things, that Herr Bergfeldt had passed away.
It was a happy release, for he had become a heavy
burden, and even Augusta had said that a peaceful
end would be a blessing for him and for all of them.
Now he was lying at rest beside Emil. I felt it
deeply—very deeply.

The only news I had to send home was that we were
all in excellent health, that Fritz and Franz had already been burnt as brown as Camerooners, and that
the youngest Spannbein looked more like a seal than
anything else with his closely-cropped hair. Augusta's
little one was getting on splendidly. The sea air
gives people appetites like a sausage machine ; then
there is the strengthening nourishment, which changes
into strong and healthy tissue in the body, by which

means fresh inclination for eating is called forth, which in its turn banishes the scrofulous element out of children, and leads back the whole of one's general organism to health. The Doctor ate so much, that he exceeded the price we had contracted for. Otherwise there was very little to happen ; we really did rest.

The longer we remained, the more enjoyable it was. The sea is always different. Sometimes like this, sometimes like that ; but it is just in its diversity that its charm consists. When the sky was clouded, the clouds were rent asunder sometimes, and the evening gold glittered behind them, so that one seemed to see a portion of the universe where the sun was shining grandly, as it always does, while we were enveloped in grey sadness. The Doctor even went to the expense of a tiny carriage sometimes, and we visited the delightfully clean villages on the island, the mountainous downs, the heath glowing in red, the lighthouse which warns ships by its intermittent glow, and I even went so far as to go into an ancient Hun cave. The Hun no longer dwelt there, but there was an old woman with stearine candles, susceptible of a gratuity. And how tame all the animals are about Sylt !—for the fowling-piece is buried there. Hares behave as if there were no stewing-pans in existence. There is much that is extraordinary about the place. But the most delightful part of all is the dip in the foaming billows, which my son-in-law rates far higher than Heligoland, which he had once visited. The air suited me splendidly ; the nerves regained their tone, and asthma vanished. The Doctor was generally to be found seated in a hole, where he devoted himself to card games ; Emmi and Ottilie made peregrinations along the beach, and I minded the children. I grew to love them as if they were my own.

I was struck by a terrible shock in the midst of this peaceful existence—a letter with a black border, which I took up in terror. "Erica!" was my first thought. But, thank God, it was not so. It was due to Frau Bergfeldt's amiability; she probably had some black-edged paper left, and so she dealt me a blow with it. I feel for everybody's grief, but no one ought to be frightened unnecessarily, and an envelope like the one I received does have that effect until one knows whence it comes and what it contains. There was not much that was rational in it. "She was gradually getting reconciled," she wrote, "and went frequently to water her husband and Emil. Just at last he had not cared to eat anything. And after all, the greatest good was to be extracted from life by means of one's teeth. When that was done with, there was no more to be said."—And to send black-edged paper for that. She shall catch it from me some time.

Upon our departure we were able, with the exception of the Bergfeldt episode, to look back upon a series of strengthening weeks, and as the steamer turned into the Watten-sea, and Sylt with its downs sank lower, we all agreed with one accord that we were able to cope with Berlin once more. But the big town eats us up at last.

HOME.

About modern Renaissance—About little Wilhelmine Fabian and a
    set-off—Why Hinnerich repents, and swears frightfully notwith-
    standing—Why the Bergfeldts never will be lost, and Frau
    Kliebisch grows younger—End.

THE first thing that met my eyes at the station was
my dear, dear Carl.   After all, nothing is worth anything without him.   How safe I felt on his arm, amid
the crowd of arrivals !   He kept on saying how the
air had browned me, and how well I looked.   " So I
am.   And you ? "—" I am glad that we have got you
back again."—Augusta, the children and her husband
came to fetch the little one.   She was so astonished
at the sight of the fresh, hardy creature, who had hung
together like a bag of bones before the beach and
sand cure !   Herr Weigelt wanted to say some rubbish, but we hastened off, and walked the few steps to
our house.

Outside it was still the old place, but it had been
changed inside, and my fear of new things made it
difficult for me to enter.   But our imagination generally pictures things wrongly, and that was the case
on this occasion.

Of course many things had changed their places,
and they looked smaller, but all the more comfortable
for that ; and it was our old furniture too, only they
had got rid of the redundancy, as they were bound to
do.   It was a cosy nest in which to grow old.

Betti's wing had been done up in Renaissance style,
but it had not been turned into a museum, so that if
one so much as coughs the little knick-knacks tumble
from their shelves and get more broken than they
were before.   Betti was so pleased at showing me

everything, and Felix kept his arm round her and looked on too. So I did not get much sitting down during the first half-hour. When I had expended all my terms of praise, I asked, "Where is Frieda?"—There was a pause of embarrassment.—"She is at Fritz's," my Carl answered, with reluctance. "We would not write to you, but the danger is over now."—"What danger?"—"We feared that we should have lost Erica."—"Erica?"—"She is over it now, and a happy mother. You are to see her and her little daughter to-morrow."—"And Fritz?"—"He does not stir from the side of his wife and child. Frieda is housekeeping for them."—"But she cannot do that." —"Yes," said Betti, "she would; and because it had to be done, she could."—"I am going off at once; nobody shall keep me here!"

And so I did.—Frieda opened the door very gently for me. "She has eaten a little bit of pigeon," she whispered; "Dr. Paber is quite satisfied with her to-day. How nice to have you here! She has often asked for you."

Then came Fritz. He looked worn out with watching. The sad earnest of life had marked his forehead —I saw the signs of it.—"My poor boy!"—"Not poor; I am doubly rich now; my wife will not leave me. Oh, sister, what days they have been!"—"May I see them both?"—Fritz went into the room, and after a pause he beckoned to me. The room was darkened, and Erica looked pale—oh, so pale!—as she lay in bed. But her glance was clear, she was looking on-wards into life again. "I was standing in front of the Dark Gate," she said; "then a voice called to me, my Fritz called, and I came back."—"No such thoughts; we will get away from it as soon as we can. There is more sense in that, is there not?"—And now I saw the wee daughter. It was a strong little thing and well made, and was slumbering peacefully. This was sufficient for the first time, but I had to convince myself, or else suspicion would have driven me wild.

So I had my hands quite full. The state of our domestic affairs was a new one, and Erica laid claims on me, which were—oh, so willingly !—acceded to. Frieda was to be depended upon, and so after a lapse of some weeks we had the consolation of seeing Erica allowed to rest for a short time in her garden-room. She might perhaps have got well sooner, but it is more difficult to recover in Berlin flats, if one's youth has been spent in nearly country air.

His wife's advance in health and strength had a visible influence on Uncle Fritz ; the tormenting memory of those terrible hours, during which mortality had shrieked its awful note of warning through the house, dwindled away—those hours during which he had felt with dreadful force that all courage and all strength is nothing but vain striving when Fate stretches out its hand for our loved ones. "However," so he said, "Erica has now entered on life for the second time, and Berlin is her home ! "—" In time she will accommodate herself to the capital," I answered.

The little daughter had been very properly named Wilhelmine, although the Krauses did think that it should have been called after the grandfather ; but I really should have been hurt if Erica had done that. The Krauses had received tidings from their Edward already ; he had to work like a day-labourer, but he was of good cheer and devoted body and soul to his profession. He had entered into life-long friendship with a negro who was on the same ship, and about the same age as himself ; he was probably the captive son of a king.—"Of course," Uncle Fritz had answered ,

" and made of such excellent wool besides, that the dye won't come off."—She must always have everything grander than other folk, even if she has to draw on her own imagination.

I was able by degrees to devote myself more exclusively to my own business, but I did it rather by fits and starts than in an undisturbed fashion ; for to begin with, Frau Bergfeldt, whom I had purposely left very much on one side, came stumbling up-stairs, and she had a request. She wanted us to take tickets for Leuenfels's tragedy, which would not be accepted anywhere, and which was now about to be performed in a booth with the assistance of some young writers like himself. " It is sheer envy which makes them strive to bring him to a fall," she said ; " but all of those who belonged to the poets' league ' New Germany ' had banded themselves together to show the world that all former poets had been idiots. You really must read Leuenfels's poems," she said ; " they used to give my deceased husband a fit of the shivers, they were so beautiful."—" No doubt they brought him to his last gasp."—" Oh, dear no ; the doctor did not understand the nature of the case. He was not properly treated."—" Not by you," I translated truth into plain language for her ; " for you positively commit murder with your envelopes." This was a set-off against what she had done.

However, as she had been giving Leuenfels an unjustifiable amount of credit on the strength of his piece, I took six tickets for her sake for the " Battle of the Nations." Her daughter joins her with her family, and intends to continue letting the rooms ; and so they hope to be able to gain a livelihood. Augusta is sure to please the people.

The tickets turned out to be a very opportune pur-

chase, for instead of leaving me in peace, the Kliebisches had come to Berlin, and as I had invited them
years ago, they visited us. Frau Kliebisch had broad-
ened out considerably. Pomerania must be a nutri-
tious country, with its smoked goose-breasts, and the
other animals they raise there. It must be admitted
that her beauty was already a matter of history, and
it may have been on this account that she wished to
have her eating department furnished anew by a den-
tist. Her husband, however, had travelled hither, im-
pelled by heavy cares; for on the occasion of a
meeting of naturalists, it had been stated in a scientific
speech that agriculture might allow itself to be buried,
as in the near future all such products as flour, meat,
milk, and bread would be manufactured by means of
chemistry, all of them from air and water, with a bit of
mineral kingdom thrown in. "In that case I am a
ruined man," said Kliebisch.—"Has that really been
announced?" asked my husband.—"All the papers
contained a statement that a golden era was dawning
for us, and that every fear about food-supply would
be removed."—"It must have been the creation of
their own imaginations."—"Not a bit of it; Virchow
was there, too, and had not a word to say against it;
and you know how he drags every mistake made by
the Imperial Diet to light, so that it must be all right.
If I could only buy a machine like that in Berlin, I
should do capitally; we have excellent air, water, and
sand about us for the manufacture of artificial nourishment."—"I wonder whether it would agree with
me?" I suggested.—"And then there is the question
as to what the cost of production would be," said my
husband. — "That is just what I want to inquire
about."

Frau Kliebisch had become an out-and-out agriculturalist, and knew more about potatoes than she used to do about music. Her dairy left her no leisure for music, and her·children did not learn either, as they were quite devoid of talent. "Instead of their learning, we have taken the money the lessons would have cost," she told us, "and paid it into a military insurance office for the boys; that will produce a nice little sum if they are obliged to serve. If farming should get into still greater disrepute, owing to the new air discovery, that will be a great assistance to us. Hinnerich is greatly disturbed, and regrets bitterly that up to now he has not paid sufficient attention to science."

Herr Kliebisch's brother had come with them also; he was a farmer too, and a widower—tall and handsome. When he said good-day to me, I really thought that a small bundle of faggots had been put into my hand. He said, "And if the whole staff of professors set to work to turn the machine, they will find it hard work to produce a good fatted calf." A very sensible man.

We made the Kliebisches come with us to see Leuenfels's piece, "The Battle of the Nations," into which not only all the Leuenfels-Bergfeldtian acquaintances had been introduced, but also some others of the public. Amanda had been ready with her support, and the Doctor and Emmi as well. We made up a large party, and Frau Bergfeldt sat beside me, and said the piece would bring in thousands, because the spiritual, aided by a guitar, would triumph over the material. She ought to know something about it. The first act was capital. They played in animals' skins, in order to represent the savage days of yore; then the scene was changed, and songs and lute-playing introduced us to the civilised haunts of humanity.

They sang and declaimed one Leuenfelsian poem after
another. "Is it not wonderfully fine?" asked Frau
Bergfeldt.—"I like it," I said. When the curtain fell
there was some applause, and Leuenfels appeared,
looking very important. There were a great many of
us there who were friends ; and then the Kliebisches,
with their big hands !

Now came the second act. It was very much the
same thing as the first, for the savages went off on
predatory excursions, and just as I thought they came
to the people with the guitars. And the rude things
they said to one another ! My word ! The audience
yelled " Da Capo "—" Once more,"—and when the one
man took his lute and banged the leader of the savages about his horns with his old instrument so that
the splinters flew about and he tumbled down dead,
the noise was no longer exactly pleasant. One set
hissed, others applauded and stamped their feet, and
some even whistled, which caused a good many to
retire from the scene. However, we stayed, for we
wanted to see the fluttering shroud. But it did not
blow about on the flagstaff as it ought to have done,
and made no great impression. Frau Bergfeldt asked
me softly, "Am I likely to get my rent?" I did not
know.

According to our agreement, we went to the Rath-
skeller after the piece was over, where Leuenfels's
triumph was to be celebrated. He was awfully abusive. "His piece was too nearly akin to the Titans to
be appreciated by the blockhead multitude, to whom
true poetry was a sealed book. But he was a real
poet, notwithstanding the noise and cat-calls of his
enemies."—"You have covered yourself with immor-
tal renown for the whole of your life," I said.—"Certainly," he answered. "It does one good to discover

that some power of discrimination is still in existence. We shall go on writing."—The Doctor remarked below his breath that he would prefer being prompter to a performing ape.

But he is not conversant with the drama. On the other hand, he informed Herr Kliebisch that artificial nourishment is still in the theoretical stage ; that it is, so to speak, the amusing side of science, for it was correct enough, but not to be reduced to practice. Upon this Herr Kliebisch let fly an awful oath at the theoretical and ordered some champagne. My Carl did his share in having some bottles, but Kliebisch out-did him in the finer qualities, and promised the Doctor a ham for his household.

The Doctor paid no heed to the opportunity afforded him of standing a bottle in return. Amanda merrily kept up a sturdy conversation with Kliebisch's brother, while Leuenfels discoursed exclusively about his piece, and waxed mightily enthusiastic about himself, until the cashier arrived from the theatre.

"Produce the reward of honour," Leuenfels exclaimed boastfully ; "there will be no lack of princely presents for the poet !"—"He brings the rent," said Frau Bergfeldt.—"Is this the settlement ?" Leuenfels asked after reading the note the man handed him. "What does it mean ? What is that ?"—"The tickets for your own use, and your share for this evening, just balance, but six marks have still to be paid for the lute."—"How is that ?"—"You insisted on having a real 'ute to be broken, and a second-hand one costs six marks."—"I have to pay out some more ?"—"Six marks."—"They can be deducted from the proceeds of the next performance."—"'The Battle of the Nations' has been removed from the bills ; it was too badly received."—My Carl lent Leuenfels the money,

and he marched off dejectedly with Frau Bergfeldt.
It seems as if tragedy had its drawbacks. Well, Augusta knows where we are to be found.

When we reached home, Felix and Betti were waiting for us. News had arrived from Max.—" Well ?" I
asked.—"He will not believe what I wrote to him,"
said Felix, "that Frieda had become quite another
person."—"If only he could see her!"—"Quite my
idea," said Felix.—"Excuse me ; mine."—"Mamma,
Felix has thought out a plan already. When Max
arrives the day after to-morrow, he will take him to
the Residenz Theatre, and go to a box, where nobody
will be able to see him easily ; then you and the Kliebisches must go there too, and take Frieda with you."
—"I have had enough of theatres for the present."—
"Mamma, Friedrich Haase plays the King's Lieutenant—his most celebrated part; and just think how
elegantly arranged Director Amos's stage is—the Kliebisches really ought to see it ! Frieda will go quite
unsuspectingly."—"Children, how about my nerves ?"
—"You left them behind you at Sylt."—"We will
go."

That evening will remain engraven on my memory.
Between the first and second acts Frau Kliebisch informed me that her brother-in-law intended making
Amanda.Kulecke an offer. What did I think about it ?
She pleased him extremely.—I looked him carefully
over. He was something like Uncle Fritz, only more
substantial. "Try your luck," I advised him. After
this, the great artist's marvellous acting held my
attention entirely captive, so that I neither thought
about Amanda nor Frieda. He had to come forward
in the middle of the act, and the people shouted their
enthusiastic "Bravos." Suddenly Frieda gave a start ;
"*His* voice," she cried, then got up and looked about

her. And as she discovers Max, she sinks unconscious into my arms.

The gentlemen nearest me showed great kindness in helping me to lead Frieda out, the box-keeper fetched some water to revive her, and when he came with it he stood in astonishment to see a young man kneeling before a young girl, who clung round his neck in tears. While the people inside there were watching the play, we were having our drama in the passage. However, it came to a happy end; and even if there should be an occasional interchange of harsh words later, my own impression is, that Max may calculate on more happiness than most other people. I know Frieda now. She will learn to see more and more clearly that contentment is the highest gain, the happiness that all seek for and the fewest find, because it is too dim for them.

Before the end of the act we were all in a fly on our homeward way. I then left the two alone, for it is very annoying when two people wish to exchange confidences and the third cannot betake herself elsewhere.

Frau Kliebisch called on me one day, looking quite rejuvenated; she could smile freely without shielding her mouth with her hand, as she had done before, and her Hinnerich recovered all his former tenderness for her. If he had fallen in love with her dazzling pearls in his day, it was her duty to attend to their renovation; for how often love vanishes with the outward charms!

Amanda was engaged, even before the Kliebisches left. She visited us with her athlete, and called him her file-leader. "He shall have an awfully good time," she confided to me. And I am sure that he will, too.

As the first snow fell the time was approaching when

we had to bethink ourselves of the day of presents.
Year by year they had increased in number, those to
whom my heart clung, but the love it contained was
not less. Oh, no ; the more it was distributed, the more
it grew. It must be true that it is inexhaustible.

I thought the old puppet-show would be suitable
for Fritz and Franz, and it was getting ruined in the
lumber-room ; to mend and paste it together was an
agreeable evening occupation for my Carl and myself.
Notwithstanding the factory, he had less work to do
now, as Felix took most of it off his hands. We had
found a real treasure in him.

So we sat there and pasted kings and queens, knights,
counts, peasants, and beggars, and fastened new wires
on to the figures.

"It is extraordinary," I said, "I cannot do without
work, with the best will in the world."—"And yet,"
answered my Carl, "there was once somebody who
wished—I mention no names—to retire into complete
tranquillity."—"Carl, people often have ideas, only
they can't help running their heads against them.
How is it possible for Grandmamma Buchholz to insist
on tranquillity ? What would become of the children
and grandchildren ? Ah, Carl, I never can see Uncle
Fritz's little Wilhelmine without the thought,—I was
just as helpless once as the sweet little being that
bears my name. Will she grow up as I did, with just
the same plaited hair and apron with sleeves ; will
she once have as rich a blessing as has been bestowed
upon me here below ; will she find sometime a true
heart like yours ? We shall hardly live to see it."

"The day is drawing near its close," spoke my Carl,
"the great Sabbath of peace of our century. Its rosy
hues are fading softly away, but what will the morrow
bring us ? "

"Carl, do you know, man must leave what he loves some time? But a strong hand leads those who are left behind, through chance and change, towards their home. When we wish to direct, we find that we have not the right wire to do it with. Just when we fancy that we have set to work particularly craftily, we can see our mistakes afterwards; and if things do turn out as they should, it happens without our intervention. Just look back on our life. How sunny it has been, owing to you, husband of my heart, owing to you, whom He, our Father in Heaven, gave me!"

We were both silent. Time stole gently past us, and our thoughts followed it.

THE END.